Issue 19
February - March 2020

Lezli Robyn, Editor
Shahid Mahmud, Publisher

Published by Arc Manor/Heart's Nest Press
P.O. Box 10339
Rockville, MD 20849-0339

Heart's Kiss is published in February, April, June, August, October and December.

www.HeartsKiss.com

Submissions to *Heart's Kiss* magazine are now closed. We thank all who submitted and wish you well on your future endeavors.

Available by subscription (www.HeartsKiss.com) or through your favorite online store (Amazon.com, BN.com, etc.).

ISBN: 978-1-61242-493-4

Contents

OPENING EDITORIAL

by Lezli Robyn

While I sit here, sipping an Australian hot chocolate "Milo" drink, reading wonderful romance for this wonderful magazine, I cannot help but be proud of what Tina Smith and I have created with *Heart's Kiss*. We have been dedicated to celebrating love in all forms, and this issue is no different, with one of my favorite pieces, "Threshold of the Heart," being a second chance romance between two gifted women who just cannot stop thinking about each other. Not only have we published "own voice" stories, and diverse writers over the years, but we also publish all the tropes readers so love to curl up with in a romance book. We wanted to show our readers that *everyone* deserves their happily-ever-after story to be published.

Which means it is with great sadness that we announce the closing of *Heart's Kiss* magazine. While Tina Smith had recently left the magazine to go back to being a practicing psychologist, it is still true that we both absolutely loved editing this magazine, and our publisher, Shahid Mahmud, loved supporting it. However, we discovered after three years of publication that a magazine format was just too unusual for a genre that is not very used to romance in the shorter form.

Fear not, for you haven't seen the last of us! The feedback from *Heart's Kiss* has been intensely positive, and while a magazine was not the right format to be displayed prominently in bookstores, we've realized a series of themed romance anthologies would allow us to distribute romance fiction nationally, on a level the magazine format limited us from. The romance book world is much more used to seeing romance in novella or novel format, so our future anthologies are guaranteed to reach a much wider audience. It also means we can continue to deliver diverse romance fiction to our loyal readers several times a year. While one door is closing, another is already open for us to step right through and discover new love stories.

Along with the aforementioned second chance story by newcomer T. Thorn Coyle appearing in this last issue, we interview celebrated romance author, Rick R. Reed and regular contributor and Harlequin author, Melinda Cutis (who is having a UPtv movie made from one of her novels as we speak!). We also welcome back to our pages paranormal romance author Kate Pavelle with "Upon a Bed of Bones," and Harlequin author, Kayla Perrin, with another installment in Dante and Bella's bumpy road to love in "One More Night With You." Anna J. Stewart also delivers a new novella, "In Wraith Danger," depicting an unexpected paranormal romance set on a cruise ship. (She also just had one of her recent Harlequin novels turned into an UPtv movie! Our writers are so talented!)

We're also delighted to publish two great flash fiction pieces in this final issue, showcasing newer talent. In "Making the First Move," by Ian Cai Mercer, we relive the jitters and exploration of chemistry when a non-date turns into a first date. And in "The Unexpected" we are gifted with this heartbreakingly beautiful story about treasuring your loved ones and doing everything you can to celebrate important milestones, in a piece that brought this editor to tears. So understated in words, yet so impactful in its delivery.

Julie Pitzel once again delivers a thought-provoking piece in her "You Read That?" column, showing how perceptions of romance fiction can generate more criticism than other genres, and C.S. DeAvilla returns to us one last time with books she recommends our readers devour while they are waiting for our first romance anthology, "Thankfully in Love," to hit the shelves later this year. (Bookmark *www. heartskiss.com* to keep updated on all our release news.)

And with that, I thank you, dearest readers and writers. What a wonderful love story we have had with you, and hears to many more romances in the future!

Rick R. Reed draws inspiration from the lives of gay men to craft stories that quicken the heartbeat, engage emotions, and keep the pages turning. Although he dabbles in horror, dark suspense, and comedy, his attention always returns to the power of love. He's the award-winning and bestselling author of more than fifty works of published fiction and is forever at work on yet another book. Lambda Literary has called him: "A writer that doesn't disappoint…" You can find him at www.rickrreedreality.blogspot.com. Rick lives in Palm Springs, CA with his beloved husband and their fierce Chihuahua/Shiba Inu mix.

HEART'S KISS INTERVIEWS RICK R. REED

by Lezli Robyn

Lezli Robyn: Good afternoon, Rick. It is an absolute pleasure to be able to interview you for our magazine. We should start off with the first obvious question: how did you start your writing career?

Rick R. Reed: My love for writing began with a passion for stories that began when I was probably about four years old. I wrote my first short story when I was about six, first play in fourth grade, and I kept my fifth grade classmates enthralled by reading to them aloud a serial novella I wrote about a young girl's kidnapping. My first publication came in 1991 with *Obsessed* in Dell's lauded horror line, Abyss. *Penance* quickly followed. Since then, I have been writing what I cared most about: gay themed romance and sometimes, romance with a dark twist. To date, I have more more than forty books in print, with digital-only shorts and novellas doubling that number.

LR: Since your start in 1991, how many novels have you now written?

RR: Novels only (I've also done digital shorts, anthologies, and short story collections): Let's go with 40 novels and several short story collections.

LR: Which book have you written has had the most impact on you, in the writing of it, and why?

RR: My most recent, *Unravelling*, because it's based on my own coming out in the 1980s. It was painful to go back and revisit the pain of that time—plus it was the era when AIDS was a death sentence and that was always a dark cloud on the horizon.

LR: What is your writing process?

RR: I aim for 1,000 words a day when I'm writing a book. I usually surpass that, but it's a bar I know I can meet. I'm a morning person, so I like to work then with no music or other distractions (other than my dog Kodi, who's always on the chair behind me, usually sleeping and inspiring). I can't write for more than two or three hours because I know the quality would suffer.

LR: What is the hardest part of the writing process to you?

RR: Getting started. I can find a million things to do other than just getting started on my creative work for the day. I learned procrastination at my mama's knee.

LR: What made you want to write romance, as a genre?

RR: I wanted to tell stories drawn from my life and people I knew. I wanted my romances to be marked by a genuine connection to real gay life, which is why I consider myself an #ownvoices writer.

LR: If you had to pick a favorite book of yours, what would it be? Why would it be your favorite? (I know they are all your babies but let's pretend you HAD to pick one.)

RR: I'd pick the ones that are drawn most closely from my own life and experience, because they're closest to my heart. So, in no particular order: *Caregiver*, *Blink*, *Unraveling*, *Raining Men*, *Legally Wed*, and *The Perils of Intimacy*.

LR: What is next for you? What is your next book to be published and when? What are you writing next?

RR: I have a slew of books coming out in 2020 because of the implosion of the publisher I was with for a decade (and more than 30 books). I asked that my rights be returned on all of them when they were failing to pay me (and still are, as well as hundreds of other authors, but I don't really want to delve into that). But all of those books will be coming back out this year, mainly from Nine Star Press and JMS Books. New editions will be released more than once a month.

As far as new, *Unravelling* was just published on January 13, 2020 and has been getting a great response.

And, last but not least, I'm currently almost finished with *The Man from Milwaukee*, a literary horror novel about a young man in Chicago who becomes obsessed with serial killer Jeffrey Dahmer the summer of his arrest. It's…different.

Copyright © 2020 by Lezli Robyn.

Melinda Curtis is an award-winning, USA Today *bestselling author of over sixty romance titles. She writes sweet romance for Harlequin, sweet romantic comedy, and fun, sexy sports romances. Sign up for her book release newsletter and download two free reads.*

HEART'S KISS INTERVIEWS MELINDA CURTIS

by Lezli Robyn

Lezli Robyn: Hello, Melinda. Thank you for agreeing to be our last interview for Heart's Kiss magazine. Your contributions to our magazine gave us some wonderful happily-ever-afters and we're so thank you for your stories. The best way to start off this interview is to ask you, how did you start your writing career?

Melinda Curtis: I read a horrible book by an author who shall remain nameless and wondered if I could do better. Not knowing how to start a writing career, I then read a lovely book by Susan Crosby, who happened to have a PO Box listed on her reader appreciation page. She lived thirty miles from me (and I live in the middle of nowhere). I sent her a card, asking her how to begin a writing career and she mentored me.

LR: Since your start in 2002, how many novels have you now written?

MC: Now you're making me feel my age. I've written, published or sold over sixty titles.

LR: Which book have you written has had the most impact on you, in the writing of it, and why?

MC: The book *Summer Kisses* is very personal to me. The hero had never had anyone close to him die until his grandfather became ill. At the time I wrote the book, my husband was going on the same emotional journey with his sister, who had terminal cancer.

LR: Which writing accomplishment (award, sales, recognition, milestone) has affected you the most? Why did it have such an impact on you?

MC: This is a hard question to answer. I've won awards (Holt medallion for best first book), sold to two different traditional publishers (Harlequin, Forever Romance), and had a book made into a movie. I guess if you stick around long enough, something good is bound to happen.

LR: What is your writing process?

MC: I approach writing like many people approach dieting—a different method for each book. Sometimes I need to noodle a book before beginning to write. Other books spring to life on page one. And others refuse to come to me without me drafting by hand.

LR: What is the hardest part of the writing process to you?

MC: The middle of the book. Invariably, the closer I get to page 100, the more I feel it's the worst book ever written.

LR: If you had to pick a favorite book of yours, what would it be? Why would it be your favorite? (I know they are all your babies but let's pretend you HAD to pick one.)

MC: At the moment, I'm particularly fond of *And Then He Kissed Me*. It has my trademark humor with sassy (sexy without sex), and an Ecuadorian billionaire hero who needed a plucky heroine to take him down a notch.

LR: If you were able to pick one of the romances in your novels to have as your own, which would you pick?

MC: I think *Doggone Christmas*, which has magical dog biscuits and a matchmaking Saint Bernard. Falling in love can sweep you off your feet and hearing a dog's voice in your head—dispensing love advice, no less—would be crazy-good fun.

LR: When you write romance novels, you create the two leading characters to fit each other perfectly, even if they are opposites. What if you had to pair two people from two separate novels you have written? Can you think of a heroine from one novel and a hero from another you would put together as a couple? Why would they work?

MC: Shane Monroe from *Lassoed by the Would-Be Rancher* would be a handful for any of my heroines, but if he had to be matched with someone other than Franny Clark, I'd put him with someone who'd exasperate him, like nerdy scientist Lorelei Spencer in *You May Now Kiss the Bridesmaid*.

LR: So like your close friend, and fellow Harlequin author and *Heart's Kiss* contributor, I hear one of your novels has been turned into a movie! That must have been quite the thrill for you. How did that come about?

MC: I had absolutely nothing to do with it! I heard the production company was looking for a winery book and Harlequin proposed *Dandelion Wishes*. I do have two other indie novels being looked at for translation into either movie or TV series. Very hush-hush, exciting stuff.

LR: What was it like to be on the set of this movie? I cannot imagine how it must feel to see your characters come to life.

MC: It is very surreal to watch the actors bring my characters to life. What was truly mind-blowing though was the depth to which they researched their character's backstory without having read the book. I was able to watch them be interviewed for promo spots and they talked about their backstories as if they had read the book! Truly amazing.

LR: When can we watch this wonderful movie of yours and on what channel?

MC: Coming this spring to UPtv.

LR: What is next for you? What is your next book to be published and when? What are you writing next?

MC: Last year was a big push for me. Translated, this year I'm feeling a little over-exposed. I have 10 books releasing from January 1 to June 1, and another 5-6 in the second half of the year. My first full release from Forever Romance, *Can't Hurry Love*, is dropping March 31. This is a small town rom-com where the meet-cute is the sheriff responding to a call of a woman burning her dead husband's underwear in a bonfire in her driveway.

Copyright © 2020 by Lezli Robyn.

Kayla Perrin *is a multi-published, award-winning* USA Today *and* Essence® *bestselling author with over 50 novels and novellas in print. She is a trailblazer in the African-American fiction arena. She has written for many major publishers including St. Martin's Press, HarperCollins Publishers, and Harlequin. In 2001, after only four years in the business, Kayla was awarded the* Romantic Times *Career Achievement Award for excellence in multicultural romance. In 2007, her novel,* Midnight Dreams, *was the Borders bestselling multicultural romance of the year. In 2011, she received the prestigious Harry Jerome Award in Canada for excellence in the arts.*

ONE MORE NIGHT WITH YOU

by Kayla Perrin

CHAPTER ONE

In an instant, my world was shattered.

I'm pregnant.

Clarissa's declaration sent me falling from Cloud Nine and into the depths of hell.

I was numb as I exited the taxi and somehow made my way into London's Heathrow airport. Numb as I checked in and went through security. Numb as I sat in a chair at the gate waiting for my flight with my knees pulled up to my chest.

I'm pregnant.

I stifled a sob and tried to force my thoughts away from Andre. Away from Clarissa. I was in a public airport, with lots of people around me. I didn't want them looking at me and speculating what kind of hell was going on in my world.

I'm pregnant.

Oh, God. A lump lodged in my throat as I heard Clarissa's devastating words in my mind again. Those words were like a bomb, blowing up my world.

Why was this happening? Why now, when I had fallen in love with Andre? Despite my reservations over our age difference and my fear that he might be a player, I'd taken a leap and had given him all of me. And what I'd found with him had been nothing short of amazing.

Until Clarissa's bombshell.

I didn't even remember getting on the plane. All I could think about was how one moment had changed everything. I'd started this trip with such elation. Now I was ending it in despair.

On the plane, I curled up on my seat and closed my eyes. I didn't want to talk to anyone. My pain was intense, overwhelming. I was in a dark place, and I desperately wished that I could turn back the clock and change things.

If I could, I would turn back the clock and not have Andre meet me in Paris. Because that's where it all had started.

Where I'd started to fall for him.

My heart ached at the very thought of erasing what I had shared with Andre. No, there was no way I would do that. Despite what I was feeling now, I couldn't bring myself to really wish that we hadn't connected the way we had. What I'd shared with him was too special. No, if I had the power, I'd erase Andre ever being involved with Clarissa. Because it had taken me forty years, but I finally found the man that I knew I wanted to spend the rest of my life with.

Except that wasn't going to happen now. Because the hopes and dreams I'd put in the future were crashing and burning.

When the plane landed at Baltimore Washington International, I debated turning on my phone. I knew, just knew, that Andre would have reached out to me. And the rational part of me—the part that wanted to spare myself any more pain—didn't want to hear from him. But the other part—the part that loved him—*wanted* to hear his voice. It wasn't like I was walking away from him because I didn't want to be with him. Which made the reality of the situation that much harder.

The man sitting beside me on the plane probably thought I was a snob, because I had turned toward the widow and stayed that way for the entire flight. I wasn't in the mood for any small talk with a stranger.

The ping sounded, letting all of us on the plane know that we were now free to rise and gather our luggage. While people around me began to open the overhead storage compartments and gather their belongings, I finally decided to turn on my cell phone. I needed to reach out to my friends, hopefully see them as soon as possible.

I was going to need their support.

Once my phone had powered up, I heard the familiar chirps letting me know that I had a number of text messages. I scanned my notifications. I had four text messages from Andre, which didn't surprise me. But the six texts from Vivica did.

Six texts? My eyebrows shot up as concern filled me. Vivica knew I was in London for the weekend. Why would she have contacted me so many times?

I quickly accessed my message log. I saw the last message first.

> I KNOW, I KEEP TEXTING AND CALLING. SORRY, IT'S JUST THAT YOU NEED TO CALL ME ASAP. OKAY?

I frowned, then scrolled upward to see the first of her string of messages.

> BELLA, I'M NOT SURE IF YOU GOT MY RAMBLING VOICEMAIL, BUT I FIGURED MAYBE YOU'RE CHECKING YOUR TEXTS. I HATE TO DISTURB YOU WHILE YOU'RE OFF ON YOUR ROMANTIC GETAWAY, BUT YOU NEED TO CONTACT ME AS SOON AS YOU GET BACK. SOMETHING BAD HAS HAPPENED. HOLLY NEEDS YOU.

What? I quickly read the next message.

> I SWEAR, MIKE IS AN ASS. YOU WON'T BELIEVE WHAT HE DID. ALL I CAN SAY IS THAT HOLLY IS A WRECK. SHE'S COMPLETELY LOSING IT AND SHE NEEDS YOU. WE BOTH DO.

And the next message.

> I HOPE YOU CHECK YOUR MESSAGES BEFORE YOU GO HOME. I HATE TO BE THE BEARER OF BAD NEWS AFTER SUCH AN AMAZING TRIP, BUT YOU REALLY NEED TO COME OVER HERE AS SOON AS YOU LEAVE THE AIRPORT.

Her second to last message read:

OOPS, FORGOT TO SAY WHERE *HERE* IS. WE'RE AT MY PLACE. CALL ME AS SOON AS YOU CAN, AND PLEASE COME OVER AS SOON AS YOU CAN.

Good God, what had Mike done? The messages were cryptic, but it was clear that he had done something to jeopardize his and Holly's marriage.

An affair? Holly had been concerned that he was stepping out on her. Or had he done something else?

As other passengers began to disembark, I got to my feet. I had a focus now, and I was grateful for it. As much as I was grieving, this was a distraction.

Not that I wanted to see my friend suffering. Not at all. But I was glad that I didn't have to go home or to a hotel room and wallow. I could focus on being there for Holly.

Once I was off the plane with my travel bag, I punched in Vivica's number, then put the phone to my ear. She didn't answer. The phone went to voicemail.

"Viv, it's Bella. Just touched down and got your messages. No need to call me back. I'm on my way to your place."

CHAPTER TWO

When I got to Vivica's house and she threw open the door, it hit me just how bad the news was. Vivica's eyes were puffy—indicating that she had been crying—something I didn't expect.

"Sweetie," I said without preamble. "It's that bad?"

Vivica nodded. "First, my divorce this year. Now this. I'm emotional."

I stepped forward, and drew her into an embrace. "My God, what happened?"

"Oh, Bella. If it was just an affair, that'd be one thing. But Mike wants out of the marriage."

I released her, saying, "What?"

"Holly took your advice, planned this romantic getaway for her and Mike for next weekend. Only Mike up and told her he couldn't go. When she demanded to know why, he point blank told her that he's not in love with her anymore. And get this—he said he's leaving her for his secretary." Vivica snorted in disgust. "How freakin' unoriginal."

My jaw damn near hit the floor. "Tell me you're lying."

"I wish I was."

"It's over, just like that?" I asked.

"No discussion, no counseling," Vivica said. "Fucking ass."

My heart broke for my friend. "Poor Holly. She must be devastated. Where is she?"

"She's in the spare bedroom. This all went down yesterday. She didn't sleep much, and neither did I."

"I can imagine."

"I think she finally fell asleep from exhaustion, though," Vivica said.

"I'll go check on her anyway."

But as I stepped into the house, I saw her. She was descending the staircase, her hair an utter mess, her eyes bloodshot.

Emotion clogged my throat. Holly, who had always seemed so strong, stood there looking fragile and destroyed.

"Oh, hon." I started toward her immediately, my arms outstretched.

Holly began to sob, and I hurried to pull her into my arms. As she cried, I rubbed her back and held her and let her get it all out. "I'm so sorry, sweetie."

"Did I push him away?" she asked, her voice small and quivering.

"No!" I insisted. Easing back, I looked at her, surprised that she was even blaming herself. I put my hands on her shoulders and stared into her eyes. "You did nothing wrong. Nothing to deserve this."

"Why would he do this to me?"

"I don't know, Holly," I said, wishing I had answers for her. "But this is on Mike. Not you. Don't blame yourself."

Holly's body trembled. "I gave him *everything*. How am I supposed to go on?"

Then she buried her head against my shoulder and started to cry again. As I held her tightly in my arms, I couldn't think of anything to say. All I could think about in that moment was Andre, how I had given him everything, only to have him ripped from my life.

How was *I* going to go on?

At least my relationship with him had been short lived, and I didn't have any children with him.

Children.

I'm pregnant.

My stomach roiled.

It didn't matter that I hadn't spent years loving Andre. My heart was broken just as if I had. Because in my heart I knew that he was the one for me. And now another woman was having his baby.

Holly raised her head and stepped out of my embrace. "I hate him. I want to claw his eyes out with my bare hands."

"Girl, I hear that." I put my arm around her and led her to the nearby sofa, where I sat her down. "But let's concentrate on you. Have you eaten?"

"I'm not hungry," she replied, not missing a beat.

"She's refused food all day," Vivica said.

"You need to eat something," I told her.

Vivica said, "I've got turkey and ham slices in the fridge. I can make you a sandwich."

"I'm not hungry," Holly repeated, stressing the words.

"Hey," I said gently. "You need to eat something. If you don't want a sandwich, how about some eggs?"

"I can make you an omelet," Vivica suggested.

"I want wine," Holly said.

I glanced at Vivica, saw her look of concern. Then I faced Holly and said, "I don't think wine's what you need right—"

"That's exactly what I need!" Holly snapped. "I need wine, or beer. Or better yet, vodka. I just want to forget."

I exchanged another concerned look with Vivica, whose eyes conveyed to me that she thought we should give Holly what she needed. At least for now. I gave a slight nod.

"I've got white wine," Vivica said. "Not your favori—"

"Bring me the bottle," Holly said.

I stayed with Holly as Vivica went into the kitchen. Holly eased her head down onto the sofa's armrest and closed her eyes.

If what I was feeling was so devastating, I could only imagine how much worse it was to be in Holly's shoes. She and Mike had been married for a decade, and had two children.

Leaving Holly on the sofa to get some rest, I got up and joined Vivica in the kitchen.

"Pour me one, too," I told her.

"I don't know how to help her," Vivica whimpered.

"How can we help her?" I asked. "Mike has just pulled the rug out from under her world. There's nothing we can do to make that better for her, except be here for her. Same as we were there for you."

Vivica poured a second glass of wine and passed it to me. "It's just…I've never seen her like this."

"I know. She's always been the strongest of all of us, which makes it really hard to see her like this." I sighed softly, then downed a liberal sip of the wine. "Where are the boys?"

"With her mother," Vivica responded.

"Where's Mike?"

"Probably with his whore." Vivica snorted in derision. "He drops a bomb on Holly's world, yet he moves on, unscathed? Why the hell would he leave his wife for his secretary? Holly's brilliant, a great mom. She left a career in law to raise their kids because he wanted that. Now he does this to her? I don't get it."

It was the kind of question for which there was no logical answer. Men left beautiful and successful women all the time, and there was no rhyme or reason for it. "That's the million dollar question, isn't it?"

"Let me give Holly her wine," Vivica said. "I should probably slip something in here to help her sleep…"

I followed Vivica out of the kitchen and into the living room. She sat on the sofa beside Holly and said, "Here, hon. I've got your wine."

But Holly didn't move. It took no more than a few seconds for us to realize that she was asleep. "She's out cold," I commented. "That's good. At least while she's sleeping, she's getting a break from her nightmare."

"Unless she's dreaming about Mike."

I shook my head. "Naw, she looks too peaceful. Like she's in a dead sleep from pure exhaustion."

"I hope so." Vivica faced me. "Oh, sweetie. I can see the stress on your face. I'm sorry you had to get off the plane and head right here to this drama. How was London?"

The question caught me off guard, and for a few seconds, I couldn't even speak. Vivica looked at me curiously. "Um," I began. "It was fine."

Vivica's look of curiosity intensified. "Fine?"

"I'm distracted right now," I explained. "Given what's happening with Holly."

"I get that." Pausing, Vivica seemed to study me. "But why do I get the sense that there's something you're not telling me?"

I glanced at Holly, and satisfied that she was out cold, I wandered toward the front window and stood in front of the loveseat. I stared out at the tree-lined street. "London is beautiful," I began without preamble. "The hotel was right across from Hyde Park, and wow, talk about a stunning hotel."

"And Andre?" Vivica asked, sounding a tad impatient. "How did it go with both of you?"

"How did it go?" I repeated, and knew that the moment I'd spoken the words, Vivica would realize I was stalling.

"Now I *know* something's up," Vivica said. "You're repeating what I'm saying. What happened?" Her eyes narrowed. "Oh, no. Another woman?"

I didn't speak. Suddenly, I couldn't.

"So after all this time, he turns out to be a player—"

"No," I interjected. I spoke around the lump that had lodged in my throat. Glancing in Holly's direction, I wasn't sure if I should get into it right now. But as I faced Vivica again, saw her eyes boring into me with concern, I knew she wouldn't let the matter drop.

With a sigh of resignation, I sank onto the loveseat. Then I dropped my bomb. "Clarissa's pregnant."

Vivica's eyes widened. "What did you say?"

"Clarissa. She showed up in London. Which was amazing, by the way." I paused to keep my composure, because I didn't want to fall apart. "Everything between me and Andre was…perfect. Until Clarissa said that she's pregnant."

Vivica sank onto the sofa beside me, her forehead scrunched as she looked at me. She was speechless.

"So, there you have it." A tear escaped my eye, and I brushed it away.

"Oh, God," Vivica said. "If you don't want to be here right now—"

"Of course I want to be here," I interjected. "Holly needs me, and there's no place I'd rather be. Her marriage is falling apart. What's a lifetime compared to a couple of months?"

I said the words in part to convince myself, but it wasn't working. Two months with Andre had felt like a lifetime.

"Go ahead," I said. "Tell me you told me so."

"I would never say that, Bella."

"But you thought I was making a mistake," I pointed out. "He might not be a player, but here I am, still hurt." I sipped some wine. "I feel stupid for ever thinking things would work out with Andre."

"So what happened?" Vivica asked gently. "He found out Clarissa's pregnant and he dumped you?"

I shook my head. "He denied the baby's his. He still wants to be with me."

"Wait—what?"

"But how can I?" I pressed on. "God, the one thing I can't give him. The one thing. And this… this heifer can?"

"So you're walking away from him," Vivica said, for clarification.

"I can't come between him and his baby, Viv."

For a long while, Vivica said nothing. She sat with her wine glass raised, a frown on her face. Finally, she spoke. "This isn't the 1940s. You wouldn't be the first person to be involved with a man who has children with another woman."

I shook my head. "I can't be that person, Viv. The one who comes between a father and his child."

"But you said he still wants to be with you."

"I thought about this the entire flight back home," I said. "Andre already hates Clarissa. If I don't walk away, he'll never try to resolve this with her. He'll walk away from his child." I paused. "And who knows, maybe they can work things out."

"So you've decided to become a martyr? You're going to sacrifice your happiness for Clarissa and her baby?"

I didn't answer, just finished off my wine. Then I got to my feet. "I need another drink."

I brought the bottle back over to the loveseat, where I filled my glass, then extended the bottle toward Vivica, offering to fill her glass as well.

"No, I'm good," she said. "What you said before, about not being able to give Andre a baby—"

"Please," I said. "I can't…"

Vivica nodded slowly. "Okay. Why don't you tell me how this whole thing with Clarissa went down? Why was she even at the wedding?"

"She wasn't supposed to be." I blew out a frazzled breath. My head was beginning to throb. Just thinking about what had happened was causing me physical stress. "She just showed up in London. Uninvited, and unwanted. I guess she was originally invited to the wedding with Andre, before they broke up. And girl, you should have seen the dress she wore." I guffawed. "Trifling ho was trying to upstage the bride. You should have seen the bride's face. Andre's face. No one was happy that Clarissa was there, and I don't know what she was trying to prove. That she's still a part of Andre's inner circle?"

Vivica scowled. "The nerve of some people never fails to surprise me."

"Clarissa was like a gnat, annoyingly buzzing around and trying to get time with Andre. She said she needed to talk to him, but he wasn't having that. He told her he didn't want to talk." I paused and closed my eyes, a wave of fresh pain washing over me. "I was on my way to the taxi this morning, saying goodbye to Andre, and she came out of nowhere. That's when she told him she was pregnant." My voice cracked as I finished speaking. I quickly drank more wine.

"Oh, sweetie." Vivica rubbed my forearm. "I'm so sorry."

I tipped my head back as I finished off my second glass of wine.

"Maybe it isn't Andre's," Vivica went on. "She's a piece of work. How do you know she's not lying about being pregnant? People like Clarissa hate to lose. If she wants Andre back and you're standing in the way…"

I held up a hand to silence my friend. "And if she is pregnant?"

"Is it really the end of the world?"

"Yes, Viv. It is. You remember Cynthia, don't you?"

"How could I forget?" she asked.

Cynthia had been a friend of ours in college. During her sophomore year, she'd gotten pregnant. She learned about her pregnancy after she and Darren had broken up, but she'd hoped that Darren would be willing to work things out with her for the sake of their child. In the end, Darren—who'd already been involved with someone else—had walked away from her, his child, and his responsibility. He'd gone so far as to move across the country to get away from her. Devastated, Cynthia had moved to Buffalo, New York to live with her mother. She'd left DC—and us—behind.

"We were livid with Darren," I said. "We couldn't understand what kind of man would walk away from his baby. But he wanted his new relationship, and totally turned his back on Cynthia."

"And we were pissed with his new girlfriend," Vivica added, frowning.

"Exactly." I poured myself more wine. I needed it. "I know that there's huge animosity between Andre and Clarissa, and him being involved with me is not going to help matters. That baby deserves to have a father."

"I hate that you feel you have to sacrifice your happiness. Why don't you deserve to be happy?"

I said nothing. Just drank more of my wine.

Vivica's eyes narrowed as she studied me. "You like him. Really really like him."

"I guess I'm just destined to be forever alone," I said. And with those words, the tears fell.

"Don't say that," Vivica said. "You get your mother out of your head. Good grief, I don't know why she ever said that to you."

"Not everyone ends up in a relationship," I pointed out.

Vivica sighed. "Honestly, I don't think it has to be the end of the world if Clarissa's pregnant."

"What's the point in starting a relationship with a man who's about to have a child with his ex?" I shook my head. "I have to count my losses, and be thankful that I learned about this now before things got too serious."

"Things aren't serious now?" Vivica's question was rhetorical.

"You know what I'm saying."

Vivica leaned forward on the sofa, resting her arms on her knees. "Find out first," she said. "Clarissa could be lying. Hell, she probably is lying. And even if she is pregnant, who knows if it's Andre's? Seriously?"

Slowly, I shook my head. "I can't be that woman. The one who gets involved with a guy who's recently knocked up some other woman. No, I have to step aside, give them a chance to work things out."

"Exactly."

At the sound of Holly's voice, both Vivica and I looked in her direction. I was stunned that she was awake.

"If Andre's ex is pregnant, you have to walk away," Holly went on as she sat up. "Look at my situation. Mike's secretary knows that he's married, that we have two young boys, and yet she's taking him away from me. Taking him away from his kids."

My chest tightened. Even though that was the same conclusion I had come to, I felt a fresh wave of pain when I heard Holly say it.

"I think Bella should find out first," Vivica said. "Find out if Clarissa is really pregnant with Andre's child."

"Cut your losses," Holly said. "Cut your losses and move on."

The words were direct, and what I needed to hear, and yet they made my eyes fill with tears again.

"Clarissa's crazy," Vivica stressed. "Why let a crazy person keep her from the man she loves?"

"That's another reason to walk away," Holly said, matter-of-fact. "You want that kind of drama in your life? Not to mention the age difference. Bella, I thought this was just a fling."

"Holly!" Vivica scolded.

"No," I said. "It's okay." I needed to hear the harsh truth so that I wouldn't waiver from my decision.

"Walk away," Holly said. "Walk away, unless you want to end up hurt like me."

CHAPTER THREE

I finished off that bottle of wine and had half of another one. Then I went to bed on the pullout sofa in Vivica's basement—where I hoped that sleep would give me peace.

Holly's directness—even during her own pain—had me facing some hard realities. Wasn't my relationship with Andre supposed to be a fling? How had I gotten so attached? I was ten years older. When had I started thinking I could plan a future with him?

But despite every negative thought I had, I couldn't deny the truth. I hadn't planned to fall in love, yet it had happened. I hadn't planned to fall for a younger guy, but why did age matter? It wasn't like I was forty years older.

Then there was Vivica, encouraging me not to walk away. I didn't know what I should do.

I only knew that I wasn't yet ready to hear from Andre, so I kept my phone off, because I knew he was bound to reach out to me. He loved me. I didn't doubt that. And I knew he would try to convince me to stay with him.

The next morning, I had a pounding headache in addition to my aching heart. A new day only brought the reality home that my life had irrevocably changed.

I'd weighed the pros and the cons. And I'd come to the conclusion that it was best to end things with Andre now. I had to. And though my head knew that it was for the best, my heart…oh, my heart.

"Keep focused," I told myself as I got ready for work. "It's better that you end things now, rather than later." If I continued to see Andre, my feelings would no doubt grow even stronger.

Holly's affirmation last night that I should end things was like an exclamation point on my own opinion. However, when Vivica hugged me at her door that morning, she whispered, "It doesn't have to be the end of the world if Clarissa is pregnant."

"Viv, you know I love you," I said, "but some things just aren't meant to be."

I remembered all too well how much pain Cynthia had gone through when Darren had walked away from her because he'd been involved with someone else. That was something that had weighed heavily on my heart as I'd tried to sleep. I didn't care about Clarissa, but the baby was innocent in this situation. The baby deserved a father.

I was glad when I got to work, hopeful that a busy day of company business would distract me from my personal life.

"Morning, Gretchen," I said to my secretary as I strolled toward my office door.

"Morning," she replied. Her eyes narrowing, she lowered her glasses down the bridge of her nose to better see me. "What are you wearing?"

Because I hadn't gone home, I was wearing one of Vivica's dresses. Vivica was more voluptuous than I was, so the only options that would work were her lycra leggings, form-fitting tops, and body-hugging dresses. I'd opted for a black dress—a neutral enough color—but it clung to me like a second skin. The flat black sandals didn't fit with the outfit, but the only other option I'd had had been my glitzy shoes I'd brought to London for the wedding.

"I thought I had my heels in the car," I said by way of explanation. And a lame one at that.

"That's some dress," Gretchen said. "Very sexy."

Apparently the fact that I was wearing a light sweater did nothing to detract from the tightness of the dress—which was not the type of outfit I wore to work.

"Oh," I said. "Just thought I'd do something different today."

"New man in your life?" Gretchen asked, her eyebrows raising hopefully. She was in her late fifties, had been happily married for years, and was constantly hopeful that I would find that special man to settle down with.

I had found him—but he'd been ripped from my life.

My chest tightening, I replied, "No."

"Keep dressing like that, and it shouldn't be long," Gretchen said, giving me a knowing look.

I offered her a small smile, then continued into my office. I closed the door behind me, slumped into my leather chair and dropped my head down onto my desk.

After sulking for a good minute, I sat up straight. "Snap out of it," I told myself.

Then I fired up my computer, hoping that losing myself in work would help me to forget about my broken heart.

I left the building only to grab a sandwich and a coffee down the street, then went back to the safety of my office. Behind closed doors.

My secretary had checked on me right after I'd returned from lunch, interrupting me to ask if everything was okay.

"Honestly, I don't feel very well," I told her. Which wasn't a lie. "And I've got a lot of work to do." Also not a lie. "I don't want to be disturbed by anyone, unless it's an emergency."

"Sure thing," she said, looking at me with concern.

My head jerked up when, just after two o'clock, the door flew open.

"Miss Sinclair."

"Gretchen, I thought I told you that I didn't want to be disturbed."

"He said it's an emergency."

"Who said it's an emergency?"

And then he came into view—pushing past Gretchen and stepping into my office. My stomach did a somersault as I stared at Andre.

"I did," he said. "The man whose calls you won't return."

Gretchen moved to stand in front of him, holding her hands up as if they could stop Andre's muscular body. "Sir—sir, I told you to wait outside. You can't just barge in here like this."

"Do you want me to leave?" Andre asked, not even acknowledging Gretchen with a look. His eyes were steadfast on me.

"Sir," Gretchen said, her tone firm. "I will call security."

"It's okay, Gretchen," I told her. "Please, give us a minute. And close the door behind you."

Gretchen looked at me, confused, and I nodded to let her know that I was okay. She walked out of the office, and Andre quickly closed the door.

My breath caught in my throat as he stalked over to my desk.

"You plan on never talking to me again?" he asked.

"I…" My voice trailed off. I didn't know what to say. Never talking to him again of course seemed illogical and unlikely, but at least for the time being it was the only way for me to move on.

"I need an answer," Andre said.

I looked up at him, at his powerful body—and at the anger brewing in his eyes as he stood over me. The way he was looking down on me made me feel small.

As if this was my fault.

"I'm not the one who got someone else pregnant," I said.

"Even if that's true, you make it seem as though it was while we were together. That I cheated on you."

I blew out a frustrated breath. "No, that's not what I'm saying. I…" I paused, inhaling a deep breath. "It's just…things have gotten complicated."

Andre rounded the desk and turned my chair in his direction. I gasped at the unexpectedness of it. And when he lowered himself onto his haunches and placed his hands on my thighs, heat spread through me. The idea of him down low like that in front of my legs, with easy access because of the dress I was wearing…. I swallowed.

"Things may be complicated," he said, "but the one thing that isn't is how I feel about you."

I stared at Andre, but didn't know what to say.

"Can you really walk away from me and not look back?" he asked.

"Sometimes, it's the best thing to do."

"You don't mean that."

I drew in a deep breath. Tried to remember my resolve. "Yes, I do."

"I look at you, wearing this dress, and I'm already damn near going out of my mind." His fingers disappeared under the hem, touching my skin. "I think about how good we are together, and how much I don't want to lose that. And you're telling me that walking away is the best thing to do?"

"I didn't say it was going to be easy."

His eyes went to where his hands were. He pushed the dress up a little, and I was powerless to stop him. "Damn, I'm distracted trying to talk to you while you're dressed like this." I heard his ragged breath. "Baby, I don't believe Clarissa. She's just trying to screw things up for us. For me. She's angry because I dumped her."

"And if she *is* pregnant? With your child? What then?"

Andre didn't speak right away. I saw disappointment and confusion and anxiety flash in his eyes. Which told me what I needed to know. With me in his life, I would give him an easy out. A way to walk away from his responsibility. I understood that he didn't love Clarissa, and there was no question as to why not. But still. A baby was innocent.

"Babies deserve to have their fathers in their lives." His fingers pushed higher, and despite myself, I uttered a little moan. "Andre, you can't do this to me."

"Why?" His voice held a challenge. "Because you're immune to my touch? Because you don't want me anymore?"

"I never said I didn't want you."

"Then don't walk away from us." His fingers made circles on my inner thigh. "From this."

I wanted to spread my legs wide and let him have his wicked way with me, right here in my office. Which was madness. Every time I was near Andre, I wanted to throw caution to the wind and let my desire overtake reason.

It was that very thought that had my mind snapping back to the real issue here—the one I couldn't hide from, no matter how much he turned me on. "Andre, we can't."

He eased up and grabbed a hold of the armrests of my chair and positioned his upper body over mine so that his face was inches away. "How can you expect me to stay away?"

Such a simple question, and it was absolutely profound. After what we'd shared together, how *could* I expect him to stay away? And yet, it was exactly the connection we'd had that made me believe that Andre would put Clarissa on the backburner and turn his back on his child. I had to ensure that he would do the right thing.

"Andre—"

His lips came down on mine, silencing my protests. I stiffened in the chair, but only for a brief moment. The next moment, my lips melted against his. Because I wanted this. From the moment he'd barged into my office, I had wanted this. I had never stopped wanting him. How, as he'd asked, could I truly walk away from him?

I snaked my hands around his neck and held on as he kissed me. His tongue delved into my mouth, urgently twisting with my own tongue. Lord, this man was so sweet. So damn fine. Everything about him stoked my inner fires.

The sudden and sharp knocking on the door caused both of us to jump apart. "Ms. Sinclair?" Gretchen asked. "Are you okay?"

Andre quickly rose, and I felt a wave of cold wash over me. Was this how I was going to feel for the foreseeable future? Cold and sad without him in my life, in my bed?

"I'm okay," I called.

"Are you sure?"

I didn't know why Gretchen was doing this. Perhaps she felt something was off with Andre and wanted to protect me. Obviously, she knew that he wasn't here regarding business.

I looked up at him. "We can't talk here. We just can't. Please leave."

He held my gaze for a long moment, and I thought he was going to ignore my wishes. But then he gave me a slight nod and headed toward the office door. I quickly stood and straightened my outfit. When he opened the door, Gretchen was standing there as I expected. Andre breezed past her without a word nor a glance. Gretchen turned to look at him as he walked away, then jerked her head back in my direction.

"I'm fine," I said before she could ask me again.

"I thought you said you weren't seeing anyone," she said.

He's not just anyone, was the thought that popped into my mind.

"Gretchen—"

My cell phone rang then. Glancing at it on my desk, I saw Holly's face flashing on my screen. I was glad to have a way to escape Gretchen's questioning. Though she was my secretary, she could be very mother-like. Sometimes too much so. There were times she wanted to know if I was eating enough, if I'd met someone nice, and even if I was getting enough sleep. Things that were not even close to being in her job description.

"Gretchen, I have to take this call. But trust me, I'm okay."

She nodded, then excused herself from my office and closed the door. I quickly swiped my cell phone to accept Holly's call. "Hey, sweetie. How are you?"

"Someone needs to tell this motherfucker that he needs to go."

My back straightened with alarm. "What?"

"I just came back to the house to get something for the kids and Mike is here, trying to steal everything of value!"

"Oh my God."

"You put down that vase," Holly yelled. "You didn't even want it!"

"Call the police," I said.

And then I heard Mike say in the background, "We both know you're not going to stab me. Put the knife down."

"Shit, Holly," I uttered. "You have a knife?"

"He can't just come in here and steal marital property. I have a right to protect what's mine."

Good God, have mercy! "Where are the kids?"

"At my mother's."

"I'm on my way."

CHAPTER FOUR

My office wasn't too far from Holly's house, and I only hoped that World War III didn't break out before I got there. It was never easy navigating through DC traffic, but at least it was early, before rush hour, so I was able to get to Holly's house without too much of a delay.

It was quiet as I made my way up the steps. Eerily so. My heart began to pick up speed. Had the worst happened between the time Holly had called me and I'd gotten here?

I tried the door. It opened, and I stepped inside cautiously, calling out, "Holly? Mike?"

"In here," came Mike's gruff response.

I went forward and turned left past the foyer and into the living room. And that's when I saw Mike sitting on the sofa, his hands folded neatly in his lap. Holly stood in front of him with a butcher knife held out threateningly.

"My God!" I hurried over to her. "What are you doing?"

"He thinks he can screw around on me, then come in here and take my favorite things? If you don't want to be married anymore, why do you care about that vase we got on our honeymoon in China?"

"Because I bought it. And it cost a small fortune."

I glared at Mike. "Don't you do that," I said. "Don't pull that 'I bought this' crap. Marriage is about partnership."

"And I gave up an amazing career for you, asshole," Holly piped in. "I should just stab him right now. I don't care if I go to jail."

My gaze whipped to Holly. "You *do* care if you go to jail." Then I looked at Mike again. "I'm pretty certain you can't start taking things out of the house before any sort of settlement."

"I bought most of the things in this house," he retorted.

"And I gave up my career for you!" Holly shouted. "To raise your children!"

Glaring at Mike, I said, "You're a lawyer. You know better than that. And do you want to get hurt? Because you keep saying stuff like that, and I'm not sure I can hold Holly back."

"Damn straight," Holly quipped.

I understood her frustration, but I needed to do everything in my power to keep her from losing control. So I said gently, "Sweetie, I know you don't want to go to jail today. Don't throw away your future because of an ass." I cast him a sidelong glance. "Now, I'm sure that Mike will agree to leave, and stay somewhere else, and allow you guys to deal with this legally. Because that's what an educated lawyer does. Right, Mike?"

"Whatever," he snapped.

"And you're not going to call the police, either." I gave him a pointed look. "This is the mother of your children, and you did her wrong. Men don't realize how they can screw up a woman's brain by cheating on her and taking her love for granted. You did this, Mike. And you know it. So I expect you to accept your responsibility for the mess you created here, and not be vindictive by calling the police. "

"Fine." Michael glared at me. "Fine, I'll just leave."

"I should just cut him," Holly said. "Make him feel the pain I feel."

I'd never seen Holly like this before. Her world was in a tailspin, all because Mike had devastated her with his betrayal. "I know this hurts, Holly. But he's not worth it."

"I wanted that special fortieth birthday celebration," she said, her voice quavering.

"And you'll get it. Viv and I will make sure you have a great time. I know that right now everything sucks, but we're here for you. Girl, I've got your back."

Holly began to sniffle. Then she lowered the knife from its threatening position.

Mike jumped to his feet. For a moment, I was terrified that he was going to leap forward and grab for the knife, or perhaps tackle Holly to the ground.

But instead of escalating the conflict, he quickly shuffled toward the right, heading toward the front of the house.

"Don't bother coming back," Holly told him. "I'm gonna change the locks."

"You do that, and you and I will have a problem," Mike told her.

"We already have a problem, genius!" Holly yelled.

"Wait, Mike," I said, walking toward the exit of the living room. When I got to the entranceway, I saw that he had paused at the door to listen to what I had to say. "Just in case you're thinking of ignoring what I said and decide to contact the police about what happened here today, I'm a witness. I can attest to the fact that you came here and tried to steal items from the house."

Mike glowered at me. I thought he was going to say something, but he stalked off, slamming the door behind him.

I quickly locked the door, then went back into the living room. With a gasp, Holly dropped the knife and it clattered against the hardwood floor. Then she started to cry.

I took her into my arms and held her, offering her the only comfort I could. "He's not worth it, sweetie. I swear, he's not."

"I gave him everything."

"And what are you thinking? That killing him is going to be the solution to end your pain? You have two kids to think about. Thank God they weren't here."

"I know," Holly said, her voice seeming so feeble. My friend who had always been incredibly strong had been reduced to a vulnerable and weak woman because of Mike. I hated it.

As I led Holly to the sofa and sat with her, I wondered what it was about the power of love that could destroy you so completely. You could go from incredible highs to devastating lows.

As I had with Andre. It was exactly this devastating low that I was trying to spare myself by leaving him now.

But was I really sparing myself any pain when doing the right thing hurt so damn much?

I went into the bathroom and called Vivica once Holly had settled down. I got her voicemail.

"Viv, it's Bella. Call me back as soon as you get this. Holly has pretty much had a meltdown. I got to the house and thought she was about to kill Mike. And that's no exaggeration. She was threatening him with a butcher knife." I sighed. "Look, I think at least one of us should stay with her. I don't think she should be alone."

When I returned to the living room, Holly was still curled up on the sofa where I'd left her. I found a comedy for her on Netflix, and put it on to play. After about twenty minutes, she drifted off during the movie, and I was grateful that she was now at peace. At least for a short while.

Sleep would give her a chance to rest and recuperate, and hopefully she would awake with a new sense of acceptance. With how volatile things were right now, I didn't imagine there was any chance of a reconciliation. And given what Mike had done, I didn't see Holly forgiving him, even if he begged. So she was going to have to try to find a way to make peace with what had happened so that she could let go and move forward.

Easier said than done. And didn't I know it. Although, I wasn't walking away from Andre because of a betrayal. But nonetheless, I had to find a way to let go and move forward as well.

After Holly had been sleeping for about half an hour, I decided to call a locksmith. I didn't know if doing this was legal or not, but for the sake of peace, I figured it was best to change the locks. If Mike was intent on taking items from the matrimonial home, nothing would stop him—if he had a key.

As I waited for the locksmith to arrive, my phone chirped. I thought it was Vivica texting me, but when I looked at my screen, I saw Andre's name.

OUR CONVERSATION ISN'T OVER. CAN WE TALK TONIGHT?

My stomach tightened. This would be so much easier if he just agreed to stay away. At least I had an excuse to avoid him for now. I sent him a reply text

CAN'T. A FRIEND IS HAVING AN EMERGENCY.

It took only a few seconds for his response to pop up on my screen.

EVERYTHING OKAY?

I didn't lie.

NOT REALLY. BUT IT WILL BE.

Seconds passed, and I figured Andre was done texting me. Until my phone chirped again and I saw a new message from him.

IF I CAN HELP IN ANY WAY, LET ME KNOW. I'M HERE FOR YOU, NO MATTER WHAT HAPPENS BETWEEN US.

My heart ached with an intense pang of loss, and my eyes misted. Leaving Andre was going to hurt a lot more because he was being so nice to me.

He was still the man I loved. Unlike my ex, Steven, I didn't have a reason to hate Andre.

And with his words, he was telling me that even if we could only be friends, he would still be there for me.

Had I ever met a man like him? How had Clarissa blown it with someone so incredible?

My fingers poised over the screen of my phone. I wanted to say something, but I didn't know what.

And when my fingers constructed the words, they weren't what I planned.

I APPRECIATE YOUR CONCERN, BUT I'M FINE. THERE'S NOTHING ELSE TO DISCUSS. AS LONG AS CLARISSA IS HAVING YOUR BABY, WE CAN'T BE TOGETHER.

My thumb hovered over the SEND button. God, I couldn't send that to him. It was too harsh.

The doorbell rang.

I peered through the window and saw a van with the locksmith's logo.

I quickly pressed SEND, then put down the phone and headed to the door.

CHAPTER FIVE

Vivica came to join me after she finished work. We both agreed that someone should stay with Holly for the night. I would have stayed, but I really needed to get home and into my own clothes.

We both wanted to make sure that emotionally, Holly was okay. And in case Mike showed back up, we knew she'd need at least one of us there.

"If there are any issues at all, call me," I said to Vivica as I was heading out the door.

"I will," Vivica said. "And I think she'll be able to relax. That pill I gave her…I wasn't quite honest. Sure, it will help her sleep. But it's also an antidepressant. I had a leftover supply after my divorce."

"Very clever," I said. Vivica had produced a pill, told Holly that she needed to take it, and Holly hadn't argued.

"Just call me Dr. Viv." Her smile didn't quite reach her eyes. "When I was going through my divorce, I needed those. I'm leaving Holly with my leftover stash."

I hugged Vivica. "I hope today was the worst of it. And I seriously hope Mike stays away."

Vivica shook her head. "I wonder if Mike feels bad. This kind of animosity—especially when you've got kids—is it worth it?"

"What's worse is that this whole thing came out of left field for Holly," I said. "Mike should have been honest about how he was feeling a long time ago."

"All we can do now is try to keep her sane," Vivica said. "And focused on Jamal and Kwame. The boys are going to need her to be strong."

"Absolutely," I agreed. Then I hugged Vivica again. "Keep me posted."

Thirty minutes later, I was driving into my neighborhood. As I turned onto my street, my stomach tensed. Would I see Andre out, cutting his grass or talking to a neighbor?

I didn't, and I was able to drive into my garage and enter my house without incident.

The first order of business was a shower. As I stood under the spray of warm water, I thought about Andre's words. How he would still be there for me, even if only as friends. I should have felt better, comforted by those words. But strangely, I felt even more pain.

Andre was everything I'd ever wanted in a man. I knew I couldn't be just friends with him. How could I see him and make nice with him? It would be torture. Or, God—seeing him with Clarissa's baby? That would absolutely crush me.

Maybe just breaking up with him wouldn't be enough. Maybe I would also have to sell my house and get out of this neighborhood.

Well, if that's what it took, I would do it.

"Good," I said to Vivica on the other end of the line a couple of hours later. I was in a robe, curled up on my sofa, a glass of wine on the coffee table in front of me. "I'm glad she's calm."

My doorbell rang, and I looked up. Then my pulse quickened.

"It's a rollercoaster for sure," Vivica said. "One minute angry, the next crying. But she's down now, and I think she will be for the night."

I was up and walking to my door, planning to peer through the side window. The doorbell rang again.

"Is someone at your door?" Vivica asked.

"Yeah." Now the knocking started. And as I was able to look through my side window, I saw Andre's unmistakable form. "Um, I have to go."

"Andre?"

"I'll talk to you later."

As I ended the call, Andre knocked the door again. "I know you're in there," he said. "I just saw you looking through the window."

My heart was pounding and butterflies were frantically flying around in my stomach. Taking a deep breath, I opened the door.

Andre's lips parted, as if he'd been about to say something, but stopped when his eyes settled on me. They roamed down the length of my robe, then back up. I tightened the folds around my body.

He met my eyes, looking at me with concern. "You okay?"

I nodded. "I'm okay, but one of my best friends is going through a tough time. She and her husband are splitting. It's gotten ugly."

"Sorry to hear that," Andre said.

"Ten years of marriage, two children." I shook my head, remembering the ugliness I had witnessed today. "It's awful."

"Can I come in?"

I opened my mouth to speak, then halted. "Andre, I don't think that's a good idea."

"So that's just it? You're ready to throw our relationship away, just like that?"

I glanced down, unable to look at him. "Not just like that," I said softly. "Nothing about this is easy."

"Please let me come in."

What he was asking was more than to simply come into my house. He was asking me to let him back into my life. But how could I let my guard down with him, only to be more hurt in the end?

"Andre, I can't."

"Clarissa is lying. I'd bet my life on it."

I looked him in the eye. "That's what you want to think, but you're not sure."

"What if I get you proof, then?" he asked. "Will you stop pushing me away? Or is this your convenient way to dump me after making me fall in love with you?"

The words were like a slap, and I flinched. How could he say that? "No. Of course not."

"Dammit, Bella. I love you. This makes no sense."

Hearing him tell me that he loved me made me think of all that I was losing. I blew out a frazzled breath. "I'm just trying to do the right thing. But if you do get the proof that Clarissa is lying, then that will change things."

"Or maybe it won't."

Confused, I met his gaze. "What does that mean?"

"You were always unhappy about the fact that you're older than I am." He shrugged. "Maybe this just makes it easy for you to walk away from me."

"You know that's not true."

"Do I?" he asked.

"If I didn't love you, I wouldn't be torn up by this. I don't care about our age difference. But I do care about being the reason that a father is not involved in his child's life." My stomach began to clench painfully, just thinking about the reality again. Maybe in a few days or a few weeks I would be better able to handle this. But right now, I couldn't. "I at least…I at least need time. To process everything, to deal with it."

"I'm going to prove that I'm telling the truth. I know Clarissa better than you do, and I don't believe that she's pregnant with my child. I'd bet my house and every penny I have in the bank that she's lying. I wish you would trust me."

"This isn't about trust," I said. "It's about the truth. Either she's pregnant, or she's not."

"All right." He dragged a hand over his face. "As long as you're telling me the truth—that you're not gonna walk away from me if I'm right—I can deal with that." Pausing, he edged closer to me. I thought he was going to kiss me, but instead he stroked my face. "I can't lose you, Bella."

Then he turned and walked down my steps, and I wanted to cry. God help me, I wanted to call out to him, invite him in, and spend the night making love.

I was so damn conflicted. It would be so easy to be selfish and go for what I wanted. Have him in my life, the consequences be damned.

But instead, I watched him walk away.

CHAPTER SIX

It's one thing to tell yourself that you're doing what's right. It's another thing to live with that decision.

I was glum at work over the next two days. In a funk that I couldn't quite shake. Respecting my wishes, Andre didn't try to contact me. But that two days without him in my life felt like an eternity.

If this was how I was feeling now, just being without him for a few days, how was I going to get through the coming weeks and months?

But I had been heartbroken before. I told myself that this too would pass—if this was what was meant to be.

The knock on my office door had me quickly putting my phone face-down on the desk. I'd been looking at a photo of me and Andre. It was a picture of us in London, at the wedding, when I had been spectacularly happy.

Before my world had crashed.

Clearing my throat, I said, "Come in."

Gillian, one of my colleagues, opened the door and peered inside. "You busy?"

"I've got a minute," I told her.

"You okay?" she asked as she began to step into my office.

"Why does everyone keep asking me that?" I'd been hearing non-stop queries of concern over the last couple of days.

"Because you look like your dog died."

"I don't have a dog."

"What's going on?" Gillian asked. "You seem… depressed."

I debated what to say. Clearly, I wasn't very good at hiding my emotions. "A friend of mine is going through a rough time. Her marriage is breaking down. It's got me feeling glum."

"Are you seeing anyone now?"

The question startled me. I hadn't expected Gillian to say that, not after what I'd just told her. My jaw flinched, but I said, "No. I'm not."

"Good." Gillian smiled. "Remember the cousin I wanted you to meet?"

I blinked, confused. She had mentioned a cousin? Suddenly, it came back to me. "He's a director or something?" I asked.

"He produces documentaries."

"Yes, that's right." Gillian had mentioned that she wanted me to meet this cousin, thought he would be perfect for me. The problem was that he lived in LA. However, she figured that we should get together whenever he came to Washington. "He lives in LA, right?"

"Yes, but he's coming to DC this weekend. And he's hoping he can take you to dinner."

For a moment, I was like a deer caught in the headlights…stunned and unsure of how to respond. I didn't want to go on a date with anyone. My heart was breaking.

"I don't know, Gillian," I said. "I'm not really interested in dating."

"You're not getting any younger," she said, then smiled to soften the blow. "Come on. Dexter is *really* looking forward to meeting you. And did I mention he's gorgeous? *And* he's a successful filmmaker?"

I groaned softly. "I don't know, Gillian…"

She narrowed her eyes, looking at me with suspicion. "Are you secretly seeing someone?" she asked. "Maybe that explains your bad mood. Maybe you've got some relationship drama going on."

I did my best not to react to her comment. She was far too intuitive. Or perhaps she'd spoken to Gretchen? "No." I stressed the word, and it wasn't a lie. "I'm not seeing anyone."

"Then why not go to dinner with Dexter?"

Gillian didn't know what I was going through, but maybe she was right. What would it hurt to say yes to dinner? It would certainly help keep my mind off of Andre.

"When does he get to town?" I asked.

"Thursday."

"That's tomorrow."

"He's got a couple of meetings here with lobbyists. He's working on a film about…. Well, he can tell you all about it. He said Friday would be a good day to meet."

I drew in a breath. I didn't want to lead the man on, but what if I liked him? I couldn't pine over Andre forever.

"When he gets to town, have him call me at the office," I said.

Gillian beamed. "He's great, really. You're gonna love him."

I doubted it. But on the other hand, maybe a date was exactly what I needed to help distract me from Andre.

❖

As I drove up to my house after work, I was startled to see someone sitting on my porch. It took only another moment for me to realize who it was.

Clarissa!

I pulled into my driveway and stopped. And I blinked a couple of times before looking at the porch again. Indeed, she was still there.

Clarissa was at my house? Why?

She was already making her way down the steps toward me. I put the window down and said without preamble, "You need to leave."

"We need to talk."

"I have nothing to say to you." She was Andre's problem, not mine. I wanted nothing to do with her.

I noticed that as she descended the steps she put a hand on the small of her back, as though needing extra support. It was then that I also noticed a small belly. She was wearing one of those pregnancy tops, and it looked as though she had a small bulge beneath.

Already? At the wedding in London, she'd been wearing a tight dress, meaning that her pregnancy was not so far along that she was showing. Had her body changed so much in a few days?

It seemed unlikely, but what did I know about pregnancy?

"We can either do this inside your house," Clarissa began, "or here on the street where everyone can bear witness."

I looked through my rearview mirror. Saw Janine standing across the street with her dog. I gritted my teeth. "Give me a second. I have to go inside and open the door."

I pressed the button to put the window up, then hit the remote garage key. The seconds it took the garage to open seemed like hours. But finally, I was able to drive my car into my garage and park.

For a long moment, I sat behind the wheel, breathing heavily. I was livid. How dare Clarissa show up at my place and give me an ultimatum? Was that her modus operandi? She'd done the same thing with Andre when we were in London.

That was the kind of woman she was. A bull in a China shop. If she had something to say, she *would* be heard—no ifs, ands, or buts.

It was a stark reminder of the fact that if I stayed with Andre, I would always have to deal with Clarissa. And she'd be nasty, I was sure.

When I was good and ready, I went into my house. I had not invited Clarissa here. And how dare she threaten me.

I sauntered to my front door. She stood there with her arms folded over her chest, clearly impatient.

I opened the door and held it wide, not saying a word to her.

She walked in and looked around.

"What do you want?" I asked.

She met my gaze, looking me dead in the eye. "You need to stay away from Andre."

"Really?"

"Yes, really. You know I'm carrying his child." She rubbed her small belly.

I swallowed. But I wasn't about to put up with this. "First of all, you don't get to come to my house and tell me what I *need* to do."

"I'm having his baby," she quipped. "With you in the picture—"

"And I get that. But don't think you can boss me around, control me, or use your baby as leverage. Talk to me woman to woman."

I saw her jaw flinch. "Fine. Will you please stay away from Andre? My baby—our baby—deserves a chance to have his father in his life."

My stomach roiled. I wanted Clarissa gone so I could curl up on my sofa and grieve. "For the record," I began, somehow keeping my voice calm, "I have stayed away from Andre. I told him that as long as you're pregnant, we can't be together."

I didn't know why I was telling her this, and when she grinned almost in a gloating manner, I hated even more that I was giving her what she wanted.

But this wasn't about her. It wasn't about her winning and me losing. It was about a baby that deserved a father.

"Well, I'm glad to hear that," she said, and there was definite smugness in her tone.

Just seeing Clarissa here with her pregnancy top and holding her back like she needed support was an utterly painful reminder of the fact that I couldn't have Andre. I wanted her out of my house, and the sooner the better.

"For future reference," I began, "you should always try being nicer to someone when you want something from them. I don't have to back away from Andre. He loves me." I let the words sink in, giving her a small taste of her own medicine. "But I'm gonna do the right thing because that's who I am. You need to be grateful for that."

Her lips tightened, and I could only imagine that the words *Thank you* had rarely ever escaped that mouth of hers. But even as a clear look of discomfort passed over her face, she said, "I appreciate that."

"I know that you and Andre need time to work things out. Just know that I'm not standing in your way."

"I didn't give you any credit," Clarissa said, her tone softening. "You're different. I can see...see why Andre likes you."

I'm not sure why she added the last part, because the look on her face told me that it pained her to say it.

"I appreciate you doing this for the sake of the baby," she went on, and smoothed a hand over her belly.

Something about her made me want to claw her eyes out, but of course I wouldn't. I couldn't. She may be trash, but I wasn't.

"If that's all..." I gestured toward the door.

"That's all." Again, she put her hand on the small of her back as she walked toward the door. I rolled my eyes. Seriously? She wasn't several months along and she was playing this act? It was for my benefit, no doubt. Rubbing salt in a wound.

She opened the door and saw herself out, and I quickly closed it behind her.

After taking a moment to draw in a deep breath, I went to my purse and retrieved my cell phone. Gillian had given me her cousin's number before leaving the office. I'd saved it in my contacts. Now, I dialed it.

It rang three times before he picked up. "Hello?" came the deep voice on the other end of the line.

"Hi, Dexter." I exhaled softly. "Your cousin, Gillian, gave me your number. I'm—"

"Bella," he supplied, and I could hear a smile in his voice. "I thought I was supposed to call you when I got to DC."

"I thought I'd touch base myself. You come to town tomorrow?"

"Next Tuesday, actually," Dexter said.

"Oh. I thought Gillian said Thursday."

"I was supposed to be Thursday, but I had to change things."

"Aw, okay." I was disappointed. I wanted to see him as soon as possible, push Andre and that trifling Clarissa out of my mind.

"I wish it could be sooner," Dexter said. "I'm definitely looking forward to meeting you."

He had a deep and sultry voice. He sounded attractive. "How long will you be in town?"

"Tuesday til Friday morning. I've got meetings with lobbyists, the Board of Education..."

"Sounds like you'll be busy."

"Not too busy for dinner with you," he said. "What night works best for you next week? Tuesday? Wednesday?"

"I'm flexible any night," I told him. "But why don't you touch base with me when you get to town. We can make plans then."

"Sure thing," Dexter said. He sounded decent enough, easy going. Reasonable.

And sexy. Yes, he had one of those voices.

I wasn't looking to make a love connection, just to forget. But I also knew that I couldn't be foolish and close off all possibilities. Not now that Clarissa had shown up on my doorstep, telling me that I needed to stay away from Andre.

"Talk to you soon," Dexter said.

"Absolutely. Bye."

Ending the call, I felt satisfied.

There was no time like the present to put Andre in my past.

CHAPTER SEVEN

"I have a date," I told Vivica on the phone later that evening.

"Wait—what?"

"A date."

"I assume you're not talking about with Andre."

"You're right. I'm not."

"Bella, what are you doing?" Vivica asked me. "You've only been home from London for three days. Now you're going out with someone else?"

"Clarissa came to my house today. I got home from work and saw her waiting on my porch. I'd already made the decision to stay away from Andre, but she showed up to drive the point home. It pissed me off. And it also made something else very clear. If I stay with Andre, I'm going to have to deal with her. And she—well, to put it nicely, she's a piece of work. I don't think I have the mental fortitude to deal with her."

"Back up a second. What did she say to you? And what did you say to her?"

I made a sound of derision. "She told me that I need to stay away from Andre, that she's having his baby and that I need to respect that. Trust me, I wanted to give her a piece of my mind. She showed up at my house, with neighbors across the street watching. I can imagine what they were thinking. They probably think there's some sort of love triangle going on."

"My God."

"Anyway, I didn't fight with her. I told her that I'd already made the decision to break up with Andre so that he could work things out with her."

Vivica tsked. "You're letting that heifer win."

"Like I said, I don't have the mental strength to deal with someone like that in my life. The date isn't until next week. I wish it could be sooner, but…" My voice trailed off, then I started speaking again. "One of my colleagues, Gillian, told me about her cousin ages ago and wanted me to meet him whenever he came to town. Well, he's coming to town next week. And honestly, our date can't come soon enough."

"Bella, I don't like this."

"He's a documentary filmmaker," I went on, undeterred. "He sounds accomplished. And Gillian says he's a great guy. And gorgeous."

"That's all good. But he's not Andre."

Her words made me halt. "Look," I said. "I'm not about to sit around pining over Andre. He's got his life to live, and I need to move on. I can't become like Holly, all caught up in one man to the point where my whole life falls apart when things end." I paused. "How is she, by the way? She hasn't gotten back to me." I'd sent her a few texts from work earlier, and also called. Her phone had gone straight to voicemail.

"She staying at her mother's for a few days. I spoke with Mrs. Simpson tonight, and she said Holly's resting. She and the boys will be staying in Laurel with her for a while, and that's good. It's time for her to refocus."

Laurel was in Maryland. It was far enough away to put distance between Holly and Mike, but close enough that we could see her without issue. "Yeah, that's good," I agreed. "Maybe we can all go out on the weekend." If I couldn't go on a date with Dexter, I still wanted to go out. "That old school group, The Fly Boys, is performing Saturday night. Holly loved them back in the day. I can look into getting tickets for the show. Might do her some good."

My cell phone beeped, indicating that I had a call on the other line. I pulled it from my face to look down and see who was calling. It was Andre.

My heart fluttered, a reaction I was becoming accustomed to. Would I ever see his name or see him and feel nothing?

"Viv, I've got to go. I have a call coming through."

"Okay, girl. I love you."

"Love you, too." Then I quickly pressed the button to access Andre's call. It was better that I talk to him on the phone, rather than have him show up at my door. "Hi," I said, my voice soft and fluttery.

"I talked to Clarissa earlier today, told her that I want her to have a test to determine paternity ASAP."

Did that explain why she had shown up at my house? "All right."

A beat passed. Then Andre asked, "How are you?"

His voice was low, full of concern. Why couldn't he just be a jerk so that I could hate him? You weren't supposed to dump someone you were in love with.

"I'm okay," I told him. "Keeping busy."

"So if I were to come to your door—"

"That wouldn't be a good idea," I quickly said. Exhaling sharply, I decided to tell him why I'd been so abrupt. "I don't know how Clarissa took things when you talked to her, but she came to see me."

"What?"

"Early this evening. She came to my house and told me that I need to stay away from you because of the baby. She threatened to make a scene outside if I didn't let her in to talk with me."

"This is unacceptable," Andre said. "She had no right—"

"In her mind, she does," I said, cutting him off. "And if she is carrying your baby, I can see why she wants to fight for you."

"That doesn't give her the right to harass you. I'm going to talk to her."

"What's the point? You talked to her today, and by the evening she's waiting at my door? Clarissa's not going to let you go easily. And that's the problem, here. If we stay together, Clarissa's going to be a headache. And I can't handle the stress and drama right now. I hope you understand that."

Seconds of silence passed, and I wondered if Andre had hung up. Finally, he spoke. "This is a bigger mess than I thought. But I'm going to determine once and for all that she's lying."

I said nothing.

"I was hoping to see you because I'm heading out of town tomorrow."

Andre paused. I supposed he was hoping that I would change my mind about my decision, tell him that he could come over, but I continued to stay silent.

Andre spoke again. "One of my former teammates lives in San Antonio, and he's invited me out there to help with the launch of a camp. It's for underprivileged kids. I told him I'd be there for him."

"Oh, that sounds great."

"I might not be able to resolve the situation with Clarissa until I'm back, but you need to know that I'm going to do it."

"I hope so," I said softly. "Goodbye."

I quickly ended the call, because it was just too hard hearing Andre's voice. Too hard holding out any sort of hope. I wanted to believe that he was right, but I had been disappointed before. So I knew better than to delude myself.

I couldn't allow myself to get my hopes up, only for them to be shattered.

CHAPTER EIGHT

"I don't know," Holly said. "I've been a hot mess. I'm not sure I'll be good company."

"Well," I told her over the phone, "you're going. I already bought the tickets. Come on, don't you remember how much fun we used to have stepping to The Fly Boys? You need a break from all the shit going on in your life right now. And truth be told, so do I. Come on, Holly. It'll be fun."

"All right, girl," Holly said. "You've twisted my arm. I'm in."

Saturday couldn't come soon enough. I was excited about going out with my girls. And I was especially excited about seeing The Fly Boys, a three-man old school hip hop group that had been all the rage when Holly, Vivica and I had been in college.

The venue was packed, but not so crowded that people couldn't get a seat. Not that people were sitting. Everyone was on their feet, jamming as The Fly Boys were on stage, dazzling us with their old school flavor. Holly, Vivica and I were dancing as though we were twenty again.

It was a mixed crowd ranging from people in their twenties to sixties, with most of the people being around my age. I was surprised at the diverse crowd, but groups like The Fly Boys were timeless. It only proved that so much of the music today was forgettable, while some of the classics would live on forever.

"I'm so glad you dragged me out!" Holly said above the music.

"I'm glad you're having a good time," I told her.

"I am," Holly said. "You're right. I totally needed this."

Holly had driven from her mother's place in Laurel to Vivica's place, and I'd picked them both up. My plan was to be the dedicated driver. But Vivica was having none of that. "You need to forget, too," she'd told me as we were driving to the club. "You and Holly let loose, have a good time."

We decided to spring for bottle service so that we could have a table. Our bottle of Veuve Clicquot champagne was chilling on the table, and Vivica had agreed to have one glass. Holly, who'd already had two glasses, reached for the bottle to pour herself some more.

There was a huge round of applause as The Fly Boys stepped off stage. Some people started yelling, "Encore!" and "That wasn't long enough!"

The host of the event, an energetic heavy set man with dreadlocks, went up to the mic and announced, "Don't you worry. The Fly Boys will be back for another set in fifteen minutes. Eat, drink, and mingle til then!"

"Another bottle?" Vivica asked me and Holly as the waitress came toward us.

"Absolutely," Holly said. "And don't be mad, Bella. I had the waitress swap out your credit card for mine. Well, for *Mike's* credit card. Our night out is on his dime." She grinned from ear to ear.

"Holly," I said, frowning. "You really want to piss him off more?"

"Fuck him," Holly said, and sipped her champagne. "I can only imagine how much money he's been spending on that little tart. This is nothing."

Shaking my head, I rolled my eyes playfully. Oh well. It was Holly's money, too. If she wanted to spend it to have a good time, why shouldn't she? It was certainly cheaper than therapy.

"How are you guys doing over here?" the waitress asked as she reached us.

"Another bottle, please," Vivica told her.

"Sure thing." The waitress smiled brightly. The more money we spent, the better the tip for her.

"Woo!" Holly put her hands in the air and began to dance as though carefree, and it made me smile. She was a bit tipsy, sure, but she was having fun. At least for now, she had a reprieve from the drama with Mike.

I moved my body to the upbeat mix flowing through the speakers. I was feeling a lot better than I had over the past couple of days. Even though I knew my relationship with Andre was over, I was still missing him badly. Knowing that he wasn't down the street at his house made it even worse in some way. It was clear that as much as my brain knew I had to forget him, my heart was having none of it.

"Ooh, they're cute," Holly said, and pointed in the direction of the front of the club. Two taller than average men had just entered. They were well over six feet. Like closer to seven feet. The way they were dressed oozed money.

"Wait, I think those guys are pro basketball players," Vivica said.

"Really?" I asked.

"I think so, yeah."

And even before Vivica had spoken, I saw the reaction of the people around them. There was a buzz of excitement. All heads turned in their direction.

Vivica had to be right. They were professional athletes.

And suddenly, I was thinking of Andre. How these two men had nothing on him when it came to sex appeal. But no matter how cute or unattractive, an athlete with fat pockets would always attract a ton of women.

Women like Clarissa. There was no doubt in my mind that she was interested in Andre's bank account.

My eyes went to the right, to a trio of women who were now approaching the athletes. The women were young, dressed almost identically in black jeans and sleeveless tops. The three of them slowed as they passed the athletes, and one of them turned to say something to the men. Then the women continued on, giggling with each other.

My stomach clenched. Was that…Clarissa?

Or had I conjured her because I'd just been thinking about her golddigging ass?

The woman in question looked over her shoulder at the two athletes again, clearly flirting. And when she turned her head forward, I knew without a doubt that it was Clarissa.

But wait…what was she wearing?

I took a few steps forward to get a better view of her. At my house, she had been wearing a pregnancy top that made it look like she was already showing. But from this vantage point, she didn't look as pregnant as she had before.

"What is it?" Vivica asked, coming to stand beside me.

"Clarissa. She just walked past the two pro athletes with her friends."

"Which one is she?" Holly asked.

I pointed. "That's Clarissa. Right over there. The one in the white top."

"She's supposed to be pregnant?" Holly sounded doubtful.

"You don't think she is?" I asked. My pulse was racing.

"She could be." Holly shrugged. "She could have a little belly under that top."

I wasn't close enough to truly see her belly. Her top hugged her unnaturally perfect breasts and flowed outward from her breastbone. It wasn't exactly maternity wear, but given that it wasn't form-fitting, it could be something that a pregnant woman with a small belly would wear.

"Oh, look," Vivica said. "She's going back to talk to the players. I thought she was supposed to be into Andre."

I scoffed. "I'm not surprised. She'll probably sell herself to the highest bidder."

"I know her type," Holly said, and made a sour face. "Just like Mike's secretary. They show enough tits and ass to try and sink their claws into men with money."

My throat suddenly dry, I swallowed. Clarissa had snagged a man with status and money. Why had she let him go?

Maybe, like one of Andre's friends had said at the wedding in London, Clarissa was just too young and immature. She didn't know what she had until it was gone, and now she was determined to get it back.

But would she lie about being pregnant to do so?

"She would have to be really stupid to lie to Andre about being pregnant," I commented. "Wouldn't

she? I mean, that's the kind of lie that will blow up in your face."

"Maybe she's not too bright," Vivica said.

Clarissa and her friends continued walking. Clarissa had a strut that said she thought she was the sexiest woman in the place. "I remember when I was pregnant, I couldn't wear heels like that," Holly commented. "But hey, it's a different generation."

I turned back to the table. "I need a drink."

I filled my glass, then sipped liberally. The cold, bubbly beverage felt satisfying as it went down my throat.

"Pass me my water, please?" Vivica said.

I grabbed her water bottle and handed it to her.

I didn't realize that Holly was no longer beside us until I saw her weaving through the crowd. "Oh my God," I said, my heart starting to pound. "She's going over to Clarissa!"

CHAPTER NINE

I held my breath, wondering what she was about to do. But suddenly, she stopped in front of a guy. It was a man I had noticed looking in our direction before.

"What's she doing?" I asked.

Vivica shrugged. "Maybe she knows him?"

Holly slipped her arms around the man's neck. By the time my jaw was hitting the floor, she was tipping up on her toes and kissing him.

I gasped. "What the hell?"

"Oh, fuck," Vivica said. "She's making out with a complete stranger!"

For some reason, my gaze went to the right. I saw Clarissa heading my way. Her eyes met mine, and she stopped dead in her tracks.

"What should we do?" Vivica asked.

I didn't respond. My eyes were on Clarissa. She was closer now, but I couldn't see her side profile. I could only get a view of her belly from head on.

"Bella—"

"Clarissa's right there," I told Vivica. "She just saw me."

Vivica looked in Clarissa's direction. Clarissa, who had been heading toward us, suddenly took her friends by the arms and turned.

"They're leaving," Vivica said.

"Maybe not."

"No, I'm talking about Holly!"

I quickly looked back in Holly's direction, saw her walking toward the patio exit with this stranger. Had she lost her mind?

"Come on." I took Vivica by the arm, and we made our way through the crowd. We hustled, hurrying to get to Holly as soon as possible. Just as they got to the patio door, I was able to reach out and put a hand on Holly's shoulder. "Holly."

She whipped her head around to look at me. Beamed. "Hey."

"Holly, what are you doing?" I asked.

"Oh," she said brightly. "This is John. I used to work with him years ago."

"That's nice," Vivica said in a cautious tone. "But why are you leaving with him?"

"He wants to show me his car," Holly answered.

"You can't just take off like that," I said.

"I wasn't leaving forever." Holly giggled.

She was three sheets to the wind. "Okay, I think we need to get you back over to the table," I told her. "Get some water into you." I had no clue who this John guy was, nor why he and Holly had just been kissing. But I didn't like the fact that he was trying to get her out of here.

"Hello," he said, his voice deep. He extended a hand to me. "I'm John Neale. An associate at—"

"Why are you trying to leave with our friend?" Vivica asked.

He chuckled softly. "I'm not stealing her. I only wanted to show her my new car."

"We weren't born yesterday," Vivica quipped.

"Scout's honor." He raised a hand as though doing a pledge and held up three fingers. "I promise I'll bring her right back."

Holly's eyes danced as she looked at us, and I could see in her gaze that she was interested in this guy. "You two, stop being mother hens," she said. "I'll be back in a minute."

I wanted to grab her and drag her back over to our table, but I didn't. Instead, I said to John, "Don't be long."

Vivica and I headed back toward our table, and as we did, I searched the crowd. I looked for Clarissa or her friends everywhere. But I saw them nowhere.

Just as we were getting back to our seats, The Fly Boys returned to the stage. The crowd started to cheer. "I think Clarissa's gone," I said to Vivica. "She took off."

"Maybe she didn't want you to get too close. Because maybe if you got too close, you'd be able to figure out her charade…"

I poured myself another glass of wine, and tried to forget about Clarissa and Andre as The Fly Boys began to perform again. Vivica lifted her bottle of water and took a sip. "And what's with this John guy?" I asked. "Holly ever mention him before?"

"If she did, it was ages ago. She stopped working at the firm what, eight years ago? She got married two years before that. And she'd only been with the firm a couple of years. I don't remember this guy."

Five minutes later, Holly came back over to us, her hands linked with John's as she shimmied her body to the music. I eyed them with suspicion. Then I said, "That was more than a minute."

"John showed me his new Porsche. It's black. Gorgeous. Just how I like my men."

Oh, Jesus. She was flirting with John. I looked at him. He was all smiles. Probably because he expected to get lucky.

Holly poured herself more champagne, then downed it. As she put the glass down on the table, she giggled like a schoolgirl.

Then, she turned to John and slipped her arms around his waist. "John wants to take me for a ride in the Porsche."

"I'm sure he does," I said, rolling my eyes. I shot Vivica a knowing glance.

"You two, stop looking at me like that," Holly said. "John and I go way back. We were in law school together, ended up at the same firm. But then I got married, had kids, and lost touch with my old work friends. I'm so glad I came out tonight and saw him again!"

"Would you ladies like something to drink?" John asked.

"The waitress just put another bottle of champagne on our table," I told him, gesturing to the carafe with a jerk of my head.

"I'm having water," Vivica said.

"How about a round of tequila shooters?" Holly suggested.

"No," I said.

"Yes!" Holly exclaimed. "Come on, I'm having so much fun. I'm not thinking about Jackass at all."

She looked up at John. "Will you get us some tequila shooters?"

The only reason I didn't protest was because if John headed off for shooters, then Vivica and I would have a moment to speak with Holly alone.

And the moment John was out of earshot, I said, "Holly, what are you doing?"

She looked at me as though I had grown a second head. "I'm having a good time. Isn't that why we came out?"

"So, we're hanging with John now?" I asked. "Who did he come here with?"

"He was a third wheel. Came with his brother and sister-in-law. It's kind of perfect that I ran into him. He totally needed someone else to hang with."

"Why did you kiss him?" Vivica asked.

"Did you see him?" Holly countered. "Tall, dark, and handsome. Bald. *Mmm.* I always liked him—but we never got it on. Because I was involved with Mike." She frowned as she said her husband's name. "But tonight—I'm going home with him."

My eyes bulged. "No!" I said. "Holly, you can't."

"I'm grown. I can."

"Holly, you know that's the alcohol talking," Vivica said.

"I don't care. I'm having a good time, and I feel good, and John is sexy. I always thought he was sexy. But I never crossed the line with him. Don't go thinking that I messed around. But now, there's no reason not to."

"How about the fact that you're married?" I asked.

Holly threw her head back and laughed hysterically. "I'm not married. It's over with Mike, and there's no going back. If he can screw some young tart, I can certainly get my groove on. I'm not cheating. Dammit, maybe I'm finally living."

I looked at Vivica, imploring her to say something. Vivica merely shrugged.

"Maybe I was hard on you because of the fact that you had something I didn't," Holly suddenly said. When I looked at her, she continued. "You and Andre…. It was obvious how into him you were. I know that wasn't one-sided. And it made me…. It made me miss that kind of intimacy in my marriage. Who cares if he's younger? It was so clear that with Andre you felt alive."

I swallowed. *Now* Holly decided to speak favorably about my relationship with Andre?

"It's not cool that he got someone else pregnant, however," she added.

Seeing John approach, I looked beyond Holly. She quickly looked over her shoulder, and seeing John as well, she smiled. He was carefully holding four shooter glasses together. He lowered them onto the table.

Holly pushed one shooter glass toward Vivica, one toward me, and lifted one into her hand. "Don't you dare say you can't drink, Viv. This is one drink. Well, in addition to your champagne. But that and one shooter won't make you too drunk to drive."

"All right," Vivica said, not arguing.

Holly raised her glass. "To partying like we used to twenty years ago, and still being as hot as we were then!"

"I'll drink to that," I said.

An hour later, Holly and John came back to the table. They had spent a good amount of time on the dance floor. The only positive thing about being ditched by Holly was that she wasn't drinking as much—at least I didn't think so—so hopefully she had sobered up.

But her announcement when she reached the table had me questioning how sober she was. "I'm leaving with John."

"Oh, no you're not," Vivica said.

"Yes, I am."

The look of disapproval I leveled on John was swift. "Can I speak to you for a moment?" I asked him.

"Sure," he said.

I walked several feet away with him, so we were out of earshot of Holly. Then I said, "I don't care if you and Holly go way back. You should not be trying to take advantage of her right now."

"Trust me, I'm not planning to take advantage of her. Now, I don't know what her intentions are—but I plan to spend the evening catching up. And I'm sure she's going to need to get some sleep sooner rather than later. She's had a lot to drink."

"You let her keep drinking?" I asked.

"She had a few shooters from passing waitresses while we were on the dance floor. I couldn't exactly wrestle them from her hand."

And I'm sure you didn't want to, I thought.

"Which is exactly why I'm concerned," I said, giving him a pointed look. He wouldn't be the first guy who claimed he only wanted to take a girl home to a safe bed—then made moves on her.

He held up three fingers one on hand. "Scout's honor."

"Just because you were a boy scout—" Feeling hands encircle my waist, I jumped, startled. Then I heard Holly's voice. "What are you saying to John?"

I angled my head to face her, deciding to tell her the truth. "That I don't want him to take advantage of you."

"Girl," Holly said as she separated from me. "You are too cynical. John's good people."

I looked up at him. "He better be."

"He is." Holly linked arms with mine and walked with me a short distance away from John. "When have you ever known me to be reckless?"

"Never," I answered.

"In fact, haven't you and Vivica gotten on my case in the past about being too uptight? About not living in the moment?"

"I certainly wasn't thinking of this," I told her.

Holly laughed. "I swear, you are worrying for no reason." She paused, then asked, "Hey, whatever happened to Clarissa?"

My stomach tightened. "I don't know. I guess she left."

"And on that note, I'm leaving too." Holly looked into my eyes, and I could see she wasn't as drunk as I feared she was. She was letting me know that she was making an informed decision. A decision that she had the right to make as an adult.

I hugged her. "Okay," I said softly. "But you call any time if you need us. Any time. Okay?"

She nodded.

I looked at John, and he met my gaze. I gave him a pointed look. "I'm holding you to your word," I told him.

He surprised me by wrapping his arms around me. "Don't worry, Bella. Scout's honor."

As much as I was wary of Holly leaving with John, I had to admit that as they walked off hand in hand,

she seemed happy. And Lord knew, she deserved to be happy.

I only hoped that when she woke up in the morning, she would have no regrets.

CHAPTER TEN

Going out on Saturday night had been the highlight of my weekend, but as Monday rolled around, I was back in the dumps.

Hope was a dangerous thing. I kept hoping that I would hear from Andre, and that he would have the proof that Clarissa wasn't pregnant with his child.

I knew that he'd been busy with the launch of that camp for underprivileged kids, but the longer it took to hear from him, the less I believed that the situation with Clarissa would be ever be resolved favorably.

But he was heading home today. Maybe he'd have good news?

I sent him a text just before noon. I needed to know *something*.

NOT SURE WHEN YOU'RE GETTING BACK. WONDERING IF YOU HAVE NEWS ABOUT CLARISSA...

Just before three, he called. The moment I saw his name flashing on my screen, I quickly answered my cell phone. "Andre?"

"Hey."

I closed my eyes as I heard the sultry sound of his voice. I'd missed him so much. "You have news?"

"I'll get right to the point," he said.

My stomach lurched. It was bad…

"Clarissa said it's too early in her pregnancy to get a paternity test. There *is* a test we could do, something called CVS, but it's invasive this early on and Clarissa doesn't want to do it. She says she doesn't want to put the baby at risk."

"Of course she doesn't," I muttered. "My God. Why is she doing this?"

But I knew. It was a stalling tactic. A way to keep her claws sunk into Andre even longer.

"So you won't know for months," I went on, stating the obvious.

"I refuse to be held hostage by her," Andre said. "This is a game. I know it is. You're the one I want to be with."

"Andre—"

"No, I need you to hear me. Even these five days I spent away from you, I missed you like crazy. Are you gonna tell me you don't miss me?"

"This isn't about me. This is bigger than me and it's bigger than you."

"It doesn't have to be." He paused. "I'm at the airport waiting for my flight. I get back later tonight. I want to see you."

I wanted nothing more. But I couldn't say yes. I couldn't build a life with Andre while the Clarissa cloud was hanging over our heads.

"Don't," I told him. "Don't come over." I sighed wearily, emotion clogging my throat. "I love you but…I can't deal with this."

Before I lost it, I ended the call. Then I buried my face in my hands and drew in several deep breaths. It was all I could do to keep it together.

❖

Andre respected my wishes and didn't come over that night. Didn't call. I felt both relieved and depressed.

So in the morning, I texted Dexter. Reiterated that I was looking forward to meeting him, and asked him to let me know what day he thought would be good for us to get together. I added that I was free any evening that worked for him.

I'd actually been contemplating canceling the date with Dexter, but Andre's update regarding Clarissa had me changing my mind. Clarissa wasn't going to let Andre go, and I couldn't allow myself to get caught up in that drama.

Maybe the best way for me to move on was to meet someone new. Someone who could distract me from Andre.

And who knew? Maybe I would like him.

❖

"Yes, I'm still going out with Dexter," I said to Vivica the next day while I was at work. "In fact, we're getting together tonight. He's traveling today, but said he wants to see me as soon as possible.

This is the one evening that he knows he has clear. I'm excited."

"Are you?" Vivica asked doubtfully.

"I am," I told her. "I wish you would be happy for me."

"How can I be happy for you when I know you're trying to convince yourself of something you don't believe?" Vivica asked.

"Viv, I have to move on. You know that."

"All I know is that you're unhappy, Holly's unhappy. And I wish I could fix everything for both of you. Holly hasn't even spoken to me since she left with John Saturday night. When John dropped her off to pick up her car, she didn't come to my door. I texted her about it, and all she said was that she was fine."

"I wonder what happened with him," I commented. "I was expecting a call with juicy details. I mean, I was *hoping* she didn't do anything crazy. But still, I thought she would've told us about it."

"You think he was an ass?" Vivica asked.

"I wish I knew. I warned him. Of course, that didn't guarantee he would listen." I paused as I considered what could have happened. "Maybe things went badly, and she's embarrassed. Maybe she doesn't want to hear us tell her that we told her so."

"Yeah, probably." Vivica paused. "I don't want to have to tell you I told you so, too. Cancel the date, Bella."

"Viv, I've got a call coming through on my office line. I have to go."

"Perfect timing," Vivica said wryly. "We'll talk about this later."

I sure as hell hope not, I thought, then ended the call.

❖

When my phone rang just before 5 PM and I saw Vivica's number, I answered and said without preamble, "No, I didn't cancel the date. Dexter has been looking forward to getting together with me for months. It's just going to be dinner, no pressure. I'm certainly not rushing into any—"

"You need to get to Holly's place."

"What?" I asked, startled by the comment.

"All hell is breaking loose at Holly and Mike's. I just got a frantic call from her. I'm on my way there now."

I was supposed to head home to change and meet Dexter for 7 PM. But whatever crisis my friend was experiencing took priority.

I was going to have to cancel my date with Dexter after all.

❖

Getting reservations for Founding Farmers, a restaurant in Foggy Bottom, was not always easy. So I hated that I had to call Dexter and tell him that I had to cancel.

"I'm really sorry. Something's come up and I have to cancel for tonight."

"Oh, no," he said. He sounded disappointed. "Tomorrow night, I have a dinner meeting. Tonight really is probably the best night for me."

"Well, maybe we can still get together later," I suggested. Hopefully the situation with Holly and Mike would be resolved in an hour or two. "I think that 8:30 or 9 o'clock could work. If that's not too late for you. I don't know about getting another reservation at Founding Farmers, however."

"Why don't I touch base with them, see if I can push our reservation back. I've heard a lot about Founding Farmers. I was hoping to check it out."

"I'm really sorry," I said. "A friend of mine is in crisis. That's the only reason I have to put this off."

"I'd expect no less. I'll call the restaurant, and you deal with what you've got to deal with and get back to me."

"Sure thing."

I ended the Bluetooth call, my thoughts on getting to Holly's place as fast as possible.

CHAPTER ELEVEN

When I got to Holly's house, I could hear the yelling before I even stepped inside. But thankfully Vivica was there. God only knew what had happened before she'd arrived, but she was there now, standing between Holly and Mike.

"Thank God," she said when she saw me.

"You better leave," Holly said to Mike.

"You think you can call your army here and they can save you?"

"Mike," I said, "what the hell are you doing?"

"As if you don't know," he scoffed. "You probably all were part of this."

"Leave them out of it!" Holly yelled. "I already told you they had nothing to do with it."

"Nothing to do with what?" I asked.

"I don't know what's going on," Vivica said. "I just got here. All I know is that Mike forced his way into the house. Holly was terrified. She was hiding in a bathroom."

"Oh my God," I uttered.

"Relax," he snapped. "If I wanted to hurt her, I already would have."

"As if you haven't hurt her!" Vivica exclaimed.

"Stop acting like Holly's the victim here," Mike said. "After what she did…" He glowered at Holly. "I wanted her to face me. Own up to what she did."

I crossed the room to stand in front of Mike. "Whatever you think you're doing here, you need to stop. You can't come barging into a house and threaten a woman to the point where she's cowering in a bathroom."

"This is my house!" he bellowed. His nostrils were flaring, and his eyes were bulging like they would pop out of his face. I'd never seen him so enraged.

"Enough of this," Vivica said. She pulled her cell phone from her purse. "I didn't call the police earlier out of respect for you, Mike. Though God knows why I have any respect for men like you. But now, I could care less if you get arrested."

Mike's jaw flinched. I could see in his eyes that he was weighing the gravity of the situation. He knew Vivica wasn't bluffing.

He shot an evil glare in Holly's direction. "Your friends can protect you now," Mike said, his voice eerily cool. "But they won't always be here."

"That's enough, Mike," I said firmly. "You can't come here like you're ready to kill somebody. We *will* call the police. And if you think I'm joking, try me."

Mike gave me a look of disgust, then shot another look in Holly's direction. I glanced at my friend, saw that she was standing with her arms crossed over her chest. And for moment, a smug look of satisfaction came onto her face.

What had she done?

Vivica held up the phone. "I don't see you moving, Mike."

"You're lucky your friends are here," he spat out. "Really lucky."

"What are you gonna do?" Holly challenged.

Mike lurched forward, and I jumped in his path to stop him. "Not another step," I warned him. "I swear to God, Mike. If you don't leave now, you're gonna regret it."

His breath coming in angry bursts as he stared down at me, he looked unhinged. So much so that I wasn't sure what he was going to do. Was he about to snap and totally lose it?

Tension filled the air, and the next few seconds seemed like minutes. Finally, reason won out over anger, and he took a step backward. Then, pointing a finger in Holly's direction as though he wished he were actually holding a gun, he yelled, "You're not gonna get away with this, bitch!"

When Mike stalked out of the house, I followed him, shut the door and immediately locked it. Then I blew out a frazzled breath.

This was what happened when love turned to hate.

Peering through the side window, I made sure that Mike had gotten into his Mercedes and was indeed leaving. Then I faced Holly, who had come to stand beside me and look out the window as well.

"What's going on?" I asked her. "How did he even get in the house?"

"He sneaked in through a back window," Holly said.

"Shit." I shook my head, dismayed. Maybe Holly was going to have to have an alarm system installed with triggers on every window. "What the hell was he talking about?" I asked. "Did you do something to piss him off?"

And though minutes ago Holly had been undeniably smug, I now saw a mix of conflicted emotions cross her face. Suddenly, she seemed remorseful.

"Holly?" Vivica prompted. She was now standing beside us at the window.

"I gave him a taste of his own medicine," Holly said. She forced a defiant smile as she faced me and Vivica. "He's destroyed my world. And this morning, I learned that he sneaked into the house to steal valuable items while I was at my mother's. He's playing dirty, so I did, too."

I had a sinking feeling. "What did you do?"

"I sent pictures of his penis to the people he works with," Holly announced.

I gasped.

"What?" Vivica asked, stunned.

"I know it was childish," Holly said. "Completely immature."

"You think?" Vivica asked sarcastically.

"I wasn't thinking," Holly said. "That's the point. I was just so livid."

"How could you do that to him?" Vivica went on. "I don't care what's going on bet—"

I squeezed Vivica's arm to silence her. Whatever Holly had done, she needed our support right now… not a rebuke. Besides, I could see in her eyes that she regretted her actions. That the gravity of what she had done had hit her.

Holly wandered the short distance into the living room and slumped onto the armchair. We followed her.

Biting on her thumbnail, Holly looked crestfallen. "Why did I do it?" she asked, looking up at us. "Because I'm pissed off. He thinks he can just leave me, then screw me over financially as well?" Holly shook her head, her eyes growing wide with anger. "No. No way in hell. He doesn't get to do that to me and walk away unscathed."

"Well, there's no wonder he's livid," I said softly.

"It's not like I set out to do it," Holly said. "But I came home and found my favorite painting gone this morning…I was fuming. I…I just reacted in a way that I knew would hurt him. And I guess I knew he'd be unpredictable, because something told me to take the kids back to my mother's place. Then I was worried he was going to come here and destroy the place, so I came back home…"

"You're lucky he didn't kill you," Vivica quipped.

"Mike is making me so crazy!" Holly cried. Suddenly, her face crumbled. "God, he was so angry. So hurt." She looked at me and Vivica, a pained expression streaking across her face. "Did I really send a picture of his penis to his colleagues?"

Neither Vivica nor I spoke.

"What did he expect, damn it? That I'd sit here and let him walk over me? The locks were changed, and you told him not to take anything from the house. But he got in here anyway, and stole that painting I ordered from Paris. I was the one who discovered that artist. I'm the one who found the gallery in Paris." She paused. Whimpered. "God, I can't undo what I did."

"You're right," I said softly. I sank onto the sofa beside Holly and put my arm around her shoulder. "You can't undo it. But I hope you can live with it."

"I get that you're pissed with Mike," Vivica began, "and you have every right to be. But what you did was low down and dirty on a whole other scale. It's the kind of retaliation that leads to more ugliness."

"Please, Viv," Holly said, her voice cracking. "I can't hear that right now."

Holly broke free from me and jumped up from the sofa. Then she started toward the staircase at the back end of the living room. "I need to be alone."

"Don't push us away," I said. "We're here for you."

Holly turned and stared at me first, then Vivica. "What about you, Viv? Are you here for me, too?"

"You know I love you," Vivica said. "That's why I'm worried about you. Worried that Mike is going to retaliate. I don't want to see things get even worse between the two of you."

"Fine," Holly said. "You both think I'm a horrible person. I guess it's no surprise why Mike left me."

I took a step toward her. "Holly—"

"No, Bella," she interjected. "You don't have to lie anymore."

"I never said you were a horrible person," Vivica said. "We don't think that."

"I'm done with this conversation," Holly snapped. "I need both of you to leave."

"I'm not sure that's a good idea," I told her.

"It's not a fucking question."

Vivica looked at me, concern flashing in her eyes.

"You heard me," Holly said. "Leave, you two. I love you, but I need to be alone right now."

I began to nod. "All right," I said. "But if you need me, I'm a phone call away. No matter how late."

"Holly, I wasn't trying to judge you," Vivica said. "I'm just worried."

"We've never bullshitted each other, and I don't want you to start now," Holly said. "I fucked up. I get it. But I feel like I'm losing my mind." She exhaled sharply. "Right now, all I want to do is rest. Please, I need you both to leave."

I took hold of Vivica by the arm. "You heard Holly. Let's go."

I kept my hand on Vivica's arm as we walked to the front door. After I opened it, I turned to face Holly, who had walked to the foyer behind us. Quickly hugging her, I said, "Call any time. I mean that."

"I will."

Holly and Vivica then exchanged a brief, tense hug. Then Vivica and I exited the house. Holly closed the door behind us, and I heard the lock click almost immediately.

"Bella, I'm totally worried about her," Vivica said.

"I am too. But she knows what she did was wrong. Hopefully this is the straw that breaks the camel's back and she knows she's got to stop."

"But what if Mike comes back? And you and I aren't there?"

The words caused a chill to crawl down my spine. "We have to hope and pray that doesn't happen."

CHAPTER TWELVE

Because Holly kicked us out earlier than I expected, I was able to call Dexter and tell him that we could meet for any time after 7:30. He was able to rearrange our date for 8 PM.

"Why don't I pick you up?" Dexter suggested.

"That's not necessary. I can meet you there."

"It's tough enough to park in the city and I have a car with a driver. It'll be easy enough to get you."

I was going to insist that I drive, but I was tired, and emotionally ragged after the incident at Holly's. Besides, being in the car with Dexter would give us more time to get to know each other. "All right," I told him. "That'll work."

At least he had a driver, which made me feel more comfortable about being in a car with him—something I typically never did on a first date with a guy.

I had followed my gut where Dexter was concerned in terms of traveling to the restaurant with him, and I wasn't disappointed. My initial impression of him was that he was a gentleman. He opened the car door for me, greeted me with a big smile and a hug. He was pleasant, and unlike some men, knew how to talk. So there were no uncomfortable gaps in the conversation.

He also was, as his voice sounded, sexy. Tall, with golden brown skin, he had classically handsome features. And he had a great smile.

In the car, he started to tell me about his work as a documentary filmmaker. I learned that his latest project was on fast food in America. His goal was to open the eyes of the average consumer so they could see the truth behind the products they were putting into their bodies. He was particularly concerned about the alarming rate of childhood obesity. Lack of exercise, too much sugar and processed foods, and he felt compelled to make a change.

"One of my nephews is eight and has Type II diabetes," Dexter said. "Too many electronics and far too little physical activity…. Things aren't the same as when I was a kid. I hope my film changes that."

"I love that you're passionate about this topic. It's something I haven't really considered, but yes, it's obvious that things have changed over the last twenty years even. When I was young, we played outside. Now, kids want to be at their computers."

"My film follows five families. I focus on two children, one a teenager, the other under ten. And also three adults in different age ranges. I highlight the problem with diet and obesity and really hope to inspire change."

"Wow. I'm impressed," I told him. And I was.

"And speaking of food—looks like we're here." Dexter smiled.

As we exited the car, Dexter came to stand behind me and put his hand on the small of my back. He was tall, probably an inch shorter than Andre. He also wasn't as muscular as Andre…. But then, he wasn't Andre. And wasn't that the point?

"With all I've said, I don't want you to think I'm fanatical or anything. I'm not the kind of guy who eats the best meals all the time, has to always have organic, etc. Don't get me wrong, I eat a mostly clean diet. But I will have chips and junk food. From time to time. I just make sure that I also work out."

I looked up at him and grinned. "Good. Because I was planning to order everything deep-fried, and to wash it down with a few sodas. I hope you won't give me any strange looks."

He chuckled warmly. "No, I won't give you any strange looks. But I'm sure you know how to burn off all those calories. Because you are in amazing shape."

I looked up at him and offered him a little smile. It was nice that he thought I was attractive.

"What do you do for exercise?" he asked. "Run? You look like you have a runner's body."

"Yep. I love it. It's a great way for me to clear my mind and get exercise at the same time. And I get some fresh air."

Soon, we were in the restaurant. We were led to a table near a large fireplace. The place was filled with people, and there was a buzz of chatter in the air. I liked it. It wasn't too intimate, and yet wasn't too loud that we couldn't hear each other.

Though Dexter, quite frankly, did most of the talking. I loved that he was passionate about his film and his work, but as we shared the devil-ish eggs seafood combo for an appetizer, I began to tune out a little bit. I was thinking about Holly, wondering if she was okay.

And truth be told, I was thinking about Andre.

Clarissa had made sure that she found a way to keep us apart. Was it really too soon for her to have a paternity test done? And if she honestly believed that Andre was the father, why wouldn't she? She had to have her doubts, clearly.

"Wow, this looks amazing," I said when the waitress brought our meals. I had ordered the boneless rib eye, while Dexter opted for the barbecue braised pork.

Dexter topped off my glass of wine from the half carafe he had ordered. "Let me know if you want me to order more wine. Since neither of us is driving…"

"I should be good with this," I told him.

We both began to eat, and the taste of the rib eye blew me away. I'd heard of this restaurant before, but had never actually made it here. "This is outstanding," I told him. Then, I teased, "I wasn't sure you were going to go for barbecue pork. All those extra calories."

"I'll be hitting the gym at the hotel in the morning."

We ate, and Dexter told me more about his work. His first film had been about war veterans and the lack of dignity they were afforded. How many of them ended up homeless, barely surviving, after serving their country. He was definitely into causes, and I liked that. These days, so many people cared only about the superficial things in life, and the issues that mattered were forgotten.

"Why don't you tell me about you?" Dexter said. "I feel like I've done all the talking."

It was true. He *had* done all the talking. But I'd let him, because I'd been distracted. I probably should have told him no to getting together tonight, given what had happened with Holly. And I kept thinking about Andre, wishing he were sitting across the table from me as opposed to Dexter.

Not that Dexter wasn't a perfectly nice guy. He just wasn't Andre.

"I'm enjoying hearing you talk," I told him. "It's refreshing to meet someone who is so passionate about what he does."

"Thank you." Dexter gave me a skeptical look. "But I feel like you're distracted. Am I wrong?"

There was no point in lying. "I admit, my mind is not totally here. That emergency earlier…a dear friend of mine is going through a breakup. She's having a really hard time."

"Boyfriend, or husband?"

"Husband. They were married ten years. Things have become incredibly nasty between them. It's hard to believe that two people could love each other so much, then treat each other like they despise no one worse in the world."

"The flip side of love is hate. You only hate passionately when you loved deeply."

I nodded as I lifted my wine glass and took a sip. "You're absolutely right about that."

And then I thought about Andre. Would he hate me? Hate me for pushing him away? Would the time come when he couldn't even stand to look at me in the neighborhood? Or would we be able to move past our breakup and become friends?

"Are you sure there's nothing else?" Dexter asked.

"No." I began slicing my beef. "Nothing else."

When he said nothing, I looked up. Found Dexter staring at me.

"What's his name?" he asked.

My eyes widened. "Excuse me?"

"It feels like there's a wall between us. Now, I get that we just met. But I sense hesitation. And I'm guessing it's more than what's going on with your friend."

"I…" My voice trailed off. "A lot's going on."

He said nothing, just continued to look at me with those eyes that seemed to see right into my soul. I knew there was no point in continuing to lie. "All right." I sighed softly. "I recently broke up with someone. So I'm still…dealing with the aftermath. Maybe I shouldn't have agreed to this date

with you, but Gillian spoke so highly of you, and I know you're not often in DC…"

"No, I'm glad you did agree to meet me. And I understand. Jumping into a new relationship is probably the last thing on your mind."

"Exactly," I told him. "I'm not against getting to know you. I just…"

"Want to take things slowly," Dexter finished for me.

I smiled. He seemed to know exactly how I was feeling. "Yeah. I realize we don't even live in the same state, so the idea of rushing things is not really an issue. It's just that with my ex, things happened quickly. Against my better judgment, I rushed into a relationship with him. In hindsight, I know it was foolish. Now I'm nursing a broken heart." I quickly drank more wine. "But you don't need to hear about that. It's a typical story, and the bottom line is we're not together anymore. I just don't want to be as foolish the next time around."

"I'm glad to hear you say that. Because I feel the same way."

"You do?" I asked.

"Absolutely." Dexter reached across the table and gently stroked the back of my hand with the pad of his thumb. "Good things come to those who wait."

CHAPTER THIRTEEN

"Well," I said when Dexter's driver pulled up in front of my house. "Thank you for dinner."

"Let me make sure you get inside okay."

I guess the look on my face was somewhat suspicious, because Dexter said, "Don't worry. I meant what I said about taking things slowly. But I'd like to say goodbye to you with a bit of privacy. Is that okay?"

I swallowed. Though I supposed there was no need to be nervous. With his driver waiting for him, I didn't imagine him trying to push things too far.

So I said, "Sure. That's okay."

I opened my door, and by the time I was stepping out, Dexter was already there, offering me his hand. He'd slipped out of his own door in a flash so that he could be a gentleman.

A smile touched my lips as I looked at him. I liked him. I liked his manners, his respect.

I led the way to my door, and unlocked it. I stepped inside, and Dexter followed me in. He glanced around with interest. "Nice place."

I turned to look at him. "Thank you."

"I really did enjoy meeting you. I'm in town for a couple more days. I hope we can see each other before I leave."

"Let me know your schedule," I said. "I'll try to make it happen."

"I'm going to be busy, but I will definitely try to make time for you."

A few beats passed, with him looking at me and me looking at him. It was as though he didn't want to say goodbye.

"Why are you single?" I suddenly asked him. With everything we talked about, we hadn't discussed this. "I know you told me that you've never been married, and you seem so…nice. Like a good catch. I just wonder why you've never found the right woman."

"Is it so hard to believe?"

"Most men who are successful and available don't have a hard time finding a good woman. Women on the other hand…"

"I was engaged," Dexter admitted. "For two years, actually."

"Wow. And you're saying this now when you're at my door, as opposed to during dinner?"

"They say you shouldn't talk about your exes on your first date." He gave me a little smile.

Ouch. "So I guess I failed that test."

"No, I asked you. And I'm glad you told me what's going on. With me, I've been broken up for over a year. So it's really a non-issue. But it has made me cautious. I loved her, thought I was going to marry her. But things fell apart. Kind of like what you said about the guy you were dating, things started hot and heavy. It was exciting. We dated for about six months before moving in together. Things were probably good for another couple of months after that. I proposed. And slowly, things started to change. We weren't getting along as well anymore, not having as much sex. She hated how I did this. I hated how she did that. You know, the common gripes. The kind of stuff you can never really know before you live with someone."

"That caused the split?"

"We grew apart. But mostly, she seemed to hate that I had to travel for work. It's not like I traveled excessively, but she didn't like being alone. At all. That wasn't something I realized in the beginning. But in hindsight, I can see that's why she wanted to move in quickly. There was a time when while we lived together, she lost her job. She'd show up at the office, bring me lunch. Sometimes she'd bring baked goods and other treats. Everyone at the production company loved her. And at first, I loved her thoughtfulness as well. Then came a point when it became too much. I realized she was clingy."

"Ahh. That will always destroy a relationship."

"We tried to talk about it, tried to work things out. But we never could. When I made the decision to end things…all I can say is that it was hard. Real hard. And she was livid."

"It's never easy."

"Yeah, well, it got worse. She talked about wanting to kill herself, not being able to live without me." Dexter grimaced. "She even called some of my colleagues, told them the same thing."

I gasped. "Oh my goodness. What happened?"

"I had to call her family. They were in a different state, but they came and they got her, and I hope she's getting help."

"You don't know?"

"I realized that with someone like Emma, I had to completely sever the ties. She became obsessed with me. The first couple of times I reached out to her, it only made things worse. When she learned I wasn't going to take her back, she threatened suicide again. Her mother told me I had to cut all ties. So I did."

Was that what Andre and I would have to do? Cut all ties?

Suddenly, Dexter was wrapping his arms around my waist and pulling me close. "I hope you don't think badly of me."

"No," I told him. "Of course not."

He stared down at me, and I swallowed as I saw his eyes darken. "I really liked meeting you," he said softly. "And I really, really want to kiss you. I know it's only the first date, but would that be okay?"

Dexter was a different breed of man. Respectful. Intriguing. And didn't I want to get over Andre?

Suddenly I knew that I had to kiss him. I had to kiss him and see if Andre had forever ruined me for any other man. This man was attractive and successful. Certainly a good catch. Maybe he could help mend my broken heart.

"I guess that would be okay," I whispered.

Grinning, he tightened his arms around my waist and lowered his head.

As his lips met mine, he moaned softly.

And Lord, I wanted to feel something. I really, really did.

But I felt nothing.

As Dexter broke the kiss and eased back to look at me, I saw that he knew it too.

"I'm sorry," I said. "I thought I was ready, but I'm not." I drew in a deep breath, shuddering as I exhaled. All I could think about as Dexter had brought his lips down onto mine was Andre. All I could wish was that Andre was the one holding my body close to his right now.

"It's okay," he whispered, looking into my eyes. "I understand. We're going to take things slowly, see where this might go."

I nodded. "Okay." There were no promises. We'd stay in touch and see how things played out. Maybe in a couple of months…

"I'll call you before I have to head out of town. Maybe we can get together for coffee, at least."

"Sure."

Dexter turned and walked the few steps to the door. "Paul's probably wondering what's taking me so long."

"I'm sure he is."

Dexter opened the door, then looked over his shoulder and gave me one last smile. "Talk to you soon."

As Dexter started down the steps, I watched him. I looked at his fit body, thinking that he certainly was attractive. He would be perfect dating material…. If not for Andre.

At the car now, he turned and waved at me. I waved back, then closed the door.

I went right to the kitchen and opened my fridge, because I needed a glass of wine. I was pouring it when I heard a knock on my door.

Dexter?

I hustled back to my front door. I opened it, saying, "Dexter—"

But his name died on my lips when I saw who was standing there.

It wasn't Dexter. It was Andre.

CHAPTER FOURTEEN

My eyes widened, and my heart started to pound. My lips parted, but I couldn't say a thing.

"You're already seeing someone else?" Andre asked without preamble. An accusation, really.

"Andre…"

"Is that what's going on here?"

I said nothing. All I could do was look at the fury in his eyes—and the unmasked pain.

He stepped into my house uninvited. "You sleeping with that guy?"

His voice held an almost desperate note, as if the idea that I was involved with someone else terrified him. "He's a friend of a friend," I explained.

"That's why he's coming out of your house at this hour?"

I stiffened my jaw, defensive. "I don't owe you an explanation. Another woman is carrying your baby."

He advanced, slipping his arm around my waist and immediately moving to the wall with me, pinning me there. "I didn't agree to break up with you. You sent me away. If another man is really the reason you want nothing to do with me—"

"It was a blind date," I explained.

"So you're already dating?" he asked, his tone filled with disbelief.

"I only said yes because…because I need to forget about you." My voice cracked, and I hated that. I wished that I sounded more resolved.

"You want to forget about me?" His voice was softer, and held a hint of pain.

"No," I whispered. "I don't want to forget about you. I can't…"

Andre's body relaxed, and he exhaled sharply. I could hear his relief as well as feel it. "Baby…"

No longer tense against me, I could feel the warmth emanating from his body to mine. He lowered his head, then trailed his nose along the side of my face, his warm breath fanning my skin.

Oh my God…

"Tell me you're missing me as much as I'm missing you," he whispered.

Heat was spreading through my veins as surely as if someone had injected me with lust. Dammit, why did I find him so irresistible?

"Andre," I began, but I couldn't think of anything else to say. When I was around him, my thoughts turned to mush. My brain turned to mush. The only thing that mattered was how he made me feel.

His lips skimmed my cheek as he smoothed one hand down my back and onto my ass. His other hand went down my arm, and he linked hands with mine. He took our joined hands and raised them high, pinning me to the wall even more effectively.

"Oh God," I uttered. "Andre, I don't—"

"Are you going to tell me to leave?" I heard a hint of a challenge in his tone.

I wanted to lie. I wanted to tell him yes, that I wanted him to leave. I wanted to stick to my resolve, save my heart the pain that would come from continuing to be involved with him.

But I couldn't lie to him. And it was time I stopped lying to myself.

"No," I rasped.

With a growl of satisfaction, Andre's lips came down on mine. Heat washed over me instantly. It was as though we hadn't been together for years, instead of just days. His tongue delved into my mouth, tangling with mine. And Lord, did he ever taste sweet.

Gripping my ass, he pulled me close, urging my body against his so that I could feel just how much he wanted me. All the while, I kissed him back with desperation, my own hands snaking around his neck and clinging to his broad shoulders for dear life.

Andre tore his lips from mine and dropped down onto his haunches. The next instant, he was bunching my dress around my waist and pushing my panty aside with urgent fingers. My womb tensed with pleasure. And when Andre's mouth covered my pussy, all I could do was splay my hands against the wall and cry out.

"Oh, yeah, baby." His voice was low, ripe with desire, and that intensified my lust. I didn't care if there would be no tomorrow. I didn't care if my heart would be in shreds in a few days. I needed this. Needed it desperately.

His tongue flicked up and down my nub, driving me wild. My pleasure multiplied when he began to fondle me with his fingers in addition to his tongue. I all but stopped breathing, shutting down every sensation but this. Slowly suckling me, Andre slipped two fingers inside of me.

Nothing had ever felt this good.

"Andre…oh, baby."

We were in the foyer of my home, and he was feasting on me, as though it had to be here, now. As though we couldn't even take the time to head to the bedroom.

And I didn't want to. I wanted to come. Come right now. Come so hard for this man I loved.

His fingers moved slowly, going deep while his tongue tantalized and tortured at the same time. My knees began to get weak. My breathing came in hot gasps.

And then I glanced down, saw him looking up at me. Looking up at me as his lips suckled me. That's when I vaulted over the edge into utter bliss. I came hard. Andre lapped at my essence, ate the passion that I had for him.

"Oh baby," I whimpered. "Oh…" My voice trailed off on a passionate sigh. My body was on sensory overload.

Andre gripped my hips and kissed a path up my belly before meeting my mouth. And he kissed me again, slow and deep. I could taste myself on his lips and tongue. It felt as though I had branded him with my essence, and he was now branding me.

He was mine and I was his.

"I love you," he whispered.

The words made tears come to my eyes. I was so confused. I didn't know what was right. I *wanted* to concentrate only on what I was feeling and not worry about anyone else. And yet there was a helpless baby on the way who deserved his father.

"Tell me you love me," Andre said.

"I love you," I rasped. I needed this moment, if only this. I did love him. And I wanted him.

I tightened my arms around his neck. "Take me to bed."

Not wasting a second, he swept me into his arms and whisked me up the stairs to my bedroom. With his lips on mine, he eased my body down so that I was standing, then began to drag down the zipper at the back of my dress. I grabbed at his shirt, pulling it from the waist of his jeans.

We had to break apart so that he could pull his shirt over his head. Our ragged breathing filled the air. I looked at his gorgeous physique, at those strong arms and washboard abs. A fresh wave of lust shot through my body.

He began to undo the button on his jeans, and I shimmied out of my dress. When he dropped his pants, his erection was large in his boxers.

I wanted to ride him all night long…

"God, I've missed you," he uttered, and started toward me. He framed my face and began to kiss me. I slipped a hand into his boxers. When my fingers stroked his shaft, he groaned into my mouth.

I tore my lips from his and began to lower myself. Holding his cock, I laved my tongue around the tip.

I felt Andre shudder. "No," he said, and pulled at my shoulders. "I need to be inside of you. Now." He urged me up. "Take off your panties."

I did as he instructed, pulling my thong down. I slipped it off my legs, and heard his moans of delight. Our connection was off the charts. I knew that he would always turn me on.

"Damn, Bella. You're killing me." His eyes drank in my nakedness, heating my skin as effectively as his touch.

I sat on the edge of the bed. Slowly spread my legs. Touched myself.

A carnal sound rumbling from his chest, he advanced. And in the next instant, Andre was positioning himself between my thighs and securing my legs upward behind his arms. I reached for his cock and guided it to my center. I was wet, more than ready. And with one thrust, he filled me.

"Andre!" I arched my back and cried out from the delicious pleasure as he filled me. It had been far too long. "Oh my God!"

He stayed deep inside me for a long moment, and just stared into my eyes. He pulled back slowly and thrust deep again, our eyes connected the entire time.

His movements were slow and deep and oh so tantalizing. Our sighs of pleasure filled the room. I wanted to stay here forever with Andre like this. The two of us loving each other.

Andre's thrusts picked up speed, and my body filled with sensations of heat. Then he eased forward, seeking my lips. His kiss was filled with meaning. With love.

He was mine. I was his. How could I fight the truth anymore?

Each thrust of his shaft inside of me filled me so completely, touching my soul and my heart. I loved

him. And I wanted him in my life. Right now, that was all that mattered.

As his breathing became more ragged, he bit down gently on my bottom lip. Heat filling my womb, my head began to get light. Another orgasm was building.

"Andre, baby, I'm close."

He thrust hard and deep, groaning as he did. Then he eased back and did it again, and again. I looked at him, my eyes holding his. And I saw in his gaze the same thing I felt. A desperate need. But also, love.

"Ohhh." I moaned. "Baby, I'm coming…"

Andre thrust into me fast and deep, groaning long and hard as he did. We both went over the edge together. And together, we rode that wave into the sweetest abyss.

CHAPTER FIFTEEN

We made love again that night. And again.

Our lovemaking was amazing. I felt every touch, every kiss even more intensely than I had before. My breasts and every part of my body were extremely sensitive to Andre's touch.

Perhaps our coming together again had been utterly sweet because of the fact that we'd been apart.

Being with Andre felt comfortable. Right. Just as it always had.

I looked at his naked body beside mine in the bed. He was on his side, facing me, and sound asleep. In his face, I could see the little boy he'd been. My eyes ventured to his chest and all those hard muscles. There was nothing boyish about that body. Not at all.

I touched his face, and he stirred. Seconds later, his eyes opened and flew to mine. Then a smile came onto his face.

"Morning, sexy," he said.

"Good morning."

He reached an arm out and placed it on my hip, then urged me close. As my naked breasts pressed against his chest, his lips found mine. He gave me a soft kiss.

Just a quick peck, a simple morning greeting, but my body tingled nonetheless.

"I hate to kick you out of bed," I said, trailing my fingers down his arm. "But I've got to get ready for work."

His hand tightened on my hip. "I can't seduce you into skipping work today?"

I wanted to say yes. He was entirely irresistible. But I couldn't. "I wish. I really do. But I've got a meeting with the CFO today, and—"

"It's okay," Andre said.

A beat passed. "So," I began. "About last night."

"Don't," Andre said. "Don't push me away again."

A small smile tugged at my lips. Being with Andre last night had proven to me that I couldn't push him away. Trying to live without him was like trying to live without air. I simply couldn't do it.

"I'm not pushing you away," I said. "Not anymore."

His eyes lifted, filling with sweet surprise and happiness. And just seeing that look on his face filled my own heart with a sense of fullness that I could barely describe.

"I love you, Andre." The words were simple, and the truth. I smoothed my hand over his strong shoulder, remembering how last night we had clung to each other as though it was the last night we would ever have together.

But I was done denying myself. I loved this man.

"I guess it's not the end of the world if someone else is having your baby." As I spoke the words, I cringed. I hated the reality, but what could I do? There was a huge chance that Clarissa was lying, that she was just saying she was pregnant as a ploy to keep Andre in her life. But if she wasn't?

Andre's eyes widened with surprise. "You mean that?"

"These couple of weeks trying to live without you have been excruciating. And it's obvious that anything you had with Clarissa is over. But Andre…" My voice trailed off, and pain filled my heart. "If you *are* the father, I want you to embrace this child. There's nothing more that I want than to be able to give you a baby, but I can't. Which means that if we stay together, this might be your only chance to have a child of your own."

Andre's eyes narrowed and he looked at me with a confused expression. "Is that why you pushed me away? Because you can't give me a baby?"

Until I had said the words, I hadn't fully acknowledged the truth in my heart. Clarissa being pregnant hurt more because I knew she would be able to give Andre the one thing I couldn't. I would always look

at Andre with their baby and feel a sense of failure because I could never share that joy with him.

"It's just…you deserve to be a father."

Andre's arm tightened around me, and he looked at me with an indescribable expression. I couldn't tell if he was disappointed with me.

"I want *you*," he said. "I want it all with you. If we can't have our own biological children, so be it. There are other ways. A lot of great kids out there need homes. I'm not against adopting. In fact, it's something I'd love to do."

"But I'm sure you want a child of your own," I said. "To see him or her grow up. To be a part of his life."

"Everything I want is right here in this room," Andre said. "If I can't have you, I have nothing. The rest…. We'll work it out, babe. And no, I won't walk away from Clarissa's baby—*if* I'm the father. But were you going to walk away from me because—what?—you didn't feel good enough for me?"

"I just don't want you to have any regrets," I whispered.

"Regrets over choosing you?" He stroked my face, and I could see the emotion in his eyes. Hear it in his voice. "You're my everything. And the fact you care so much about me being a father—enough that you would step out of the way—makes me love you even more. I've never met a woman like you, Bella. And dammit, I'm not gonna lose you."

Then he kissed me, a deep kiss filled with love. His fingers smoothed over my hair as his tongue delved into my mouth. With a sigh, I wrapped my arms around him and held him tight.

And just like always, that spark of heat quickly consumed us. I felt his member grow hard against my body.

Breaking the kiss, Andre said, "I can handle anything—as long as you're in my life."

His words melted my heart. "I feel the same way. That's what I was trying to tell you. I wanted to walk away, but I can't. Because I love you. And even if the road isn't going to be easy, I'm going to fight for you. For us."

Andre stroked my cheek. "You know how badly I want to make love to you right now?" he asked. He tweaked one of my nipples, and my lips parted on a soft moan.

I bit down on my bottom lip, then said, "Not as much as I want to make love to you." I wanted nothing more than to stay in bed with him, naked, the two of us loving each other heart and soul. But I had to get to work. "But we'll have tonight, Andre. And tomorrow, and the next night…"

He grinned from ear to ear. "Yeah, we will. I love you, Bella."

"I love you, too, Andre."

Andre left, and I got into the shower to get ready for work. My heart was full. Never in my life had I ever felt so complete.

And what I'd said to Andre had been like a weight lifting off of my shoulders. It had suddenly become very clear to me that a big part of my wanting to walk away from him had been about wanting to make sure that I didn't stand in the way of his happiness as a father—because I couldn't give him a child.

I didn't doubt for a second that Andre loved me. I'd had a knee-jerk reaction to Clarissa's bombshell, but I'd now had time to think. Time to reflect on what I needed, wanted, and deserved.

It had been less than two weeks without Andre in my life, yet I'd missed him terribly. It was clear to me that I would always miss having him in my life, in my bed. The passion between us was the real deal.

And it was worth fighting for.

I'd never met such an amazing man. And didn't I deserve to be happy? Why should I walk away from him and sacrifice my own happiness? What we had together was the kind of love that came along once in a lifetime.

As I exited the shower, I couldn't stop smiling. I would be smiling at work today, not sulking as I had since returning from London. Everything was right in my world again.

A short while later, I was dressed and ready for work, and backing my car out of the driveway. I glanced in my rearview mirror—then hit the brakes. "What the heck?"

I whipped my head over my shoulder to see if I had actually seen what I thought I had.

Oh my God. I *had*.

Clarissa!

CHAPTER SIXTEEN

Clarissa was standing on the sidewalk, blocking the path of my car. What the hell?

She started walking down my driveway. I debated whipping out of the driveway before she could talk to me, but I could just see Clarissa jumping into the path of my car so that I could clip her. Then she could run to the police and play the victim.

She walked toward the driver side window—waddled was more like it. Her face looked crestfallen as she faced me, one hand on her hip.

I put the window down. "Clarissa, what are you—"

"You told me you were going to stay away from Andre. Why was he coming out of your house this morning?"

"Are you *spying* on us?" Good Lord, it wasn't even eight in the morning!

"Answer the damn question," Clarissa said.

This bitch was getting on my last nerve. I blew out a frazzled breath. I didn't have time for this. "Don't you have better things to do with your time than stalking?"

"I needed Andre last night," Clarissa went on. "He was nowhere to be found. So I came here early this morning. I was…I was sick." She whimpered. "But he wasn't around to help me. Because he was with you."

She put a hand on her belly, and I couldn't help but look at it. Since the last time I'd seen her, her belly seemed to have grown even bigger. Unnaturally so.

"Are you even pregnant?" I asked.

Her eyes widened, and I saw her jaw tighten. And I saw something else.

A bit of panic?

"I hope you enjoyed yourself last night," Clarissa spat out. "Because that was the last night you'll ever spend with Andre. The last night you'll ever spend with *my* man."

"Are you done?" I asked.

"You lied to me," Clarissa said, looking at me with disgust. "You had no intention of staying away from Andre. Did you, bitch?"

She wasn't in my path anymore, and I hit the gas and backed out of the driveway. The car squealed. I was done with Clarissa. Done with her antics. Done with her thinking she could control my life.

I drove out of the neighborhood, not looking back.

The stress of the situation with Clarissa was getting to me. Because at the office, my stomach was roiling so much that I thought I was going to throw up. I didn't feel better until I ate a toasted bagel and drank some peppermint tea.

During my lunch break, I called Vivica. I'd filled her in on my reconciliation with Andre, and was now telling her about Clarissa's latest antic.

"That bitch is getting on my last nerve," I said. "And how creepy is she? She was watching my house? She knew Andre was there for the night? That is straight up crazy."

"Girl," Vivica said, "be careful. She sounds nuts."

"Her belly was even bigger than before," I said. "Obviously, pregnant women get bigger. But from last week until now she's grown so much? And when we saw her on Saturday night, she was barely showing." I paused, thinking of all the reservations Andre had about her. What he told me about why he didn't trust her. "I'm starting to wonder if she's really pregnant. I think she's just desperate to keep Andre at any cost."

"I have an idea," Vivica suddenly said.

"What?"

"A way for you to find out once and for all if Clarissa is pregnant."

I sat up in my chair, leaning my elbows on my desk. "What are you thinking?"

"Remember when Craig was cheating? Well, I never really told you and Holly this, partly because I was embarrassed. But I hired an investigator. He followed Craig around, watched him. Saw who he met up with after work. And he's the one who found the proof that Craig was screwing around. The investigator was *very* good. In fact, I was surprised at some of the pictures he was able to capture. It was like he was in the room with them. Maybe he can help you out?"

I bit my inner cheek. Hire an investigator? Did I really want to go that far?

"If Clarissa is lying, it will come out soon enough," I said. "I guess it doesn't really matter right now. Andre and I have worked things out. We're not letting Clarissa come between us anymore."

"I disagree," Vivica said. "It *does* matter. Because the longer it takes to find out the truth, the longer she'll be a pain in your asses."

"You're right about that."

"So why wait?" Vivica asked. "She's already making your life hell. Showing up at your place whenever she wants, giving you grief about Andre because of the baby. I'd get the proof you need to end this as soon as possible. Because as long as she has the pregnancy to hold over your heads, she's going to continue to hijack your life and Andre's as long as she can."

Vivica had a point. Clarissa was that kind of person. The sooner I knew the truth—whatever it was—the better.

"What's this investigator's name?"

An hour later, I had it all arranged. I'd spoken to Henry Balfour, the detective who had been able to capture pictures of Craig with his mistress. He assured me that he'd be able to get close enough to Clarissa to determine the truth. I didn't have Clarissa's phone number nor her home address, but Henry said that he'd be able to learn everything about her by just her name.

All I had to do now was wait.

When I saw Andre's name flashing on my phone near the end of the day, I quickly answered the call. "Hey," I said, my voice husky.

"Hey, beautiful."

My heart melted. I loved hearing his voice.

"What time are you getting home?" Andre asked.

"Why? Are you planning to have your wicked way with me again?"

"You complaining?"

I giggled. "No. Not at all."

"I was thinking I could make you dinner. *First.*"

Already, heat was filling my womb. I couldn't wait to make love to Andre again. "I'll be home around six," I told him. "But Andre…" Remembering how Clarissa had accosted me this morning was like cold water being thrown on my happy feelings. "Did you speak to Clarissa today?"

"How did you know?" he asked.

"So you did?"

"Yes," Andre answered. "I was going to tell you about it tonight. She came by, said she wasn't feeling well. When I suggested she go to the doctor, she refused. She said she would feel better if I gave her some tea. So I did. I think—I think she was playing games, trying to get me to spend time with her. Because then she started asking me what I wanted to name the baby. I told her that until we knew for sure if I was the father, I didn't want to have that conversation."

God, Vivica was so right. Clarissa would continue to hijack our lives. "Well, she accosted me again this morning when I was leaving for work," I told him. "She *knew* that you'd spent the night at my place."

"What?"

"She was angry that I wasn't staying away from you. Seriously, it's like she's stalking us."

"All right," Andre said. "I can't ignore this any longer. I have to talk to her, tell her to stay the hell away from you."

"Maybe I shouldn't see you tonight," I said, my thoughts whirling inside my head like a hurricane.

"Bella—"

"No, hear me out. Clarissa is deranged. If she's watching what we do and sees that we're still seeing each other, maybe she'll come unhinged. Who knows what she's capable of?"

"No," Andre said. "I'm not doing this. I'm not letting Clarissa scare us into staying apart. If we ignore her, she'll go away."

"I hope so," I said.

"I know so," Andre insisted. "I'll see you after work. Okay?"

"Okay."

CHAPTER SEVENTEEN

I glanced around the neighborhood to make sure that no one was lurking, then rang Andre's doorbell. Several seconds later, the door opened.

Andre's lips grew into a grin when he looked at me.

"Hey," I said softly.

"Come here, baby," Andre said, and pulled me into his arms.

Now inside the house, he closed the door behind me and turned the lock, then brought his lips down on mine. Instantly, heat engulfed us both. Every time we came together, it was electric.

Moaning with pleasure, I slipped my arms around Andre's neck. He lowered his hands to my breasts and squeezed.

"Ooh," I uttered.

Easing back, he looked at me oddly. "You all right?"

"My breasts…they're very sensitive." I grinned up at him. "They've missed you."

"Is that so?" he asked, and started to undo my blouse.

"Yes," I rasped.

He trailed his finger along my bosom. "Your breasts seem bigger," he commented. "I noticed that last night."

I'd noticed the same thing. That they looked fuller, and they certainly felt heavier and more sensitive. "I'm probably ovulating," I said by way of explanation. And as I said the words, I realized that my period was late.

About ten days late, actually. I'd been due on my return from London, but with the chaos of Clarissa's bombshell announcement, I'd been too stressed to even think of my cycle.

Clearly, the stress had wreaked havoc on my body. It wasn't the first time I'd been late. It had happened on occasion in the past—also during times of stress.

Andre gave me another odd look. "What are you thinking?"

"Nothing," I replied.

"So you can't have children, but you still ovulate?" he asked.

"I don't know how it all works. But—" I slipped my hands around my back and unclasped my bra. "Is that really what you want to talk about right now?"

My breasts spilled free, and Andre groaned when he looked at them. Then he took both nipples between his fingers and began to tweak them. Sensation hit me with the force of a Mac truck. I sighed as my nipples hardened.

"Mmm," Andre moaned. Then, pushing my breasts together, he lowered his head and flicked his tongue over one nipple. Then the other. He laved his tongue back and forth over both of my nipples—hot, wet, and oh so tantalizing. My womb tightened as glorious heat spread throughout my body.

"Baby…" I uttered.

Andre pushed my nipples together as closely as possible, then took them both into his mouth at the same time. He suckled me slowly and sweetly, and I cried out, the pleasure deliciously intense.

"God, I love how you respond to me," he whispered, then drew one nipple deep into his mouth and suckled me hard.

We weren't even out of the doorway, and already I was half dressed, and he was thrilling me sexually. "Take me upstairs," I pleaded.

He scooped me into his arms and whisked me upstairs. I clung to him, nuzzling my nose in his neck and inhaling his musky scent. In his room, he placed me on the bed and began to kiss me. As his tongue tangled with mine, I undid the clasp on his jeans. And when I pushed his jeans and briefs over his hips, I moaned into his mouth.

"I need you inside of me," I said, stroking his erect cock.

Andre smoothed a hand down my neck, then down the center of my body, between my bosom. Down to my abdomen. Over my pussy. I let my legs fall apart to give him more access to my sweet spot.

Crash!

The sound of something shattering had Andre and me quickly pulling apart. My pulse racing, I felt disoriented. One minute, I'd been on a sexual high. The next—

Andre jumped up from the bed. "Stay here."

"Was that a window?" I asked.

Andre pulled his jeans up over his hips. "I'm about to find out."

Sitting up, I watched Andre race out of the bedroom. My heart was pounding.

The seconds that passed seemed much longer. I got out of bed, and seeing one of Andre's shirts on a chair, I snatched it up and slipped it over my head. Then I went to the bedroom door.

"Andre," I called.

When he didn't answer, I started downstairs. On the main floor, I turned, heading toward the kitchen and the family room at the back of the house.

When the kitchen came into view, I gasped. Shattered glass covered the tile floor.

Andre whipped his head around to look at me. "I told you to stay upstairs."

"Babe, you can't walk around on the glass like that in your bare feet."

He bent to pick up something behind the counter that I couldn't see. As he stood tall, he produced a brick. "Someone threw this into the house."

"Not just someone," I said, and felt my blood start to boil. I wandered toward the patio door window and peered outside.

"Bella, stay away from the window. God only knows if Clarissa is still out there."

"She's probably long gone," I said sourly. "The friggin' coward."

"The bitch is psychotic," Andre quipped. "She went into the backyard so she wouldn't be seen."

"I told you she's been watching us," I said. "How did she know I was in here?"

"She could have just been lashing out at me," Andre said. "I didn't give her what she wanted when she came here." He took a few careful steps toward the stove. "Shit. There's shattered glass all over the stove. Obviously it got into the pot of rice."

"Babe, please," I said. "Come get some shoes on."

Andre started toward me, then cussed when his knee sharply buckled. Instinctively, I moved toward him, but he held up a hand to keep me at bay. Bracing one hand on the edge of the counter, Andre lifted his foot. I saw the blood as he began to pull out the shard of glass.

"Andre…"

"I'm okay," he said.

"You need to call the police."

"Yeah, I'm going to. Clarissa's gone too far now. Her ass needs to be arrested. Immediately."

CHAPTER EIGHTEEN

I stayed with Andre that night. He insisted. And I didn't refuse. I wasn't interested in staying home alone—not after Clarissa's latest antic.

Unfortunately, the cop who came to take our statements didn't seem convinced that Clarissa was behind the vandalism. Neither of us had seen her do it. And I could tell that my story of a jealous ex was falling on deaf ears.

Still, the officer promised to follow up with her, while at the same time pointing out the extreme likelihood that a teen or teens might have simply been out to cause some mischief.

But in the morning, when I went home, the officer's theory seemed even less likely. I knew—just *knew*—that Clarissa was been behind the vandalism. Because on my garage door, in big, bold red paint, was the word WHORE.

"Yes, I understand that a rush order will cost more money," I said into the phone once I was behind my desk. "But I need that graffiti off of my door ASAP."

"We'll get someone out there right away, ma'am," the man told me.

I ended the call with him, then put in a call to Henry Balfour. The call went to voicemail.

"Hello, Henry. This is Bella Sinclair. I'm just wondering if you've got any information for me regarding Clarissa. Please call me back as soon as you can."

Just before three o'clock, my cell phone rang. When I saw Henry Balfour's number, I quickly answered the call.

"Henry," I said without preamble.

"Hello, Bella. I got your message."

"You have news?" I asked.

"I do have an update on the case. I'd like to meet to go over my findings."

So official. "You can't just tell me?"

"It's always better to see the evidence first hand. And that's something I prefer to do in person."

I wanted answers now. All day, I'd felt sick to my stomach. This situation with Clarissa needed to be resolved yesterday.

"Can we do this today?" I asked.

"I can meet you as early as four-thirty," Henry said.

"Five o'clock would be better," I told him.

"That'll work."

"Excellent," I said. "Where?"

I left work a little early and headed to Capitol Hill, where I'd agreed to meet Henry at a café. He told me he would be sitting at a table in the back, and what he would be wearing, and I found him easily.

He rose to greet me as I neared his table. "Bella?" he asked.

I extended a hand. "Hello, Henry."

He took my hand and shook it, offering me a business-like smile. Henry was short, stocky, and average looking. His thin blond hair was balding.

He sat, and I took a seat beside him at the four top table so that he could more easily show me whatever he had found. He had a large tablet on the table, on which I hoped he had pictures.

"Thanks for agreeing to meet me so quickly," I said.

"No problem," Henry said. "I was able to get nice and close to the subject, so I'm certain of my findings."

"Is she pregnant?" I asked, needing to know.

He pressed the button to turn on his tablet and said, "See for yourself."

Henry started flipping through the various pictures. In the first picture, Clarissa was standing in front of a restaurant with her cell phone to her ear. She appeared to have a small pregnant belly. In the second picture, she was exiting a house. My stomach sank when I saw that she *did* look pregnant.

But as Henry swiped to the third picture—this one captured through the window into a home—my heart began to pound with excitement.

Clarissa was wearing workout gear—a tank top and tights—and had a perfectly flat belly.

"In the privacy of her own home," Henry began, "Clarissa wasn't concerned about faking her pregnancy. But she should have made sure to close her blinds before working out in her home gym."

"That conniving…" I stopped short of completing my thought. No need to cuss in Henry's presence.

As I stared at the next pictures of Clarissa—drinking water, wiping sweat off of her forehead, doing crunches—I was stunned that anyone would be so manipulative. Clarissa really wasn't pregnant. Didn't she know that her lie would be exposed eventually?

"Can you send me these pictures?" I asked.

"I can do better than that. I've printed them for you." Henry reached into the laptop bag beside him, and withdrew an envelope. "Might be a little old-fashioned, but I like it this way. I prefer to give people physical evidence. Makes it easier, especially for court cases."

"How much do I owe you?"

Henry produced a bill detailing the work he'd done. "This wasn't a hard job at all. Only took me two days to get the proof you needed. You'll see I gave you a twenty percent discount."

"Are you sure?" I asked.

"No problem. All I ask is that if you know someone else who needs an investigator, you refer them to me."

Grinning, I shook his hand. "Done deal." Then I asked, "Do you prefer cash? I don't have quite enough on me. But I can go to an ATM."

"Actually, I'm able to process a credit card payment, if you want to pay me that way."

"Perfect," I said. This was the best $320 I had ever spent.

I called Andre as soon as I left the café. The call went to voicemail.

"Andre, call me back as soon as you can. Better yet, come by my place as soon as you get this message. I'll be home around five-forty-five."

Though I left Andre a voicemail, I also sent him a text letting him know that I wanted to talk to him as soon as possible, that I had some news to share.

And as for that bitch, Clarissa—I couldn't wait for Andre to show her the evidence that she'd been lying her ass off. She was playing a game, and I was simply a pawn in it. So was Andre, for that matter. I was done with her and ready to let her know.

When I got home, the first thing I noticed was that my garage door was freshly painted. Thank God the graffiti was gone. I parked in the driveway, then made my way onto the porch and to my front door.

Once inside, I checked my phone. Andre still hadn't replied to me. No text, no phone call. So I called him again. Again, his voicemail picked up. Where was he?

"Hey, babe," I said when the beep sounded and I was able to leave a message. "It's Bella, again. Where are you? I really need to talk to you. I'm home now, so when you get this message, just drop by."

I ended the call. Then I went to the kitchen to prepare something to eat while waiting for Andre to get back to me.

CHAPTER NINETEEN

When I heard the knock at my door, I put the plate of pasta I'd just shared onto the counter and hurried out of the kitchen. I should probably just give Andre a key. That would make things a lot easier.

I swung the door open.

And was shocked to see Clarissa standing there.

She stepped into the house uninvited. "I warned you," she said without preamble.

"Get out of my house."

"What kind of bitch doesn't stay away from a man when he's the father of another woman's baby?"

I laughed sarcastically. "Really? If you're pregnant, why don't you lift your blouse and show me your belly."

"I've had enough of you."

"Show me your belly," I insisted. "Then I'll walk away from Andre."

Clarissa kicked the door shut with a foot, then took a few steps toward me. The look in her eyes unnerved me.

"Enough of this," I said. "Get out of my house."

"Or else?" Clarissa challenged. "You gonna call the police again? Try to convince them that a pregnant woman is wreaking havoc in your life?" she added in a whiny voice.

"You're trespassing now," I said. "So yes, I'm going to call the police if you don't turn around and leave."

When Clarissa didn't make a move to leave, I whirled on my heel and started into the living room, where my phone was in my purse.

"Good luck making it to your phone," Clarissa taunted me.

"You want to get arrested," I said, "that's your choice."

I dug the phone out of my purse, and as I lifted it to my ear, I turned to face Clarissa. If she knew what was good for her, she'd be gone.

Instead, she was right there—in my face.

I gasped. "Clarissa, what are you doing?"

"Solving things. Making sure the problem goes away."

And before I knew what was happening, I felt the blow to the chest. As I gasped again, I saw her hand retreat. She was holding a knife, and it was covered with blood.

My blood.

My eyes narrowed. I felt stunned. Disoriented. The phone slipped from my fingers and fell to the floor.

And then it was ringing. Or was that my ears?

Clarissa shoved me, and I fell backward onto the carpet. My brain fighting to make sense of what was going on, I heard Clarissa say, "Help me! Andre—he just attacked me! Come quick! I think…I think I'm dying!"

My breaths were wheezing out of me. "Clarissa—"

She dropped my phone onto the floor and stepped toward me. "Oh, what's wrong?" she mocked me.

I pressed my hand against my chest. Warm blood was spilling out. With every ounce of strength I had, I tried to back away from her. "Stop…"

Clarissa snatched up an ornament from my coffee table. Then she advanced.

My limbs were getting weak, but I kicked at her legs with all my might. "Get away from me!"

"Die, bitch!" Clarissa yelled.

I threw a hand up as she swung the ornament down at my head.

I screamed.

Then the world went black.

Don't miss
IF THIS IS OUR LAST NIGHT,
the conclusion of the Bella & Andre
AGE OF LOVE series,
coming soon!

Copyright © 2015 by Kayla Perrin.

Ian Cai Mercer has written many poems, reviews, hiking tales, and stories for his blog at http://iancaimercer. wordpress.com. Then there is Mr. Tiglet's Travels. His Storysite has tales ranging from Pirateez, the Woozies to the Tiglet Show and Infinite Whoniverses. Infinite Tigletverses/Tigletverse Photography for his filmmaking and photography projects can be found at www.facebook. com/mrtigletstravels. While having written many SF/ Fantasy stories, he loves the irony that his first paid publication is for romance, which began as a creative writing exercise back in 2003 for his English Degree.

MAKING THE FIRST MOVE

by Ian Cai Mercer

Sometimes taking the first step feels like one giant leap.

Christa was enjoying her day off, reading while waiting for Gerry in the gym. When he said that he liked badminton, she asked him if he fancied a game and was thrilled that he had said yes. With it being a Sunday, the Physiotherapy unit was closed for the weekend. Being a deputy Supervisor had its advantages, for her at least.

She was relieved when he entered, putting her book away. In a dark blue tracksuit, he looked like a sailor. She met his gaze and waved.

He came over, a glint in his eye as he greeted her. "It's the Lady in Red!"

"Do I stand out a bit?" She struck a pose, grinning like the Cheshire Cat on a good day.

She listened as Gerry told her about his previous dayshift, remembering to nod her head at all the right places. It was difficult to just concentrate on his words, especially when they made eye contact.

Lost within those deep pools of blue, she was surprised when he stopped talking.

"Hello sleepyhead!" He waved a hand in her face. "I'm not sending you into a coma wittering on like this, am I?"

A shiver coursed through her, prickling the hairs at the back of her head. "Course not; I'm just glad to be with you," she replied.

He flushed and she wondered if she'd embarrassed him, but then he shrugged.

"Well, glad to hear it." And with that he took her hand and held it in his.

It was as if the world itself shook and came to life. As if all this time she had lived her life in black and white, then it suddenly exploded into an atomic rainbow of colours.

There was a long pause, a shifting of his feet awkwardly, then: "I really like you; in fact, I've fancied you for ages." Now he appeared as nervous as she was.

Christa watched as he struggled for words, stammering, so she used it as an excuse to hug him, a little awkwardly. "Don't worry, I won't bite," she reassured him. "I've been thinking about us for ages too." She stepped away. "Shall we try a date? How about lunch after this game?"

Now it was his turn to do a Cheshire Cat impersonation. "You're on!" he said and they began to play Badminton.

It was a ferocious game. Christa could not believe how fast it all came back to her. She easily took the lead, eventually beating him. He sat, leaning back against the wall, so she joined him, sipping from a water bottle and shared it.

"Wow, I don't think I've enjoyed being beaten so much since…well, whenever really!" He shrugged.

"Cheers, I'll take that as a compliment. Want to play again?" She lent his way, nudging his shoulder with hers. "I'll go a bit easier on you next time." She wiped the sweat from her brow. She was exhausted, but still excited at finally having Gerry all to herself, without any of the other staff around.

"I think you've humiliated me enough today."

"You didn't expect me to beat you, did you?" He laughed.

"Ah, yes, I did think I would be all gentlemanly and take it easy on you. Last time I make that mistake!"

They laughed as they got up and left the gym, making sure to lock up.

"I have to admit, I wasn't sure you'd go out with me," Christa said as they left the unit, taking a stroll through the grounds. It was as if all her senses had been enhanced. Taste, touch, smell, hearing and sight all affected. She could smell the fragrance of spring in the air; feel the wind blow gently through her hair. She heard the cacophony of birds tweeting, almost taste the blossoming of flowers as they walked past. It all made her feel so alive. It was that atomic rainbow flashing again.

He shrugged. "Hey, well…you're the only one I want to be with." They stopped and he kissed her lightly; she felt her cheek grow warm from the touch of his lips.

Christa sighed. "That's good enough for me," she said. "Because I kinda like you too."

Christa enjoyed being with him, laughing together, just the way she had imagined it.

They went and had lunch in the pub down the road. It had a nice, traditional warmth to it, which she liked a lot. They sat down at a table in the corner and ordered house steaks followed by dessert.

"I have to admit, I wasn't sure you'd go out with me," Christa said as she finished off an apple pie and custard. "Oh my, that was very tasty."

Gerry passed her a napkin. "You know, when I first saw you at the welcome party, I thought you were nice. It's just taken me a while to get 'round to doing something."

"What is this something?" she flirted to cover her nerves.

He leaned forward, kissed her lightly, lingeringly—this time on the lips. Christa's response was electric, but she tried not to let it show. He was trying to be tender, not passionate. She felt her cheeks burn from the touch of his lips.

She sighed. "That's a good something," she said, kissing him back.

They talked for several hours. Christa enjoyed just sitting with him, laughing with each other, just the way she had imagined it.

They paid for their lunch and left, walking hand in hand. Then Gerry put his arm around her and drew her closer to him. She put her head on his shoulder and smiled.

"What are you smiling about?" he asked her.

She shrugged. "I'm just really happy to be with you," she admitted. "You're a loveable old rogue, aren't you?"

"I sure am," he agreed, then stopped and kissed her. She wanted him to never stop kissing her. Then Gerry put his arm around her and drew her closer to him.

They continued walking as Gerry held her tenderly, oblivious to everything else. She was glad that she had made the first move. Even though it had been difficult for her, it had been worth it. That was the thing about relationships—making the effort, making it work despite potential problems, disagreements and upsets. That is how you find someone who will stick with you through all those rollercoaster moments, no matter what. She hoped that Gerry would be the one who would stick around. He was worth the risk. Worth making the first move for.

USA Today *and national bestselling author Anna J. Stewart writes sweet to sexy romance for Harlequin's* Heartwarming *and Romantic Suspense lines, but paranormal romance is her first love. Early obsessions with* Star Wars, Star Trek, *and* Wonder Woman *set her on the path to creating fun, funny, and family-centric romances with happily ever afters for her independent heroines. Anna lives in Northern California where she deals with a serious* Supernatural *and* Sherlock *addiction and tolerates an overly affectionate cat named Snickers. You can read more about Anna and her books at www.authorannastewart.com.*

IN WRAITH DANGER

by Anna J. Stewart

"Welcome back to *Fantasy*, Ms. Atsila. We have your regular cabin ready for you."

"Thanks, Grant." Lilith Atsila accepted her returned passport along with her keycard, and cruise itinerary with a smile. Familiar faces made her happy and her job so much easier. "They've still got you on boarding duty, huh?"

"It's better than security detail." Grant rolled his bright blue eyes that caught against the strobe lighting flashing against the cruise ship. "Nothing exciting ever happens on these cruises."

"Same old, same old." Lilith tucked her passport into her pocket. The check-in lines were going strong at just past noon. Hundreds of passengers having their documents verified, their baggage checked for cabin delivery, already scheduling spa and relaxation treatments and social events. Lots and lots of people venturing out on the six-day trans-Atlantic cruise. Lilith sighed. "Routine and quiet. So much better than flying." She turned her attention back to Grant. "That's why I keep coming back."

"Is that really why?" Grant lowered his voice and looked around as if about to be caught doing something against company regulations. "You know we actually have a bet going below decks on why *Fantasy on the Sea* gets so many repeat customers. There's a secret club, isn't there? Come on." He flashed that college-student, I-can-charm-any-woman-out-of-anything grin at her. "You can tell me."

Lilith chuckled, her hand tightening on the handle of her rolling suitcase. "How much are you in for?"

"Only a hundred. It keeps rolling over, cruise after cruise. Because none of us can find out if anyone's right."

"What's your guess?" Lilith leaned an arm on the counter as if she had all the time in the world.

"Well," Grant leaned closer, "I think it's a sex thing. Like a private sex club where you all meet up and just have…fun."

"Why do I think you have your hopes pinned on the club rather than the bet?" She reached across and patted his hand. "Sorry to disappoint you, Grant. There's no club. I don't know about anyone else, but I just prefer the water over flying.

A throat cleared beside them and Lilith and Grant both glanced over to find one of his supervisors watching them. Lilith straightened, her smile slipping as she approached the stern looking woman. She was uniformed from head to toe, definitely former military. Definitely a stickler for the rules from her perfectly bunned hair to her shiny low-heeled pumps.

"Lilith Atsila." Lilith saw the quick flinch of recognition as she offered her hand. "Just catching up with one of my favorite crew members."

"Purser Shen-Wei Zhao, ma'am." She nodded her head once. "Nice to see check-in moving efficiently for our premier guests."

"Grant's the best you have," Lilith assured her while sneaking a peek over her shoulder. That Grant deflated in relief told her Purser Zhao was someone who kept a close watch over everything that went on in the confines of the *Fantasy*. Good to know.

"May I take your bag for you, ma'am?"

"No, thank you, Purser Zhao." Used to refusing the request, Lilith dodged the approaching hand with predictable ease. "I know where I'm going. Launch is at five, correct?"

"Yes, ma'am." Purser Zhao stepped back to let her pass. "First dinner seating at six-thirty."

"Noted." She'd sooner throw herself overboard and be shark bait than eat a meal in the dining room with the passengers, most of whom were about to leave their inhibitions—and rational thoughts—on dry land.

Traversing the roped-off entrance, she bypassed the usual security screening and found herself in the main lobby of *Fantasy*. She had to admit, this ship continued to impress. The way the entire interior of the vessel had been transformed enchanted even her jaded sensibilities. The décor looked as if a Hollywood special effects team had collided with Jules Verne's Nautilus to create a truly mesmerizing experience. To call it otherworldly would be an understatement.

The misty blues and light purple hues of the walls morphed and moved across the solid paneling, giving the ship an almost life-like sensation as Lilith made her way around. Where trees and plants might have created a rain forest oasis of peaceful tranquility on any other ship, soft, anemone like creatures intertwined with pulsing jellyfish the size of cars, hovering and drifting up and down against the glass encased ceiling. Stepping onto this ship was like walking into a dream.

The *Fantasy*, one of four in the line, was Lilith's particular favorite. It was hard not to appreciate an overload of magical, mystical, unexplainable features and attributes that left passengers and employees equally…distracted.

She made a pit-stop in her room—a forward suite that would allow her an expansive view of their travel path—long enough to drop off her bags and key in a new security code to the door's lock. Less than a minute later she was closing her door and heading down the long hallway to room seven thirteen. After a quick check of her surroundings, she tapped her personal ID code into the keypad. As the panel dropped open and a small lens emerged, Lilith rolled up her left sleeve and angled her wrist to the green laser waiting to scan. The ink of her tattoo warmed slightly as her identity was verified. At the click, she grabbed the handle and pushed open the door. "Whoa."

The normally serene mobile security center for the Universal Protection Agency was anything but calm. As she expected, the usual handful of techs and UPA officers had been overrun with elite security officers, identified by the iridescent infinity tattoos on the sides of their necks. Pulse weapons and flash-cannons were stashed along the back of the room guarded by two women, both of whom looked as if they'd been trained on Themyscira.

The familiar click of keyboard keys and muted conversation, along with the hum of computer systems and the smell of leftover food and stale coffee should have felt like coming home. But none of that made a dent in the tension pulsing through the air.

"Well, look who's back." Wanda Simonson wheeled out from behind her station, her platinum blond braid and equally silver-toned eyes a sharp contrast to the Old Navy jeans and vintage "flower power" t-shirt she wore. "Hey, Lil." They shared a quick knock of knuckles. "Guess that vacation didn't work out after all, huh?"

"No kidding," Lilith grumbled without much ferocity. What was vacation to a workaholic other than an inconvenience? Disappointing her brother, on the other hand, who had reminded her it had been months since any of the family had seen her, was a different matter. She was already dodging their phone calls asking if she was going to join them on the family trip to—God help her—Disneyland. "So?" She headed to the main wall-sized screen at the far end of the room which encompassed more than a half dozen regular cabins on the ship. "Fill me in. Have you found Agent Tadeshi yet?"

"Not a trace," Wanda said. "And I mean that literally, no trace. Tadeshi's tracker implant isn't responding. It's like he's completely vanished."

"What about the micro-drones? Excuse me." Lilith usurped a keyboard from one of the techs, who seemed grateful for the reprieve as he abandoned his monitoring chair for the coffee pot. Lilith clicked a few keys, brought up additional screens. She frowned, an uneasy knot tightening in her belly as she scanned. She knew what that knot meant. She could always feel trouble coming and days before a major inter-dimensional peace conference was not the time for something, *anything*, to go wrong.

"I think I'm beginning to understand why Fry called me back in," Lilith mumbled to herself, feeling a bit guilty for having wished violent repercussions on her boss at the UPA. "When you say it looks like Tadeshi's vanished you aren't talking about from the ship, are you?" She tried a few more locations, another linked security systems, then their backups. Nothing blipped. "He's nowhere."

"Exactly."

"And they've done a sweep of the ship, including the engine room?" Just to be safe, she clicked on the security report and confirmed their routine. "We've got a lot of off-world systems trying to communicate with each other down there. It can interfere with simpler signals and futz with the drones."

"That was the first place I sent them to search." Wanda pointed to the officers behind them. They hadn't moved since her arrival. Lilith couldn't be sure they were actually breathing, but their eyes were moving, scanning the room continually and frequently landing on her. "I'm telling you, Lil. Tadeshi's gone."

"A missing agent is the least of your problems."

The voice slid over her like molten lava. Lilith rose to her full height, fighting against the fog threatening to overtake her brain. Her fingers curled into her palms, her nails digging hard into her skin. She ignored Wanda's inquisitive look and turned, slowly, deliberately, giving herself enough time to keep her temper under control. "Quincy Lennox." Even his name tasted bitter on her lips. "How did you get in here? And what the hell are you doing on the *Fantasy*?"

Six foot whatever, blue-black hair and eyes the color of the midnight sea on a full-moon, Solstice Quincy's action movie good looks and killer smile had always been enough to kick her into overdrive, and not just her pulse. Except….

Except looking closer he looked like he'd been run over by a garbage trawler. Twice. "You look like crap."

"Nice to see you, too, Lil." He gave her one of his irritating nods of acknowledgement.

Lil didn't shift her gaze. She didn't dare. "Did I miss a memo about hell freezing over, Wanda?"

Wanda tapped on the computer. "Ah, no, Lil. It's one of its balmier days, actually."

Quincy's full mouth twitched. "Haven't lost that sense of humor, I see."

"And you still move like a shadow." Now she jerked her chin up to meet his gaze. And, she admitted reluctantly, to get a better look. Had more than three years passed since they'd last seen each other? The harshness lurking behind his tired eyes, the sallow pallor to his skin. The aforementioned knots in her stomach didn't loosen; instead they tightened and left her wondering how much of her concern could be laid at Quincy Lennox's feet.

"What are you doing here?" she asked again. "The *Fantasy* is the UPA's territory. No need for any UTIs around here."

The muscle in his jaw worked at one of her many nicknames for the Interplanetary Security Bureau. "The *ISB*," he ground out, "was contacted to help with security for the peace talks. I'm here as a liaison to get the ball rolling and assist with transport."

"Don't need a liaison." She patted his arm as she walked past him and busied herself with the coffee maker. The last thing she needed was a private for profit security organization honing in on her government run territory. "We've got it all handled."

The noise level dropped significantly around the room and she spun around, the order for everyone to get back to work poised behind her lips. The techs and security officers around the room continued with their conversations. The computers went quiet. Even the undertone rumbling of the air circulator had gone silent. She glared at Quincy as he approached. "We don't need your stupid cone of silence," she snapped. "My people can be trusted to hear whatever conversations we need to have."

"I can't trust anyone at the moment,"—he hesitated at her suspicious look—"where the safety of Prime Minister Zaldenda is concerned." The half-hearted addition didn't do anything to qualm her unease. The air around her shimmered as he stepped through the safety bubble he'd established. She couldn't believe that once upon a time she'd found his ability to manipulate the elements intoxicating, not to mention thrilling. What the man could do with a waterfall….

She shook the memory free of her brain and wished him gone. Except not even her magical abilities were that strong.

"Look at it this way," he tried again. "You're going to need someone to blame when the shit hits whatever passes for a fan on this boat."

"Ship," she corrected. "The *Fantasy* is a ship. And what shit are you talking about?" She slapped her hand against the invisible shield. "Drop this thing. It's unnecessary."

"It's beyond necessary." His icy eyes went sharp. "There's a Baltaran spy in the UPA."

"Yeah, right." Lil snorted. "Earth's largest inter-dimensional government protection agency, an agency with more hoops to jump through for security clearance than a Cirque de Solei troupe, has a spy. Tell me another one." She moved to push past

him, but he grabbed her arm, his fingers pinching tight into her skin. "Get your hand off me." Anger bubbled inside her like an over-brewed witch's potion. She took a step toward him so they stood chin to nose. "Or lose it."

He loosened his hold, but didn't release her. "It's not like the UPA hasn't had issues with corruption before. They've just stopped trying so hard to cover things up. Something serious is going on, Lil."

"Said the coward who jumped ship and went private rather than face the consequences of his own actions." She resisted the urge to raise up on her toes. "What's the matter? Didn't you find a happy home with the ISB? One more time, Quince. Let. Go."

He did, but he didn't move away. "We don't have time to have this fight again, Lil." She could feel the tension rolling off him in waves. "The entire Kyrian delegation set to arrive on this ship in less than four hours. If the Intel is right, there's a serious threat against one, if not all of them. Once this *ship* hits open water, we're all sitting targets. If anything happens—"

"Okay, you're right. I surrender." Lil held up a hand to cut him off. "You being here does give me a nice big scapegoat." She flicked a finger at the shield and whispered an incantation. In an instant, the shield dropped and the noise level kicked back into normal range. "Wanda, what was Tadeshi's last location?"

"Engine room. Section sixteen eleven."

Lilith pinched her lips together so hard they went numb.

"Sixteen eleven?" Quincy said in her ear. "Isn't that where the communications system for the Baltarans is?"

Lilith stepped back hard on his foot. "Wanda, I'll be on my comm. Keep your ears open. Report any new information immediately."

"You got it, boss."

"Where are we going?" Quincy nipped at her heels as she retrieved a micro-pulse gun and a new earpiece. She slipped the gun into the back of her slacks and inserted the listening device into her ear.

"*I'm* going to the engine room." Better to check it out now rather than get stuck down there once they were out to sea. Things tended to get a bit…Alice in Wonderland down below once all the engines were engaged. The combination of multiple races' magics often caused…complications. "Tadeshi could be down there. He could be hurt." Not that that would explain his dead-as-a-zombie tracker. "Or dead."

"Given the alternatives, that would be good news." He cringed. "Sorry. That was…callous."

She planted a hand on his chest and pushed him against the wall. She shot a "leave it alone" look to two of the security guards who shifted to face her, hands poised on their weapons. "Exactly what kind of breach has there been?"

He shook his head. "I can't tell you."

"Bull."

"No, Lil, I mean it. I can't tell you because I don't know. The ISB intercepted a message from UPA headquarters to the Baltarians. I—the ISB couldn't read the message but we did manage to decrypt the attached file." His dark eyes went obsidian black. "The specs for this ship. The complete specs. The Baltarans have them. Even though they're not registered for this cruise."

"Shit." Lil backed up, shook out her hand. Why was it every time she touched him he set off every cell in her body? And how was it the IBS, er, the ISB, was in the loop and she wasn't? And by complete specs… her heart did a double beat. Did that include all the codes and spells that helped run the system? "That doesn't mean Tadeshi had anything to do with it."

She'd worked with the man for years. Since before Quincy left. There weren't many people in the universes she trusted, but Haru Tadeshi was definitely on the list.

"Doesn't mean he didn't either. Currently he's the only agent unaccounted for. I checked."

She blinked against the anger. He checked her agency's system?

"Do you really think I'd be here, back in the field, if I didn't think Tadeshi wasn't a viable suspect?" It was impossible not to hear the exhaustion in his voice. "He was my friend, too, Lil."

"Was?" She narrowed her eyes, shoving the past into a corner of her soul she never accessed. "You know something I don't?" She reached for the doorknob.

"It's a…feeling. I can't explain it. And I hope to the Powers I'm wrong. But I'm not. And before you argue,"—he slipped around her and opened the door—"I'm coming with you."

❖

A lot of crazy shit had gone down in the past few months, but the last thing Quincy Lennox expected was to find himself sequestered on a supernaturally-enhanced cruise ship with an inter-dimensional prime minister, her thirteen closest aids and advisors, and his still hot-as-hell ex-girlfriend.

Funny. He could have dealt with the first two without much issue, but seeing Lil again, being around her again, having her touch him again….

Quincy gnashed his teeth and followed her out of the security hold. Two seconds around her and he was back in the land of the befuddled, falling under the spell of the only woman who ever mattered to him. The only woman to ever convince him *he* mattered.

The woman who had betrayed him.

And yet here he was, once again, following her lead. Silently relying on her to help him figure out exactly what in the hell had happened to his life.

Faint, tinkling music that brought to mind ethereal passages through time and space emanated from the hidden speakers around the ship. The walls shifted and morphed as if made of translucent gel; a miracle of modern special effects technology as far as any of the human passengers on board knew. The idea that this ship, along with the *Fantasy's* sister vessels, ran as much on magic as it did on current human science and technology, was something even the strongest and most advanced minds couldn't fathom. The idea of spending a few days in a mystical wonderland was easily more acceptable than the truth.

Exhaustion had long ago seeped into every cell of his body. He couldn't remember the last time he'd slept for more than an hour at a time. He'd had to keep moving, keep aiming toward the only person might be able to help. That he'd managed to slip onto the ship unnoticed was a minor miracle considering his shadowing abilities were normally connected to his energy level. He'd credit sheer will alone but even now he had to wonder if he was trying to get himself killed after all. If she'd killed him on sight—something she'd vowed to do three years ago—then his problems would be over. Either he found out the truth and got his life back or Lil killed him. Either way he won. Right?

He could hear voices mingling from beyond them, behind them, and even inside the glass-like elevators sluicing their way through tunnels. Every attention to detail had been paid when it came to the unexpected on this ship. Virtually nothing on board these crafts operated in what humans would call "normal ways." The suspension of disbelief was something that was not only encouraged, but a requirement of a voyage. A disbelief that didn't always work in a paranormal security officer's favor.

"I thought there was an elevator exclusively for UPA use?" Quincy called when Lil continued to move significantly faster. "Wouldn't it make more sense…" he stopped when she did; nearly took a step back when she spun on him. The ferocious look in her eyes should have had him turning around and running. Instead, he cringed. "You do believe me."

Her face twisted and she took the last few steps to the elevator. She hit the down button three times in quick succession then held out her arm for a scan. The wall between the two established elevators shivered and shifted away, exposing a set of sliding doors. When they opened, he followed her into the transportation capsule and looped his hand into the safety tether.

"Engineering, section sixteen," Lil ordered the transport. "Slow speed."

Quincy's eyebrows shot up as Lil moved in and flattened his back against the wall. Her hand was back on his chest, holding him firm, all but branding him with the heat radiating off her skin.

"Well, this is sudden." He raised his free hand to her hip, his fingers kneading into the warm, familiar flesh. He knocked his head back when she drew her knee up and pressed it against what used to be one of her favorite parts of him. "And very familiar." Maybe he wasn't so tired after all.

He took a deep breath and instantly regretted it. She still smelled like strawberries and fire. The intoxicating combination had been one of his many undoings where Lilith Atsila was concerned. "Maybe we should save this for later?"

"If you're right about the spy," she whispered hotly against his ear, "then it's best we keep whoever it might be guessing." She rose up, waited for his exhale of breath he couldn't hold back, then lowered again. "If they're surveilling the ship, then they're going to be watching whoever is in charge of the security detail. That's me." She drew her

mouth parallel to his jawline, never touching, only teasing. The dangerous glint in her dark eyes had him rethinking his currently precarious position. "Making them lower their guard might just give us a little more freedom to,"—he snapped her mouth open and bit down on his lip. Quincy jerked his head as she drew blood—"investigate. Sorry."

"I bet you are," he murmured. There hadn't ever been a time in history where Lilith Atsila hadn't made him hard. All it took was a look, a sigh. A subtle move of her pinky finger and he was all hers. Sex and their compatibility in bed (or any other piece of furniture available for that matter), had never been their problem. His hand clenched into her hip and he bit back a groan.

Trust on the other hand….

The capsule slowed to a stop. Lil stepped back, faced the doors before they opened and left him second guessing himself for the tenth time in as many days. He couldn't believe his only recourse was to step back into line with the Universal Protection Agency. The universe had been screwing with him since the day he'd been born over a century and a half ago. Why did he ever think his life would get easier?

Except…maybe he had found a sliver of hope. He wiped the blood from his lip with his thumb. The opposite of love wasn't hate, it was indifference. And there was definite interest where Lil was concerned. For the first time in a long time, maybe his gut hadn't steered him wrong.

He needed to redeem himself, if not in the eyes of the UPA, then at least where Lilith was concerned.

He only hoped he lived long enough to enjoy it.

"Section eleven is down here." Lil led the way down and around the metal stairs and platforms. The drones wouldn't have been able to transmit any signal back to the system this deep into the inner workings of the ship. Her team should have checked it. If she found nothing, she'd accept that theory. But if her intuition was right—and it always was—someone had missed something. That knot in her stomach was growing with every silent booted footfall she took.

She clicked on her flashlight to bolster the dim bulbs burning far overhead. It always amazed her how huge the engine room was, stretching nearly from one end of the ship to the other. Shadows within shadows on top of shadows. Of course, that wasn't the case with a normal cruise ship. But normal ships didn't include varying security detection units, computer encryption hookups, and a magical power source siphoned from a supernatural supply factory on an island off the coast of southern Florida.

For the most part the engine ran itself. The head engineer was actually a contractor with UPA, a necessity to keep the less technologically based parts of the system operating at peak capacity and efficiency. With the engine having been given the all clear just yesterday, the engine room was pretty much empty. And dark. She angled her light up. Darker than normal. But the energy pulsing through the entire room pounded heavy against her ears.

"You still there?" Lil whispered as she closed her eyes to adjust her own eyesight in order to allow her to see in and around and beyond the shadows dancing around her. "Quincy?" She glanced over her shoulder, finding a hint of a shadow outlined behind her. His ability to fade into the background of wherever they were often had him disappearing in the blink of an eye.

"Where else would I be?"

"Take your shadowed self that way." She motioned to her left.

"You want to split up?" The disbelief in his voice had her gnashing her back teeth. "What if I'm actually here for nefarious reasons?"

She turned and found him in the darkness. She could see his aura if she wanted, the faint silver halo of light hovering around his form. He'd always hated she'd found a way through his natural abilities to hide in the darkness. He didn't like being vulnerable in any way. Too bad she hadn't looked deeper sooner. That would have saved them both a lot of suffering.

Like it was her fault he'd fallen in love with her, a sixth generation witch; a descendant of some of the most powerful entities to ever walk the earth. A line of what her grandmother called legacy protectors. Strong, fierce female warriors that to this day lived hidden among the reality of ordinary human beings. She carried the blood and magic of her ancestors within her; magic her brothers and father didn't. Magic her siblings knew nothing about. Her

ancestor's powers inhabited every cell of her being, giving her insight, strength, and a knowledge of magic that made her perfect for a job as an inter-dimensional security expert.

Her entire life she'd been able to sense a lie before it was even told. The ability had failed her only once.

That once now stood in front of her, silently goading her into admitting that at least for the moment, she could use his help.

Rather than rising to the bait, she blanked her face and pointed again. "Circle around and down and meet me."

"Understood."

That he didn't argue with her earned him a point or two in his favor. He always had taken orders well. Then again, there hadn't been a time she hadn't been his superior, so what choice did he have now? She'd already been with the agency for more than two years when he joined. She had, unfortunately soon after, become the UPA's poster witch for why anti-fraternization rules between co-workers existed.

Lilith took the narrow metal staircase down, then the next, keeping her eyes open and alert for anything unusual as she kept her light moving. Another two levels. Down, down…she stopped.

The smell hit her first. An acrid, sulfur-like stench that had her covering her mouth and choking down the bile in her throat. Her eyes watered as she reached back to grab hold of the railing to steady herself. Trying to breathe through her mouth, she swung the light down.

The faintest tendril of smoke drifted into the air a few feet away.

She scooted under the oversized pipes, crouching and moving, her free hand poised on the butt of her gun under her jacket. Her left foot made a squelching sound as she stepped onto a grate. Heat bubbled under her toes. She scraped her foot hard, trying to clear it of whatever she'd stepped in.

Clear of the pipes, she stood up, blinking the odd darkness from her eyes as she stared down at the smoldering puddle of gelatinous yellow goo. Her light reflected back up at her in nauseating detail.

The sick feeling in her stomach rose again as she spotted the familiar insignia ring, the smart watch sizzling, and…. She crouched down, felt the ever so subtle shift of air to the side of her. When

Quincy didn't speak, she glanced up. What she saw on his colorless face, the vacant horror reflected in his eyes, worried her even more than what she was hovering over.

She reached out to take his hand, hoping to re-establish a connection with him that would give her some answers, but he jerked away, kept his hands raised and himself at a distance.

"Quincy—"

"What is it?" Quincy demanded, staring down at the gelatinous substance.

"I don't know." Grief and disgust mingled against the dread. She didn't *know*. But she suspected.

She pulled a pen out of her back pocket, pushed the tip into the slime. Even breathing through her mouth was a problem now. She could taste the toxicity in the air. She caught the edge of what she'd prayed not to find. Flipping it over, she moved it clear of most of the sludge.

"Tadeshi's tracking chip." She tucked her hair behind her ear. "Which means that's what's left of Tadeshi."

Quincy didn't move. "What would have done that? What kind of weapon?"

"Not a weapon." She could already hear the detachment coming over her, distancing her from the scene, from Tadeshi. From Quincy. Instinct kicked in. She flattened her palm on the grate, inched her fingers slightly forward until she felt the slick remnants of her friend against her skin.

"No, don't!" Quincy dived forward, hands out to stop her, but it was too late.

She threw her head back, her eyes going glassy; the darkness pressed in as she tapped the pain, the anger, the fiery rage left behind. She could see Tadeshi's quick smile flash in the darkness, see the glint in his eyes as he'd explored the ins and outs of the engine room. She felt the horror he did when he rounded a corner and found himself face to face with—

"Pull back now, Lil. Now, dammit!"

Her head snapped back and forth as she blinked out of the vision. Quincy was stooped in front of her, hands gripping her arms as he tried to break her out of the trance.

She shook her head, irritating uncertainty coursing through her as his face came into focus. The in-stant she saw his face, she recoiled, shoved him away and spun to her feet. "Get your hands off me!"

He froze, old pain surging into his gaze as he rose to his feet and met her terrified stare. "What did you see?"

"What did I see?" Why was he even asking? He knew what she'd seen. It was written all over his pale, tense face. "It was a wraith. A wraith did this. But that's…impossible." She was shaking. Why was she shaking? She was known for her control, especially in dangerous and life-threatening circumstances. "All the wraith are dead. All but…" She swallowed hard.

"All but one," Quincy finished for her. "All of them but me."

He gave her one last, long look.

Then shimmered into shadow and disappeared from sight.

❖

Dammit!

The rage circled inside him, feeding off itself, feeding off him as he struggled to keep the violence at bay. Helpless, poisonous, toxic rage.

The rage he'd spent a lifetime trying to either ignore or contain.

Quincy lurked, out of sight, in the darkness, well above Lilith's team as they swarmed the scene. Like something out of a paranormal CSI, they swooped in, gathered their evidence, and sterilized the area. All the while Lilith stood nearby, hands shoved into her pockets, her black eyes dull against the truth of what she'd witnessed in her vision.

Neither of them had the best relationship with the truth. Especially in regards to one another. Given what was happening now, that wasn't going to get any better. He was literally watching his worst nightmare unfold before him.

He thought he'd have more time, more time investigate. More time to remind Lil of what they'd once shared before he confessed his fear. More time to convince her that despite how things had ended between them, when it came down to what was important, he could still be trusted. Unless he couldn't. Now he knew the truth: time had just run out.

Sente Mathias, the Interplanetary Security Bureau's personal banshee and punisher extraordinaire, one of his many superiors, strode through the winding trails of pipes and stairways toward Lilith. Her shocking platinum hair lay razor straight against her back, a back that was covered in a tailored suit the color of marrow deep blood. Tall, slender, and wearing blade-thin heels that could puncture a human's skin with the barest of pressure, Sente was a being who straddled two dimensions, neither of them human, with loyalties only to those who could advance her to the top of the agency. Or satisfy her unquenchable thirst for suffering.

Of course the ISB had sent Sente. That was just Quincy's luck these days. Endless weeks on the run had him starting to lose steam as well as resources. As bad a turn as Sente turning up was, it confirmed one thing: someone high up in the ISB wanted him gone.

The question was, why? What did he know? What had he seen or overheard? He didn't have a clue. And no matter how hard he tried, not matter what spell he incanted or potion he drank or shaman he visited, whatever he knew was still trapped in his head. In the missing days he couldn't recall and the endless, tortuous hours of sleep he couldn't claim.

Whatever Lil had seen in her vision was still visibly clinging to her. Her skin had gone ashy pale, but she didn't shrink away from Sente. Nor did she flinch at the intrusion of yet another organization representative moving in on her crime scene. She met Sente's gaze unflinchingly and reminded Quincy of why he'd fallen so hard for her the first time around. Nothing—well, almost nothing—scared Lilith Atsila.

He couldn't hear them. He needed to know whatever it was they were saying if he had any hope of getting through this. He swung down a level, landing silently on top of a pipe right above Lil's head.

He caught the shimmer of the golden hair sticks Lil wore to tie up her thick, curly dark hair. That sparkle of inset amber stones that he remembered had been passed down from her grandmother to her still entranced him. His fingers itched to reach out, pull it free, like he had so many times before, so he could watch the waves cascade down and around her shoulders.

Lilith hesitated for a moment, glancing up and around as if she sensed his presence.

Quincy fisted his hands, then willed them to relax. She'd always been able to pick up on his emotions from miles away. Especially after they'd become involved. Did that connection remain?

Lil shook her head and shifted her attention back to Sente and the older woman's steely, unwavering and spooky gaze.

"You said you came down here because this was the last location Tadeshi's tracking device was pinging from, correct?" Sente's questions sounded textbook predictable, which didn't strike Quincy as normal at all.

"Yes." Lil bit out the word, as if she'd already had this conversation. "We're handling it, Ms. Mathias. I told Quincy and I'll tell you, we aren't in need of the ISB's assistance."

Quincy cringed and squeezed his eyes shut. *Well, shit.*

"You've seen Quincy Lennox?" Sente seemed to grow another few inches as she straightened. "When was this?"

He felt, rather than heard Lil's hesitation. "Earlier today, yeah." She shrugged. "He said something about a security issue, that he'd been sent by the ISB and that he wanted to help. I told him we didn't need his help."

"I see." Sente's eyes sharpened and glistened against the investigation lights. "Where is Mr. Lennox now?"

"Hell if I know." Lil drew her gaze up and around again, landing for the briefest of moments on Quincy. "I had my security team escort him off the ship. Why? You guys having problems with him now, too?"

"You could say that," Sente said. "I would appreciate being notified immediately if he contacts you again. My superiors and I would very much like to speak with him about a series of security breaches within the organization."

Quincy inclined his head and frowned. They were trying to pin the breach on him?

"Happy to," Lilith said in a tone Quincy was all too familiar with. "If you don't mind, I need to check in with my team and see what progress is being made with Tadeshi's remains. Oh," Lil snapped her fingers and spun around at the last second. "I don't suppose you have any idea what type of weapon can do that kind of liquefied damage to a person? I've never seen anything like that before. A place to start looking?"

"Personally, I'd begin with the Kyrians." Sente's immediate answer smelled like complete bull. "While they have publicly professed their desire for these peace talks, it's also widely suspected their weapons production factories have been working overtime in case the talks fail. There's no profit in peace."

"Meaning they can push for peace while they hope for war with the Baltarans. Okay." Lil nodded, stepped closer. "I can see where that might be something to consider. What about the Baltarans, though? They've been reluctant to come to the peace table at all. Maybe they're looking for a way to stop them before they start?"

"You're thinking the murder of your agent is an attempt to derail the talks?"

"I'm thinking all kinds of things right now. And I appreciate being able to bounce ideas off you." Lil held out her hand. "Finally, someone with the ISB I might actually get along with."

Quincy watched Sente accept Lil's hand and knew instantly that his superior from the ISB didn't have the first clue who she was dealing with. It happened quick, a flash of a moment, but in that time he saw it on Lil's face. She'd used Sente's confidence and arrogance to ride into her mind and get all the information she needed.

Maybe information Quincy needed.

A blast of energy shot up and nearly blew him backwards. His head buzzed as his ears rang. He gripped a nearby pipe for balance, waiting for his head to clear before he could decipher the message Lil had sent him.

Once he had his balance back, he rose to his full height and shimmered into the darkness.

After checking in with Wanda and the head of her security team, Lil ripped out her earpiece and deactivated it. She bypassed a return visit to the security office and headed straight for her suite, muttering all the way. "Un-freaking-believable. I swear to the Goddess if he isn't in this suite in the next ten minutes I'm going to hunt him down Buffy style."

Her powers had never—okay, once—let her down. Which meant one of two things: either what she saw was some kind of lie or...they had a wraith on board *Fantasy*. A freaking wraith with rage issues.

Wait. That was repetitive. She massaged her temples. This was giving her a migraine.

If she ever got her pulse rate down to normal range again it would be miracle. She nearly singed the doorknob when she pushed open her door. The residual heat coursing through her body finally settled as she paced the open seating area, wishing there was more to focus on on the other side of those windows than the New York harbor.

They had five days. Five days until they reached the collection of islands off the English coast; the only place both the Baltarans and Kyrians could agree on. Five days to find out why the plans to this ship had been sent from *her* employers to a faction within the Baltarans. Five days to safely transport one of the most controversial prime ministers ever to be elected; a prime minister so despised she had more targets on her back than existed in a shooting range. Lil tried to catch her breath. She had five days to find a wraith who, from what she saw, had literally sucked the life out of one of her best friends.

Except she knew of only one wraith left in existence. And up until three years ago, she'd been sleeping with him.

The quick rap of knuckles on her door had her hurrying to answer it. She reached up and grabbed the collar of his shirt and dragged Quincy inside. She had the door closed in an instant. "You have exactly thirty seconds to tell me what the hell is really going on and why I shouldn't stake you right here."

"Stakes don't work on wraiths." He shrugged out of her hold and moved into her suite. "Besides, I'm not full wraith. Remember?"

Oh, she remembered. She also remembered her family's oath to rid the world of the creatures responsible for so much death and suffering. For centuries the wraith had been declared unkillable, but Lilith's bloodline—the Atsila witches—had found a way.

A way that was as ingrained in Lil's blood as much as her magic.

"Why are you here? Why did you tell me the ISB sent you when they obviously didn't. And why,"— she poked a finger into his chest and forced him back a step—"why the hell has you own agency sent a freaking Baltaran banshee after you?"

"You aren't going to ask me why I killed Tadeshi?"

"Are you joking?" She swung on him, wondering if choking him would make a dent in his thinking. "Are you actually making a joke out of this? And don't be stupid. Unless you've figured out how to go full-on wraith in the last three years, I know you didn't kill him. What I saw was…" she trailed off, shivering so hard her bones hurt. She eased back on her anger. It wasn't going to help either of them and it certainly wasn't going to get them closer to what killed Tadeshi. "What I saw was the nightmare my grandmother used to tell me about. It wasn't human. Not in any way. It wasn't…you."

"I need to sit down."

Lil backed out of his way as he all but dived for one of the gaudy purple and turquoise padded chairs. She could literally see his knees shaking in his black denim jeans. Even without touching him she could feel the tidal wave of relief sweeping over him. "I was afraid…I was so sure…when I saw his remains down in that engine room, I thought for sure…" He leaned back, rubbed his hands down his face. "I thought for sure it was me."

"You thought after a hundred and seventy years—"

"One hundred sixty-two."

Lil snorted. "You thought after all this time you all of a sudden went full-wraith? That's just—"

"Impossible? Stupid? Unbelievable. Please." He sat up and finally some of the color came back to his face. "We face the impossible, stupid, and unbelievable every day of our lives. Having suddenly dormant terror genes suddenly burst to life does not seem out of the range of possibility. Especially since I saw it."

"You saw it? What does that mean?"

"These dreams. Every time I close my eyes. I see these attacks. These creatures killing people, animals. Anything they can get their hands on. It's like I'm watching from inside their heads."

Lil crouched in front of him and rested her hands on his knees. Even without a push her emotions locked onto his, drew them in and around her as she tapped into what was circling like smoke inside of him. She held herself against the fear, the horror, the revulsion and despair. All the soul-crushing doubts that grew larger and heavier the longer anyone was alone. "Quincy." She waited until he drew his gaze to hers. "Quincy, it wasn't you. Whatever you're thinking and feeling and seeing, it wasn't you who killed Tadeshi. I'd know if it was. I'd have seen it." She wasn't that far away from being in love with him that she didn't remember what a good man he was. What a good…wraith.

"I'd ask if you're just saying that, but you don't do that, do you?" He was trying to joke again. Trying to find his way back. But the smile flicking across his mouth disappeared and his eyes went wide. "What did you say about Sente?"

"Sente? When? What?"

"When I first came in. You said Sente is Baltaran?"

"The crypt keeper's sister down there? Oh, yeah. She's Baltaran. Not full, obviously, since banshees are inherently human manifestations, but—hey!" She snapped her fingers in front of his face. "Focus."

She knelt in front of him, lifted her hands to frame his face. For the first time since he'd appeared in the security office, she looked at him. Really looked at him. There, far below the surface, beneath the dark, haunted eyes, she found the man she'd once loved.

"Stay out of my head, Lil."

She frowned, processing the despair, the confusion, the exhaustion seeping out of every one of his pores. The past few months exploded through her mind, like fragmented pieces of glass trying to find their way back together. "Jesus, Quincy." She smoothed a hand down the side of his face. "What's happened to you? When was the last time you ate or slept?"

"What day is it?" He gave her a weak laugh that only raised her concern. "I've been on the run. I don't know for how long. Weeks? Months? There's something I need to tell you. Something you have to know."

"I think there's a lot of somethings, but they can wait." She waved her hand, twitched her fingers and drew the curtains shut. "You need to sleep."

"I can't sleep. I've tried." But he yawned and seemed to surprise himself. "I've tried so many times."

"You'll sleep now. And when you wake up, you'll eat something. Then we'll talk." He shook his head, but she kept her gaze pinned to his and, despite his request to leave his thoughts alone, she slipped into his mind. With the brush of ghostly fingers she faded his thoughts to fog, pushing them into far into the depths of his mind that they'd take a long time to return. "Sleep, Quincy. Everything will be clearer when you wake up." She stood, gave a gentle tug, and had him on his feet. She guided him over to the bed and seconds later had him stretched out, his feet dangling over the edge.

"Can't sleep." He continued to fight her, tried to sit up, but she was already pulling off his shoes, tapping a finger against his forehead and had him falling back against the collection of multi-colored pillows. "We don't have time. Tadeshi—"

"I'll find out what's going on with Tadeshi's exam. Don't worry." Every protective instinct she'd once held for him surged, given new life by the sight of the man she'd very nearly married. The only man she'd ever wanted to marry.

The only man she could never marry.

He was part wraith. And she was sworn to destroy them.

She sat beside him on the edge of the bed, stroked his silky hair back from his face. He continued to struggle against the spell she'd implanted in his mind. "Why did you come here, Quincy? Why me? Why now?" she whispered into the room when she thought he was finally under.

"Because even though you know the truth,"—his eyes opened and she shivered—"you're the only one I can trust."

Quincy surfaced from the darkness in stages. The fog of exhaustion evaporated, leaving behind a clarity he'd longed for ever since he'd walked out of the Ometra storage and security facility three months earlier.

"Quincy, you've got some 'splainin' to do."

He nearly shot out of bed at Lil's horrible Dezi Arnaz impersonation. Then groaned and grabbed his head when it kicked like a demonic mule. "Holy hell, Lil. What did you do to me?"

"Knocked you out so I could get some work done." She appeared, almost like a mirage, balancing against the gentle rocking of the ship beside him. In the dim light of the bedside table lamp he could see she'd changed out of her usual uniform of snug black jeans and black turtleneck sweater and into a pair of plaid pajama bottoms and tank top. The color, oh, the color of the fabric was a rich raspberry

that had him licking his lips as he trailed his eyes over the curves that had only improved since he'd last seen—and touched—them. "Stop staring at my boobs, Quincy. We have a lot to talk about." She laid her hand against his forehead. An instant later the last of his lethargy vanished and his hunger appeared. And not, he realized as she stepped away, necessarily for food.

"I ordered dinner. You weren't conscious so you don't get to be picky."

He swung his legs over the edge of the bed and sat up. "I'd eat cardboard at this point."

"Lucky for you, the food on this ship is great. Well come on. I'm not serving you in bed."

His lips twitched. "You didn't used to mind doing that."

"I didn't used to mind doing a lot of things." She arched a brow at him as she flipped open a folded cloth napkin. "Up. We can talk while you eat."

He sat at the small table against the far wall of the cabin and wondered how much this snazzy little suite set the UPA back. Lil had always been very frugal with her business expenses. Never pushed the boundaries when it came to showcasing a particular lifestyle when they traveled. Of course, that was before she'd become the star of the agency. Once she'd ditched him, obviously.

When she lifted the silver cover off his plate, a wave of affection nearly pushed him off his chair. "You remembered."

"Hard to forget the number of bacon double cheeseburgers you scarfed down." Lil's smile flashed so quickly he thought he might have imagined it. "Now eat. And talk." She poured them both coffee then she sat back with a plate of fries and curled into the chair across from him.

"You first." He forced himself to slow down and actually taste his food. "Did the Kyrian delegation make it on board all right?"

"They're all snug as bugs in their little rugs," she confirmed and pointed to the ceiling. "Just one deck up."

"All together or separated?"

"They're secure." Lil's eyes narrowed. "That's all you need to know right now."

"You mean that's all I get to know until you're sure you can trust me."

"I'm never going to trust you, Quincy. And not because you still work for the ISB. How about we go with: I'm taking things hour by hour. What happened at the Ometra site three months ago?"

He ate some more and swallowed hard around the dread. "I don't know."

"You have to stop saying that."

"Believe me, I would if I could." It didn't help that watching her nibble on fries dunked in ranch dressing was one of the sexiest things he'd seen in a long time. *Shit*. He was really out of it if that's what got his motor going these days. "All right." He sat back, reached for the bottle of his favorite beer she'd ordered. "About four months ago I was put in charge of the communications unit at the Ometra facility, the ISB clearing house and head office for recruit training. The transfer was completely unexpected. Came out of the blue."

"Why?"

"Good question. Up until then I'd been training their new recruits. Taking them right off the bus, so to speak. Turning them into private soldiers. I was good at it, Lil. Really good. Until something changed. Maybe that's when all this started," he mused more to himself than to Lil.

"I don't speak secret code, Quincy. Spell it out."

"I had a few ISB recruits go missing. I was told they'd dropped out, gone home, but they were some of the best soldiers I'd seen in a long time. And they were dedicated. Obsessively so. They were… well, they would have put you and me to shame back in our day."

"Our day was only a few years ago." She scrunched her face in disapproval.

"Seven, but who's counting." He started eating again. It felt so good to finally be able to talk to someone about all this. Hell, who was he kidding? It felt good to talk to Lilith again. Like before. Before he'd told her the truth about what he was. "I didn't exactly buy the explanation they'd dropped out. Something just felt off, so I reached out to a few of the families. And that's where things get… weird."

Lil's eyes went wide.

"Yeah, I know, right? It has to be pretty freaking weird for me to call anything or anyone weird. But Lil. Their families? They didn't know who I was talking about. Parents, grandparents, siblings, you name it, everyone had forgotten them. It's like these kids never existed."

"Kids?"

"Twenty-somethings." He winced. He was well over a century so anyone under was pretty much an infant in his eyes. "I thought I was being careful, but maybe I got careless? Asked the wrong person something? The next thing I know, I'm segregated out and working by myself as a screen monitor. They literally had me sitting alone in a room, watching multiple computer screens for any glitches flying across their communications networks. That's when I started to lose time. Maybe it was the boredom, or maybe I was imagining it. I don't know." The confusion was beginning to descend again. "Did I mention that that ISP has worked for both the Baltarans and the Kyrians in the past?"

Lil stopped eating. "Don't tell me: you were the one who intercepted the transmission from the Baltarans to the UPA?"

"Not only that. I was the one who traced the transmission back to yours and Tadeshi's office."

"Frack."

He'd always appreciated her affection for classic Science Fiction TV shows. "Remember what I was going to tell you before you knocked me out?"

"It didn't take much knocking."

"Cute. I contacted Tadeshi. Off server. On a burner phone. He tells me he hasn't seen any transmission, but he's going to do some digging. He said not to contact him again and that he'd meet me today, on the *Fantasy*, and we'd figure out what to do. The next day at work, I'm hauled in for questioning regarding a security breach within the ISB. Apparently I wasn't great at covering my tracks when I was trying to trace that transmission. But I swear I wiped that terminal's memory and history, Lil. I'm not stupid."

"How long did they hold you?"

"Four, five days? They didn't let me sleep. They certainly didn't give me any burgers to eat. Just enough water to keep me alive. More like turning me into the walking dead. That's why—" He finally pushed out the fear that worried him the most. "That's why I thought maybe that wraith was me. I thought maybe they'd, I don't know, freed him."

"There is no him," Lil snapped.

"They finally let me go, but they put guards around my house. I played along for a few days, getting my plan in shape. Then I made a break for it. That was three months ago. I've been lying low and constantly moving, living on whatever cash I had left. Trying to avoid the ISB and anyone connected to it."

"When did the dreams start?"

"While I was being held for questioning. Every night. Whatever you did to my head that made them go away, thank you."

"You're welcome. You know what I find interesting?"

"Can I take my pick?"

"The ISB transferred you to a dead job, then held you for questioning for days, released you with guards on your house and yet Sente Matias didn't mention a word of this when we spoke in the engine room."

"She just called me a spy and left it at that."

"But that's my point. She just said they wanted to talk to you about a security breach." Lil tapped a finger against her cheek. "They're still trying to keep you close. If they wanted to find you for official charges, they'd have brought in law enforcement. Hell, they'd have reached out to the UPA. We could have found you in a heartbeat."

"Hardly," he scoffed.

"My point is…I don't think they're done with you yet."

"And now we've come full circle." He winced and tried to find the right words. "I need to sort this all out and I need to do it with someone who can help me puzzle it together."

"And you came to me. And here I thought maybe you just wanted to take a romantic cruise."

"You know I hate the water," he reminded her. Even as he said it he could feel the boat rocking. "I've known since I heard yesterday that Tadeshi was missing—"

"Hold up." Lil stopped him. "Even I didn't find out about that until this morning. How did you know? Oh, my god." Lil dropped her feet to the floor and sat forward. "You bugged the security office, didn't you? How long have you been on the ship?"

"A couple days. All right, a week." He shrugged off her offense. "And I didn't bug the office exactly. More like the air ducts above. The ISB developed these super sensitive microphones, ." He flashed her

a grin. "You really need to expand those protective shields up a few more feet, Lil."

"Oh, I'm going to do more than that, believe me."

"When I heard Tadeshi was off the grid, I planned to book it. Just start over and try to figure out where to go from here. Then I heard they were calling you in to replace him. I figured I'd stick around, pretend to play the ISB liaison and find out what I could. Imagine my surprise when they sent an actual liaison."

With his burger gone, he plucked the forgotten plate of fries out of Lil's hands. "I landed on something, Lil. I have no idea what. I must have seen or heard something or asked the wrong question—"

"About what though? The transmission? The peace talks? Or your missing recruits?"

"I don't know. Whatever I know, they want it to die with me. That's the only reason they would have sent Sente. She's a fixer, Lil. She's who they send in when someone needs to be taken care of. Or taken out."

"Maybe I can ease your mind about that." Lil seemed to relax. "I checked in with my superior at the UPA. He confirmed the higher-ups okayed the ISB coming on board to help with the peace talks. They're calling it a test run for a possible contracting partnership."

Quincy sat up straighter. "That's supposed to make me feel better? Lil, you know how long these two agencies have loathed each other. They live for the other's destruction. All of a sudden they're playing buddies?"

"What I'm saying," she said in an overly patient tone, "is that I think whatever is going on is bigger than you. Sure, maybe they've sent Sente out here in case you show up."

"Which you told her I did."

"It's called gaining her trust, Quincy. And you're missing that bigger bit of information we have about Sente. Something that is not in her information, either her personnel file with ISB or on the dossier the UPA put together." She tapped her finger on a file folder lying on the table between them. "She's Baltaran. She's a killer. And she's here. On this ship. With the Kyrian delegation. Who, I'm sorry to say, have to be my primary concern right now."

"What if it's in my head?" At her blank stare, he clarified. "Since I don't know what I know maybe you can…get it out?"

"You want me to go looking around your mind to try to suss out what it is you know that the ISB might want to kill you for?"

"Yes."

"No." She stood up, started to pace, avoiding looking anywhere near his direction. "No. We aren't doing that again. I can't."

"You have to."

"No, I don't."

"Do you think it's what I want?" he kept his tone even. Controlled. And as devoid of emotion as he could manage, even while the panic and fear began to swirl. "I haven't forgotten what happened the last time. Hell, we've both been living with the fallout from that for the past three years. But I'm not seeing I have much of a choice, Lil. I need you to do this. If not for me, then to find out whatever it is I stumbled on."

"There are other witches. Other…tactics—"

"No, there's not." He waited until she finally met his gaze. "I've tried, Lil. Believe me, I've tried. You're the only one who can dig out what I know."

"No." She hugged her arms around her torso. "I won't do it."

"Then I won't help you with Sente."

Her mouth fell open.

"That's my deal. Take it or leave it, Lil. I help you stop Sente and whatever plot there is against the Kyrians, and you find out why the ISB wants to kill me."

"Maybe I don't need your help."

He smirked. "Yeah. You do. Because right now, I'm the only person on this ship you can trust. Even if I am a wraith."

She shifted on her feet, squirming. "Part wraith."

"Funny. That's a distinction you could never make before."

"Yeah, well." She sighed. "Maybe some things have changed after all."

He doubted it. "What do you say? Do we have a deal?"

"Like you said, I don't have a choice." She strode over and held out her hand. "Deal."

❖

Quincy was in no shape for Lil to do a brain excavation. Not yet. At least that's what Lil told herself the next morning as she took the stairs up to the eighth deck. It wasn't often she was grateful to be summoned by a political delegate, but given the fact she had her ex-half-wraith lover hiding out in her suite, this seemed like a suitable alternative.

She took her time, however, stopping for a moment to enjoy the water-filled view completely surrounding them. All that was missing was a fourth cup of coffee, a lounge chair, and a different, placid lifestyle.

"I find the waters of your world never grow old."

Lil turned to face the statuesque woman who joined her at the railing. "Prime Minister Zaldenda." She immediately looked for the woman's bodyguards. "I was just on my way to see you."

"I thought I might, how do you humans say, head you off at the pass?" The radiant, almost translucent quality of the Kyrians skin had always intrigued Lil. Like regal jellyfish only without the tentacles. With ebony hair that fell in thick, roped curls down her back and over her shoulders, Prime Minister Zaldenda's constantly shifting rainbow eyes carried a hint of whimsy beneath the weight of responsibility. "I thought perhaps we could talk, out here. Where the beauty and silence prevails."

"Of course." Lil still didn't approve that she'd left her quarters alone. "What was it you wished to speak to me about?"

"I understand an agent of yours was killed yesterday."

"Haru Tadeshi. Yes. We're still investigating." Now it was her turn to head someone off at the pass.

"My people tell me it was not an accident. Is it true his death might be connected to the peace talks I'm participating in?"

"We have no evidence to support those theories, ma'am." Lil set herself at attention in order to make certain the prime minister understood Lil was speaking with her as a representative of the Universal Protection Agency.

"Did he have a family?" The question was asked so quietly, so lyrically, Lil almost missed it. She followed as the prime minister began to walk, the sweeping fabric of her swirling misty silver robes moving in rhythm to the ship.

"A brother. His parents are gone. And he wasn't married. Yet."

"For centuries no Kyrian lived past your twenty years. Did you know that?"

"I believe it was in the research dossier we were provided, ma'am."

"I myself am fifty-nine. One of the longest surviving Kyrians."

Lil nodded, silently envying the woman who looked closer to her teenage years than being ready to file for social security.

"Many of my people are not happy with how I am handling these peace talks with the Baltarans. Hatred and resentment are difficult emotions to move beyond, don't you agree? Especially hatred that's been taught."

Lil chose her words carefully. "Forgive me, ma'am, but the Baltarans haven't exactly made moving beyond the past easy either. Just last year they took responsibility for the mass poisonings at your most sacred temple in Kyrial."

Grief, as fresh as if the wound had been inflicted moments before, shone brightly in her eyes. "You believe they do not deserve peace?"

"Everyone deserves peace. I'm saying some people need to work harder to prove they actually want it."

Prime Minister Zaldenda stopped, hands clasped behind her back, and faced Lil. "I cannot disagree with that observation, Ms. Atsila. Tell me about your family."

"My—"

"Your mate. Your children. Those you love and keep to your heart."

"Ah." Lil smiled and ducked her head. "I'm afraid I have only my grandmother and four brothers. No family of my own."

"But you did. There was once someone you loved. Forgive me. We Kyrians, we have this ability to see into a being's heart. And we know when it has been touched by love. The feelings you retain, they are not so old that you've forgotten…him." She smiled.

"He's very hard to forget," Lil confirmed. "Prime Minister—"

"I have spent most of my life longing for love. I've often wondered if having someone beside me would have made my obligations easier." Sadness shifted across her face. "My cabinet has begun to question whether I have grown beyond my usefulness. The timing, I find interesting." When the Prime Minister smiled, her skin sparkled. "This peace between the Kyrians and Baltarans. It is my dying wish that it come to pass. The hatred, the killing, it must all stop. On both sides. You will, I think, be of a great help to me in seeing this through."

"I—" Dying wish?

Prime Minister Zalenda captured Lil's hands between hers. "Whatever differences you have with this person you love, I hope you will find your way clear of them. It is a lonely life that is led alone. Hearts are meant to love. And to be loved. Take it from an old woman, Lilith Atsila. Embrace that which is presented to you. This,"—she motioned to the ship around them—"is nothing more than temporary illusion."

He'd moved from one form of captivity to another.

Hours, endless, suffocating hours had passed since he and Lil had made their deal and yet despite her assurances, she had yet to reappear in the cabin. Duties, she'd told him, before ordering him to stay here, out of sight, and wait.

Granted there were worse ways and places to spend his time. The luxurious accommodations gentled the torture but he found his solitude torture nonetheless. The last thing he needed to be doing was spending even more tone alone. With his thoughts. With his fears. Especially when answers could be just within his grasp.

He'd just clicked off the TV screen when the door to the cabin swung open. He jumped to his feet and watched Lil shoot across the room to the dresser. "Pit stop. Just changing. Don't have time to talk."

"What's going on?"

"Nothing and everything. Sorry." She waved away his question. "I've got extra eyes watching every move Sente Mathias makes and that's on top of the now cruise-curious Kyrian delegation. They've discovered the casino. Goddess help me. All I need is for one of them to be caught cheating."

"Cheating how?"

"They're…" Lil stopped, narrowed her eyes and shrugged. "I don't know what they are. Empaths?

Not really but that's the closest I can…look, can we talk about this later? It's almost dinner time."

"Yes, I know. I'm bored out of my mind. When are we doing this, Lil?"

"Doing what?" She snatched a yellow blouse off a hanger, whispered an incantation and blew on it. The wrinkles dropped away like water off a stone. "Watch a movie. Get some more sleep. I know: start a journal." She darted into the bathroom, but neglected to close the door all the way. He stood there, waiting, watching, as she changed, and caught the glimpse of her bare skin in the mirror.

"When are you going to do it?"

"Define it."

She was stalling. Even if he didn't know her tells, he'd see it a mile off. "We need to know what's in my head and the sooner the better."

"I know."

"Do you?" He rapped his knuckles on the door and pushed it open. "Because there's every chance it could have something to do with the peace talks. We're already a full day into this journey. If something's going to happen, it's going to happen soon."

"I am aware." She had a clip in her teeth and was twisting up her hair. "We'll get to it soon."

For the first time, he heard the lie in her voice. "You're going to renege on our deal, aren't you?"

"No, I'm not…" she spit out the clip and it clattered into the sink. "Hey! Get out of here."

"Just watching." Like he used to do when they were together. He used to love how she'd look stepping out of the shower in the morning, her hair glistening wet, her skin glowing, her cheeks flushed with heat.

"Darn right you're just watching." She made to push past him, but he caught her arm and held her still until she looked up at him. "What are you doing, Quincy?"

"Wondering if it's still there." He stroked the pad of his finger down her cheek. "Between us."

"Don't." She closed her eyes. "It doesn't matter if it is."

"You sure about that?" He dipped his head, brushed his mouth feather light across her lips and thrilled at the gasp she let escape. "We're different than we used to be, Lil." Another kiss, barely a caress, but he wanted more. So much more. He wanted… everything.

"Maybe," she whispered. "But nothing's changed." Her hand gripped his shirt, hauled him down even as she shook her head. "I can't forget what you are and you can't forgive me for what I've done." She pressed her mouth to his, for longer than a breath of a moment. "We can't be more than we are now, Quincy. It's just not possible."

"I thought by now we'd both realize nothing in the real world is impossible."

"Except we don't live in the real world, do we, Quincy?" She released his shirt and stepped away. "I need to go."

"When you get back, you're getting into my head."

"Silly boy." Lil tossed him a grin over her shoulder as she pulled open the door. "I'm already there."

May the Goddess save her from the craziness that was the human race.

"Where is she?" Lil pulled up a chair and sat next to Wanda in the security center. For most of the past twenty-four hours she'd been holed up with her team keeping an eye not only on the Kyrian delegation, but tracking every single step Sente Mathias took around *Fantasy*.

"Heading into the dining room where the rest of the team is dispersed for surveillance." Wanda smothered a yawn. "Sorry," she murmured at Lil's look. "Been a long day."

"I know." Lil rubbed a hand down her friend's arm. "And I appreciate you keeping on top of this." But running her team into the ground wasn't going to do anyone any good. "Trixie back yet?"

"She went on a coffee run. Her kind of coffee. With chocolate and sugar."

"When she gets back, I want you to take a few hours. In fact,"—she glanced around the room— "anyone who's been on for more than eighteen, get some sleep. Be back here at O-four-hundred."

"I'm too tired to argue with you." Wanda yawned again. "That's going to leave you short handed, Lil."

"I'll make do. The dinner tonight is a welcome event, so it'll run long. They Kyrians will all be in one place for a good while." All day she'd been waiting for Sente Mathias to make some kind of move. Any kind of move. Instead, the ISB agent had spent most of her day roaming the ship like a tourist, blending in with the other fantastical apparitions hovering about the ship. If Sente was looking for Quincy, she was certainly going it about it wrong. The last place he'd be is on the promenade with all the shops and entertainment venue.

Lil's eyes flicked to the photograph Sente had tacked up on the announcement board. Quincy's face looked back at her almost as closely as the real one had a few minutes ago in her cabin. He'd been declared a person of interest in an ongoing Interplanetary Security Bureau issue. Anyone who came into contact with him was ordered to report the sighting directly to Sente, who, at the moment, was lowering herself into a seat at a small table in the dining room.

"Even a banshee's gotta eat," Lil murmured. Maybe she was stalling. Maybe she had…what word had Quincy used? Nefarious. Yeah, that was it. Nefarious plans. Lil peered closer at the screen. She certainly didn't act like a woman about to commit a violent act.

"What is it exactly you think she's going to do?" Wanda asked, then let out a yelp of excitement when the door swung open. Trixie Bledsoe, all four-feet of her, entered like her typical whirlwind self to a round of applause that she soon realized was not for her.

"Now that's just wrong, guys." Trixie turned her nose in the air and chugged her coffee as the security office all but emptied out, Wanda bringing up the rear. "You two, Wan?"

"Boss's orders. Sleep awaits! Later, Lil."

Trixie waited until the door closed then, at Lil's nod, locked the door. "Something's up."

"You've got that right." While Lil considered Wanda a friend there was no way she was putting Wanda at risk by telling her about Quincy. Trixie, on the other hand, thrived in tense and secretive situations. And loved sticking it to a certain security organization. "How would you like to screw over the ISB?"

Trixie's gold-rimmed eyes widened behind her thick glasses before she grinned. "Tell me more."

Much to his horror, Quincy did as Lil suggested and began writing everything down. Everything he could remember from the past months, begin-

ning with when he'd lost his first recruit and ending with finding Tadeshi's body in the engine room. He sketched out the scene as best he could recall. How the pipes intersected, the routes to and from the area. The tracker, watch, and ring that had been found on Tadeshi's…body. Wait a minute.

Quincy inclined his head and reached for his cell. The second he lifted it he swore. No cell reception of any kind. One of those quirks of this cruise line was that all their passengers unplugged. No exceptions. Probably, Quincy thought, because they had enough issues making sure all the systems operated correctly. Adding cell phone and radio waves to the mix would probably cause massive interference.

He could call Lil on the ship's phone system, but she was traveling solo. Anyone would transfer or even overhear the call would know where he was calling from. He tapped the pen against his chin. It was late. Dinner was still in progress. The majority of passengers, including the Kyrian delegation, would no doubt be there. If Lil wasn't going to fulfill her promise and get him the answers he needed, he'd get them another way.

He grabbed her flashlight and headed to the door. The instant he pulled it open he felt a jolt shoot through his system. He flexed his hand against the sudden numbness and shook it off, heading all the way down the passageway, past the elevator he couldn't access, and into the stairwell. When the staircase dead-ended on the lowest level, he carefully opened the door, waiting for the voices and maintenance crew to move out of sight, then silently headed inside.

❖

"So don't let Mathias out of my sight, got it." Trixie got herself comfortable at her computer station, and removed her glasses as the desk and chair transformed into what Lil called Trixie's control center. A headset dropped down over Trixie's face, making it appear as if she'd donned a VR helmet. She tapped a few keys, zoomed in on Mathias' face. "I've got her pinged now. She can't go anywhere on this ship without me seeing."

"Great. That gives me…" Lil's spine stiffened. Her fingers tingled as did the back of her neck. "That son of a—" She held her tongue. "Trix, I'm going to need you to feed me any reports from the team." She grabbed an earwig and shoved it in her ear, then bent over her own terminal and quickly flashed through all the screens on deck seven. She caught sight of him just as he disappeared through the staircase door. "Where in the hell are you going?"

"Problems, Lil?"

Trixie had no idea. "One I can take care of myself. You good?"

"I thrive on a challenge. Anything happens, I'll feed it to you. Oh, wow. Ew. She ordered the escargot." Trixie shuddered, her jet black ponytail bobbing back and forth behind her. "How does anyone eat snails?"

"Asking the wrong person. I'll be back."

"I should hope so!" Trixie yelled after her.

Level sixteen eleven wasn't the easiest to access given his point of entry. It took him a good few minutes to get the lay of the space before he was headed in the right direction. At least in here he wasn't worried about being detected. His wraith genetics made slipping into shadows as easy as moving behind a curtain.

"What were you doing down, here, Tadeshi?" Quincy backtracked to where he and Lil had emerged just yesterday; the same path Tadeshi probably would have taken. The roar of the engines pounded against his ears until he raised his personal shield and found himself in his bubble of silence. His eyes adjusted to the darkness almost instantly. For years he'd banked his powers and never gave them full reign for fear of discovery. The supernatural world had come a long way in the past few centuries, but there were some creatures—wraiths in particular—who were still feared. They'd become the boogey men of the dimensions, leading characters in stories for children to keep them on the straight and narrow. Or to help keep their anger and fury at bay.

He was, he knew, an aberration. An impossibility. Part human, part wraith should have never been possible, but to hear his mother tell it, his father had been just like him; born with the genetic makeup of a race of creatures who searched out death and made it their companion or ultimate goal. Wraiths couldn't control the violence coursing constantly inside of them, but Quincy, from the day he'd been born,

had been trained to do just that. Compartmentalize. Don't let the monster out. Don't let the monster win.

Instead, he'd learned to harness his wraith powers; sensing death, sensing violence and impending disaster as easily as if he opened his eyes and looked at it. Which was why, as he meandered up and down the metal staircases, in and around the pipes and tubes and conduits, he could feel that pressure building inside of him.

And it wasn't, Quincy thought as he stopped on the spot where Tadeshi had lost his life, a residual energy. It was now. It was current. And it was growing stronger.

He bent down, using the flashlight to aid in his vision, searching for the one thing he knew Tadeshi had never been without. The one thing they hadn't found on his body.

"What in the hell are you doing down here?"

Quincy pivoted, his arm striking out to catch the person behind him on the back of the knees. He knocked her feet out from under her and sent her sprawling onto her back. "Sorry." He stood up immediately and held out his hand. "Reflex. Guess I wasn't paying attention."

Lil slapped her hand into his and glared at him. "I repeat, what are you doing down here?"

"Looking for Tadeshi's cell phone."

Lil started to speak, then popped her mouth closed. "Well, shit." She scrubbed a hand across her forehead. "You're right. I guess maybe we figured it disintegrated during the attack. But then why wouldn't anything else have?"

"Or maybe it got lost and it's still around here somewhere. Don't you have a screen you should be monitoring?"

"It's under control. We need to get you back to my room."

"Not unless you're ready to do what you said you'd do."

She stared at him.

"Whether you want to or not, it has to be done, Lil. You shouldn't worry about it so much," he added with forced humor. "It's not like I have any other secrets I'm keeping from you. Besides, you're doing it with my permission this time around."

He could see her flinch as he turned the guilt knife harder. Yeah, now probably wasn't the time to have *this* discussion.

"I can send my team down tomorrow to look for the phone. Let's go."

He couldn't believe she was just going to walk away from this. "Lil, come on. Don't tell me you can't feel that. The darkness. The death. It's all over this place. It's lurking."

"You're imagining things," she said, then seemed to realize what she'd said, backtracked. "Sorry."

"I know my powers don't come with a fancy magic pedigree, that doesn't mean they're any less effective."

She was quiet for a moment. "You really feel something?"

"I really do. Down there." He leaned over the railing and into the shimmering, soft pink depths of the engine room. "This is where Tadeshi came; it's where he died. That tells me something or someone was waiting for him, to stop him from going further. Which is why I'm going to finish what he started."

"Oh, yeah, cause you getting killed is going to make things so much better," she snapped. "Since when are you suicidal?"

"I have no intention of dying, Lilith. You coming? We have a better chance together."

"You know damned well I am." She smacked his hand away when he reached for hers. "Just…give me a second." She tapped on her ear. "Trixie? You copy? Yeah. I'll be out of radio range for a while. If I'm not back in the office in…"—she glanced at her watch—"one hour, I want you to send a team to where we found Tadeshi's remains, understood? Yeah. Thanks. Out." She twisted the earpiece out of her ear and shoved it into her pocket. "You've got an hour, Quincy. Let's go."

There had to be worse ways to spend an evening on a cruise, Lil thought as she followed Quincy down level after level, short staircase after short staircase. Whatever meager light had been in the higher levels had faded now, replaced with swirling glowing yellow and pink mist. Whatever Quincy had been picking up on, she certainly didn't sense it. Then again, she wasn't the most open-minded of people with anything concerning her ex.

"You're thinking too loud." Quincy glanced over his shoulder. "And if I can hear you, probably half the ship can, too."

Lil rolled her eyes. Her shoe caught on something that rattled. She stooped down, slipped her fingers under the embossed name badge. Without it being attached to an actual person, she couldn't get a reading. People she could read. Objects? That was her grandmother's bailiwick.

"What is it?" Quincy asked.

She turned it over and her heart clenched. "It's a badge for a purser I met yesterday when I checked in. What would this be doing down here?"

"Keep it. Let's see if we can find out."

This time when he reached for her hand, she took it. And instantly regretted it. As her hand tightened around his, all the emotions, all the grief, the anger, all the memories surged back at her like a tidal wave. She tried to pull free, but he held on, continuing to pull her forward as if he didn't feel it too. As if they were nothing more than lovers strolling through the park.

She didn't want to remember how much she'd loved him. How she'd let herself fall into fantasies about what their life could be outside the UPA. How for the first time she'd let herself believe there could be more to her life than magical obligation and continuing her family's legacy. But she did remember. She remembered all of it. And it was this, she realized, that Prime Minister Zalenda must have picked up on. The feelings that no matter how hard she'd tried to banish, remained. Locked in her heart. Always with her.

Another two levels down and they were now in the thick of the mist. The engine's consistent thudding and whirring hurt her ears and pulsed against her rapidly weakening body. She could feel the energy draining out of her with every step she took through the swirling tendrils of light and energy.

"I don't think we're supposed to be down this far!" Lil yelled at Quincy's back.

A screech ripped through the air, high-pitched, ear-splitting, heartbreaking. Lil felt it surge through her and she stumbled, dropping to her knees.

Quincy dropped her hand, stood where he was, hands turned palms up as he closed his eyes and lifted his face into the light.

"Quincy, what's happening?" Lil had never felt anything like it. It was as if the air around her was hammering her into the ground, driving the breath from her lungs. The life from her blood. "What is this place? Quincy?"

A figure exploded up from below them, grey and black smoke mixing and mingling against the stark white skeletal face with glowing silver eyes. It screamed, arching its spine and throwing itself toward Lil.

Quincy dived between them, blocking the creature from making contact; stopping it for a breath of a moment as the world went still.

Lil grabbed hold of his shirt and dragged herself to her feet. She tried to push past, tried to look closer at the figure hovering in the air in front of them. She'd seen it before, she realized now. In that blink of an eye second when she'd touched what had once been Tadeshi's body. The legends hadn't come close to describing the horror staring back at her; the grotesque, misshapen face and wild, grief and fury filled eyes. Eyes that, for an instant, seemed familiar.

Her stomach rolled as Quincy stepped forward, arm outstretched to he creature as if he wanted to pet it. "No!" Lil grabbed for his hand, but he held her back, keeping himself between the wraith and Lil. "Quincy, what are you doing?"

"Showing her she's not alone."

"Are you out of your—"

"You have to trust me, Lil. Please." He ground out his plea between clenched teeth. "I can't fight both of you. If you ever trusted me, trust me now."

She lowered her arm, but didn't move away from him. Not even as he advanced and drew closer to the wraith. "I am of you," he whispered. "What courses through your spirit, courses through mine. I can help you. If you let me." His fingers stretched out and brushed against the wraith's swirling, ragged presence.

Another scream rent the air. Lilith had to cover her ears as the wraith shot straight up and out of sight, only to swoop back down, whip into a funnel. Seconds later the black and grey matter shifted, spinning and falling, and dropped onto the grate in the form of a woman.

"Shen-Wei," Lil whispered and pushed out from behind Quincy to kneel beside the naked purser.

Shen-Wei was huddled into herself, shaking, covered in sweat and a layer of sticky, grey fluid. Her breathing sounded as if her lungs were filled with liquid. Lil looked back over her shoulder to where a stunned looking Quincy stared at them. "What? What is it?"

"Cadet Zhao." Quincy shook his head. "She's one of my missing recruits. But…"

"Sir." Shen-Wei's voice trembled as she reached for him. "Help…us." She lifted a shaking hand to him, but as Lilith touched her shoulder, Shen-Wei screamed once more, threw her head back, and transformed into a billow of smoke that vanished into the light.

"Signing back on, Trixie."

Back in Lil's suite, Quincy grabbed a bottle of beer out of the mini-bar while Lil checked back in with her team. Her voice faded into the background, her words unimportant as the image of Cadet Zhao exploding into nothing rolled through his head like a demonic film strip.

It had been over a century since he'd seen a wraith. They'd been hunted to near extinction decades before, mostly by the Atsila witches who had long ago sworn vengeance on his people. Now here he sat, another wraith dead. This time by the mere touch of at Atsila witch.

The witch he loved.

"I told Trixie I'd check in in a few hours."

He flinched and shied away when she touched his shoulder. He felt, rather than saw, her wince. "You need to get into my head. Now."

"I know. I just need a minute."

He grabbed her wrist when she tried to walk away. "What part of now don't you understand?"

"The part that says I need some time to get my own head on straight first." She wrenched free of his hold. "Unless you want me turning your brain to scrambled egg."

"You wouldn't do that."

"Really? You sure about that? Because I'm not. So I need a few minutes. Just…" She waved at him. "Sit there and stew."

"I'm not stewing." Unable to sit still, he got up and began to pace. "I'm trying to get the image of that poor kid out of my head. Jesus, Lil. She was…"

"I know." She grabbed her own beer, twisted open the cap and drank half the bottle. "I keep thinking if I hadn't touched her maybe…maybe she'd have turned back into one of those things."

"One of those things." Quincy laughed. "We've just come full circle. *I'm* one of those things."

"You are not," she snapped. "You have never been that."

"But that's what you saw. That last night we were together. When you slipped into my thoughts while I slept. That's what you saw. And that's why you left."

"You should have told me." She glanced away.

"And what good would that have done? You'd only have left me sooner, Lil."

"You don't know that."

"Yes." And that was the part that still hurt. "I do."

She drank some more. "I don't want to talk about it. Not now."

"If not now, then when? When whatever is going to happen on this ship happens? You sure you're good heading into the afterlife with this still hanging between us?"

"All the more reason for us to stay alive then." She finished her beer and pointed to the bed. "Lie down."

"Now?" He needed to find some levity before the fear took over. "Not really feeling amorous at the moment, but if you insist—ow." He rubbed his arm where she smacked him. "All right. Have it your way." He stretched out on the bed. A big mistake considering the second he did all he wanted to do was sleep. "I need to stay awake this time."

She nodded and sat next to him, rubbing her hands together as if to warm them. "That'll make it more difficult. You'll resist. Even if you don't want to. Which means it'll hurt."

"Consider me warned. We're running out of time. Let's get this over with."

"Close your eyes." She leaned over him, hands moving toward either side of his head.

"No."

"No?" She arched a brow.

"I want to watch you." He grinned. "Might be the last thing I see, remember? You're still the most beautiful woman I've ever met."

"And you're still full of bull." But she smiled in a way that told him she appreciated the compliment. "Now shut up." She brushed her mouth against his. "And let me in."

He could feel her, her mind, her thoughts, her presence, pushing in through his mind. Unable to stop himself, he closed his eyes and let his mind drift, thinking of anything but what was happening outside his consciousness. He sent himself to the only place he'd ever felt at complete peace. The twilight forests of Cerello, a dimension outside their own, where Lil had always dreamed of going. The waterfalls had been cascading silver water, arcing down from hundreds of feet in the air, like spilling moonbeams into the lake below. They had stood beneath those falls, together, joined by hearts and body, for as long as they could withstand the pleasure.

The image trembled against a quake so powerful blocks of stone broke away, pushing him into the fragments of memory he'd been unable to fit together.

"Stop fighting it." Lil's voice whispered along the edges of his thoughts. "I'm here with you, Quincy. I'm here. Let me in. Let me see. Let me…" she trailed off, her voice turning to fog. He could feel her hands tense on his temples. "There's a block I can't break. Something…unnatural. I can't—"

His memories shattered. Sharp shards flew at him, spearing through him. "Lil?"

"I'm here. I have…there." A stream of heavenly scented water flowed from above, bathing the memories in comfort and light. "Let them flow along the river now, Quincy. They're all there. You have what we need. Just let them flow. And remember. Everything. Let me see."

❖

Lil gasped and wrenched herself away from Quincy.

The images she'd seen had nearly broken her. Beginning with the forests of Cerello all the way to what had happened to him in those missing days. Tears of fury rose behind her eyes, but she swallowed them like fire, silently willing him to pull out of the trance.

She scrambled to her feet, her mind racing to compile a plan as she reached out to her team. "Trixie?"

"Right here, boss."

"Where's the Kyrian delegation right now?"

"Ah, the welcome ceremony in the dining room is almost over. It's been smooth sailing. So to speak," Trixie laughed. "You okay? You sound stressed?"

"Trixie, I need you to recall our entire team that's off shift. Every single one of them and I need you to do it off com. You understand what I'm saying?"

"Uh, yeah." Trixie's frown was implied. "But that's against regula—"

"Trix! Send the message and have them assemble on deck four, outer passageway. And make sure they're armed."

"Right. Okay. Always wanted to go out in a bang."

"Keep it only to our people outside the dining room. They can't hear you. They can't know." Her stomach churned around the beer.

"Can't know what?" Quincy was standing behind her, looking none the worse for wear after her mind probe.

"Quincy." Lil grabbed for him as she swayed. "Do you remember what you saw? Do you remember what happened?"

"Yeah." He nodded, blinking as if his mind were processing new information. "They didn't have me locked up for questioning. The ISB. They had me in some kind of lab." He rubbed the inside of his arm where Lil had watched the scientists withdraw massive amounts of his blood. "They were…sorry. It's still fuzzy."

"They were experimenting on you. There were tanks all around you. Tanks filled with some kind of fluid and there were people suspended inside."

"I remember. Yeah. Eight or—"

"Nine. There were tanks. Nine subjects. Quincy." She caught his face between her hands. "And you lost nine recruits. Including Shen-Wei."

She knew the instant he understood. The rage that rose in his eyes almost had her backing away, but she didn't. She couldn't. He needed her. And she needed him. And not just the man she'd fallen in love with.

She needed the wraith he carried inside of him.

"They used us. Experimented on us. They were trying to create an artificial wraith, a dual personality housed inside a soldier. Something they could call forth to attack…oh, my god, Lil. Shen-Wei. That's what happened to her. To all of them. They turned them into wraith. We have to find them. All of them. They have to be helped."

Lil grabbed hold of his arms when he tried to leave. "I know where they are, Quincy. They're here. On this ship. My new recruits for UPA's security force. They've been on this ship for weeks. They're my team. And right now all eight of them are in the dining room with hundreds of innocent passengers."

"And the Kyrian delegation," Quincy added. "That's why they're here. They're the weapon. They're going to kill the Prime Minister and make sure she doesn't reach the talks."

"Yes. And we don't have long to stop them."

"How did you get the rest of your team here without the others hearing?" Quincy asked as he strapped on a holster for a weapon. With two dozen security officers lined up and battle ready in the maintenance corridor outside the dining room, he'd never seen a more prepared team. Other than his own.

He felt sick. They were going to go up against the young men and women he'd trained. Exceptional athletic soldiers who had been dangerous before being turned into…whatever the ISB had changed them into.

"I used a private channel," Lil told him. "Trixie," she added at his confused expression. "Her mother was a siren. She has, let's say, a talent for targeted communication. Which reminds me, Trixie?"

"Here."

Quincy watched a very small dark-haired woman step out of the crowd of soldiers. With her high-top ponytail and florescent pink skirt and shirt she looked as if she'd stepped out of an 80's Madonna video.

"You ready for phase two?"

"Ready and waiting. Humans only. Should take two or three seconds to knock them out."

"Great. Let's hope that keeps them out of the line of fire."

"Lil." He caught her before she could walk off. "When this is over, I think it's time we had that talk."

"Ever the master of timing." She looked down at the hand wrapped around her arm. Her lips curved into a smile even as her eyes sparked. She rose up and kissed him, full on the mouth, in front of her entire squad. "Anyone has any issues with us working with a rogue ISB agent, keep it to yourself, understood?"

"Yes, ma'am," came the response.

"He trained these soldiers," Lil shifted to address her team directly. "Unless he issues an order that puts the Kyrian delegation or the prime minister in danger, you follow it."

"Yes, ma'am."

"I'll be focused on the Prime Minister. You're authorized to use whatever force is necessary to secure your objective. Understood?"

"Yes, ma'am!"

"Good. Teams one and two, disperse and enter through the main door. Headphones on. Teams three and four, with me. Quincy, on my six."

"For as long as you want," Quincy agreed and followed her to the back door to the dining room. Weapon drawn, he waited as she pressed her hand flat against the door and closed her eyes.

"I've got all eight in sight. They've flanked the prime minister. We'll need to attack and distract. Shit, Quincy. We've only got one shot at this."

He gave her a sharp nod. "That's all we need. Ready?"

She held up her free hand, lowered the other to the handle. She yanked it open. "Now, Trixie!"

Quincy instantly realized why she'd ordered the headphones. His head went light when Trixie opened her mouth and let out a sound that was a cross between a scream and a song. He grabbed hold of the second door and pulled it open as Lil and her team swarmed into the dining room.

Hundreds of passengers sagged in their chairs. Some fell to the ground, others collapsed onto the tables. It was as if someone had hit a power switch and turned them all off. The Kyrians instantly leapt to their feet. Toward the back of the dining room, at a table for two, Sente Mathias rose like a glacier in the middle of a turbulent ocean.

"Quincy, the prime minister!" Lil yelled as his recruits—her plain-clothes security force—slowly stood up and melted out of their clothes. Eight

shadowy figures, spinning grey and black clouds of death shot up and into the air, hovering around the delegation.

The Kyrians ran for cover, scattering around the room, but were quickly corralled by the secondary force Lil had sent in. Quincy kept one eye on Sente as he moved around the tables, laser pistol aimed high as he shifted from one wraith to the other.

He could feel them, feel their anger, their hatred, their fury, boiling inside him. For a moment, the briefest, longest moment of his life, he hesitated. And understood.

The wraith screeched and dived directly at the prime minister.

Quincy fired. His shot had no effect on the wraith, but sent a chandelier crashing onto the stage at the front of the room. He saw Lil running, full bore, leaping over tables and chairs and unconscious passengers in her determination to reach Prime Minister ZaldFenda.

And there the prime minister stood, swirling robes and glowing, iridescent skin, watching the end of her life barreling toward her.

Quincy followed Lil's lead and leapt onto one of the tables, launched himself into the air to grab one of the wraiths. He felt the briefest brush of form before the wraith writhed its way out of his grasp and sent him dropping to the floor. He'd distracted them. He could feel at least half of the wraith's attention on him. The one he'd nearly caught spun like a top before it hit the ground and instantly transformed back into the human he'd been moments before. Quincy couldn't stop to address the young man's confusion and pain. He needed to change them back. He had to find a way to save them. He owed them. He'd failed them. He'd let them vanish and hadn't fought hard enough to get them back.

He brought down another three before he heard another screech. One that chilled his blood right down to its marrow.

As if in slow motion, he turned and found Lil standing between a wraith and the prime minister. She had both hands raised above her head, a glistening protective shield arcing over the pair of them, trying to hold off the attacking wraith.

Out of the corner of his eye, he saw four of his recruits, the four he'd brought back, begin to transform once more. The cracking of their bones, the sinking in of their features, the screams that ripped out from their very souls as they turned their attention to Lil's forces and the Kyrians.

Something inside Quincy broke. There was only one way to save the delegation. To save the prime minister. To ensure the peace talks endured. To save millions.

"Lilith." He barely whispered her name, but she heard him. She looked at him from across the room, the question, the hesitation evident on her face. "Do it."

Tears glistened behind her determination. He turned away as she said the incantation. As she worked the spell that had been passed down through generation after generation. She dropped her arms, lowered the shield, and moved into the circle of the wraith.

The creatures exploded back, shifting out of the black and grey clouds into softer silver. Lil reached out and brushed her hand through each one and sent them ash-like into the afterlife.

Quincy forced himself to watch as the four who had looked to him soared toward her, unable to stop themselves from being pulled into her light. And then they were gone. An absence of sound descended as the wraith disappeared from sight.

Muted and muffled sobs echoed around the room. The Kyrian delegation emerged from behind the protective security force and headed straight for their prime minister.

Quincy braced his hands on his knees, his emotions bittersweet as his gaze met Lil's.

He moved toward her as the soldiers began to clear a path for the delegation to withdraw. Sente Mathias maneuvered through the tables, her attention not on him, but on the prime minister.

"Lil!" Quincy yelled.

Lil spun toward him even as the prime minister began to fall. He ran as Lil and two of the other delegates caught Prime Minister Zaldenda and eased her onto the floor.

"Where is she hit?" Lil yelled, searching the prime minister's prone form for a wound. "I can't find where she's been hit." She drew her weapon and aimed it at Sente. "I know what you are. You stay back!"

Quincy reached them as Sente knelt down beside Lil. "I can help her."

"Help her?" Lil continued to place herself between them. "You did this to her!"

"It's her hearts," one of the delegation told Lil. "They're giving out. She had hoped to survive the journey, to see the place where peace would be found, but—"

"Let me help her," Sente said again.

"You're Baltaran," Lil whispered.

Sente bowed her head in acknowledgement. "A Baltaran who wants peace. Please." She pushed Lil aside and rested her hands on the prime minister's frail chest. Quincy stood behind Lil, as the rest of the delegation gathered around. Within moments, the prime minister opened her eyes.

"I am…alive?" She looked shocked at the idea. The prime minister reached for Lil's hand. "Lilith Atsila. You brought me back."

"No." Lil looked to Sente. "She did." Quincy could see the questions begin to form. "If you did this just to kill her later—"

"My people want peace. They need peace." Sente sat back on her heels. "They did not believe the Kyrians were serious about the talks. So they sent me as a sentry and report back. They will meet you on the island in three days time," Sente assured them. "You have my word."

❖

"I'm so confused." Lil sat in the security office flanked by her officers, who were celebrating a job well done. Wanda and Trixie were comparing notes while Lil and Quincy sat at her desk trying to nurse each other's wounds with stale coffee. "If Sente works for the ISB…"

"My work with the ISB was a cover." Sente walked through the door, her tailored peacock green suit shimmering under the florescent lights. "My main job is as liaison for an entirely different corporation. One who has been very interested in the two of you for a long time."

"No offense," Lil said as she repressed a groan, "but I'm on secret agency overload at the moment."

"Quincy." Sente turned to him. "I failed you. Part of my mission was to prevent the experimentation the ISB did on you. I was not quick enough to stop it. Or what happened to your recruits. Rest assured, the ISB has been disbanded. And while a few of their higher ups have escaped capture for now, they will not for long."

"So you're *not* an assassin?" Lil asked. "You said she was an assassin."

"I wonder how that pesky rumor got started?" Sente asked with a smile. "You have the Agency's gratitude, Ms. Atsila. As do you, Mr. Lennox. And if you're ever looking for a change, I believe you'd both be an asset to the work we have in front of us."

"That would depend on what your anti-fraternization rules are," Lil said.

"Love is love," Sente said simply. "And if you bring it with you, all the better. Bring Wanda and Trixie as well. I think we'd all work very well together."

As quietly as she arrived, she left.

"Please tell me we can go back to your room and order room service now?" Quincy asked and held out his hand.

"Sure, we can do that." She grabbed hold and moved in. "Thank you. For trusting me again."

"Well, I figured you deserved another chance." He linked his hands behind her back. "You want to give this thing a go again? You really up for taking on a part-wraith?"

"Quincy, after the day I've had, I'm up for anything." And to prove it, she kissed him.

Kathryn Kaleigh writes for KST Publishing. Historical Romance. Time Travel Romance. Contemporary Romance. Sometimes sweet, sometimes with a twist of psychological drama. She has written over 80 short stories set in so many different worlds and is writing her 30th novel. Kathryn is the author of the award-winning Cupid's Kiss *contemporary series and the popular time travel series beginning with* Twist of Fate. *She grew up in north Louisiana where she currently lives with her family and fur babies, but she has lived in Houston, giving her an unquenchable love for the city life. Visit her website at www.kathrynkaleigh.com.*

THE UNEXPECTED

by Kathryn Kaleigh

I'd never thought it was possible to love going to work every single day.

I unlocked the door to my flower shop, stepped inside to the happy jingling sound of the bell attached overhead, and turned the closed sign around to open.

I dropped my handbag and tote bag onto the uncluttered marble checkout counter, then took a deep breath.

Carnations. Lilies. Roses. Gerberas. And my favorite—daffodils. So many scents that created a unique synergistic fragrance that I never tired of.

Pinks. Purples. Yellows. Whites. Reds. The whole shop was one big bouquet. A bouquet that I worked in every day. My very own bouquet playhouse that belonged to me.

I'd been open for business one month today.

I turned on the computer and logged in.

Though the building was renovated, everything was new. My computer. My refrigerated displays. And so many flowers.

I had a full page of orders that had come in overnight. It still sent a little thrill through me that people were actually buying from me. That they trusted me to make flower arrangements for the important events in their lives. Weddings. Funerals. Proms.

And Mother's Day.

I glanced at the calendar, as though I didn't have it memorized. Mother's Day was in four days.

I printed out the orders. Although I had everything totally automated, I liked to work from paper.

Just one year ago, this flower shop was no more than an embryo—a glimmer in my eyes, really. I had filed the paperwork for the corporation, but it still seemed like an impossible dream.

Eddie would have liked what that dream had become.

The first order was a cascade wedding bouquet. It must be for an elopement since there were no accompanying arrangements. No groom's flowers or bridesmaids or anything to go with it.

I hummed to myself as I put together the flowers. Positive by nature. That's what I kept telling myself.

The next arrangement was for a funeral. The request was for black ribbons and deeply pigmented orchids that looked almost black. Fortunately, I just happened to have some dark orchids on hand.

Along with the dark flowers, my mood threatened to darken. I reigned myself back and rifled through the requests looking for one more cheerful in nature. I'd found that working on the depressing ones were easier to handle in small doses.

I found a Mother's Day request for an expectant mother. They wanted bright pink colors and a teddy bear. I went into my storage room and brought out one of the teddy bears I'd ordered in bulk.

The tinkle of the front door bell interrupted my work, but an hour later I had a deposit to do the flowers for a high school reunion.

I still had time to finish up the expectant mother bouquet before lunch. I had hired a college student part time. She could deliver it that afternoon.

I put pink gerbera daisies, white and pink roses, and monte casinos in a glass baby block vase. Then I attached the whole thing to the oversized teddy bear's lap.

There. I stood back and admired the lovely creation and wasn't surprised when my eyes teared up.

It was perfect. I ran a hand along my little baby bump and allowed my mind to wander along its familiar bittersweet path.

I was ten weeks pregnant when Eddie had gone hiking with three of his friends. A simple loose rock on the trail and his life was over.

Our life was over. As least life as I knew it.

Though unconscious, he'd fought for three days, but the injuries had been too extensive.

The whole thing was such a waste.

Stop. Just stop.

Some people insisted that therapy was a waste of time. But not for me. Dr. Lee had taught me how to keep my thoughts under control. And from there, I was able to regulate my emotions.

I took the teddy bear arrangement to the counter and logged back into the computer. There was no address on my printed paperwork.

There was no delivery address.

I dug further into the order, but there was no delivery address and no credit card information. No name to trace the request back to.

Just great. I'd created this arrangement for nothing. I took a deep breath. I'd put it in the shop display window. Even if no one bought it right away, it could still lead to more business.

Taking my little creation to the shop's front window, I realized that I'd sold my main display yesterday. So I had the empty space.

There was an envelope there. Right where I was about to set the teddy bear.

I picked it up and looked for a name. I almost tossed it away, but instead, after arranging the teddy bear flowers, I opened the envelope.

My dearest Mags,

My heart flipped over and dropped to my toes.

My name was Shelby Margaret. No one called me Mags other than my husband and no one ever had before him.

I was thinking you could name her Lily for one of your favorite flowers.

Happy Mother's Day, my love.

I sat down hard on the bench in front of the window.

My eyes blurry with tears, I looked out toward the street.

Eddie stood there watching me, a wistful smile on his face. His palm was splayed on the glass of the shop window.

I blinked rapidly and stood up. I held out my hand toward him.

Eddie.

The father of my unborn child.

The love of my life.

The reason I'd been able to open this flower shop.

The ghost of Eddie slowly faded.

I just stood there staring.

Staring at the imprint of Eddie's palm on the window.

I put my hand on my stomach and felt the baby kick.

And I knew. I just knew.

The teddy bear bouquet I'd made had been for me.

A gift from Eddie.

Kate Pavelle is a prolific writer of fiction ranging from romance to thriller, with urban fantasy in-between. Look her stories up wherever fine e-books are sold. This story is a sequel to "Unsavory Company," a spy suspense set in the 1991 Balkan War. Gina's all grown up now. Gone is the indecision of a stranded art student who gets into scrapes. Now she controls other people scrapes—but she just can't wash this one man out of her hair!

UPON A BED OF BONES

by Kate Pavelle

The temperature in the metro tubes was stifling and human odor, both perspiration and perfume, mingled into a disagreeable mélange so typical of Europe. The car was only half full, leaving a few open seats.

This was not ideal.

The temperature in the metro tubes was stifling and human odor, both perspiration and perfume, mingled into a disagreeable mélange so typical of Europe. The car was only half full, leaving a few open seats.

This was not ideal.

Gina would've preferred being packed in like a sardine so she could get in and out without being followed, never mind the heat and the smell of humanity.

A half-empty car made her too visible, too on display for the guy who leaned against the sliding door three seats away from her with blatant disregard for his safety, or for the laws of physics.

To escape him, she had to blend in. And to blend in, she had to endure. Endure the heat, endure the stomach-turning odors that magnified it and, most of all, endure the discipline of utter stillness.

It wasn't easy, looking tired and bored when adrenaline coursed through her veins. Her blonde wig itched and a trickle of sweat began to wend its way down the nape of her neck. She ached to scratch it but didn't dare. She couldn't risk moving the wig itself. She wondered whether her makeup was dripping.

Checking one's makeup was an acceptable and normal action, however, especially in Paris. Gina reached into the shoulder bag she had slung across her chest like a bandolier and pulled out a sleek powder compact.

She checked her face as though she really cared and blotted some of the sweat with the tired, matted-down powder poof. The temptation to glance at the man she was almost certain was tailing her by tilting her mirror ever so slightly burned hard.

But no. She resisted.

She never caught him looking, but she still felt his attention upon her like a smothering blanket.

While she was at it, she dug around and pulled out a coral pink lipstick. She touched up her lips, rolling them in and out in a gesture all girls probably learned in their early teens. Its citrus flavor made her hungry, reminding her that 3 o'clock has rolled by and she hadn't eaten since her early morning croissant and coffee. Being hungry on account of the lipstick wasn't all a waste. If nothing else, paying attention to her appearance made her fit in a little more.

Her bespoke silk skirt, a frilly blouse and the pricy designer scarf that popped with tropical colors around her throat made her fit into the ridiculously appearance-conscious world of her current mission.

She was the very caricature of a proper *Parisienne*.

The Metro car swayed as the track turned and Gina braced herself, high-heeled shoes digging into the nonslip rubber floor. Damn silk skirt with its fluffy volume and hidden pockets. It did its job hiding things, but it didn't do much to keep her from sliding off the orange plastic seat. Tumbling to the floor would only draw attention.

Daring much, she glanced at the reflection in the window across from her.

He was still there, six foot two, dark glasses, a well-trimmed pale beard. Of course he wouldn't sit somewhere on the other side of the car. His blond hair glistened from under a baseball cap in the flickering pale light of the city's favorite transportation system. Despite the stifling heat of August, the man who seemed set on tailing her since she had emerged from within the Louvre was wearing a white button-down shirt with a tan blazer over it.

In this heat, that tan blazer probably hid a shoulder holster.

She knew she would be made eventually.

Just not this fast.

Eugene couldn't decide whether he had rotten luck, or whether his whole mission was coming up roses when she showed up. The art expert who picked up a small Degas sketch of dancers didn't just receive a piece of art worth a hundred grand.

She also got an encoded message.

And, considering what he knew about her from their last two meetings, she knew the full value of that little package.

Dr. Gina Francesca Migliore was in her late twenties now, or maybe even a bit north of thirty. He didn't know.

All he knew that he had to follow the message and see who wanted it so very badly.

And that meant following Gina.

Who might recognize him—but she probably wouldn't. Not in this disguise.

Following Gina would be a piece of cake. She was an academic, a well-known expert in her field and her entanglement with the CIA was as a mere asset.

No need to worry. He'd watch his back, and he'd admire *her* back.

He suppressed a smile. This assignment was a ruddy cake walk.

❖

Two more stops flashed past and commuters began to pack in. *This was more like it.* Gina reviewed her options in the privacy of her own mental map. By now, she knew Paris like the back of her own hand.

Risk analysis, communication potential, the possibility of being seen.

All of that played in. She only knew she couldn't afford to go to the end of the metro line, because waiting for the train back meant certain confrontation.

Now she didn't mind the chafing of a webbing holster that sagged with the weight of her gun. Now, the concealing swaths of her ridiculously expensive silk skirt carried out a practical purpose.

Hiding things.

Hiding guns and spare ammo and a small, rolled up sketch of dancers by Degas.

Poised, she bided her time. The wheels screeched as the train braked.

The train's AI announced the next station.

Barely breathing, trying for that tired and slumped look which wouldn't reveal muscles ready to burst forth, Gina waited until the last possible second.

She got up, turned away from the door and from the mystery man, and wrenched the door leading between the cars open.

The air burned even hotter in the enclosed space.

A chime warned against the doors about to close.

The movement behind her was no surprise as she burst through the other door and lunged herself into the next car.

The half-empty one.

She dashed out.

Passengers flying, manners set aside.

Her feet hit the rough, yellow-painted safety strip of the platform as the doors shut behind her.

They bit her skirt.

She grabbed and yanked—safe. Safe for now and still decently dressed, in possession of her coded message and hiding her arsenal as the train hissed and sped away.

She turned and allowed herself to breathe a little deeper. Her tail was securely on the train and on his way to the over-populated Parisian suburbs to the south.

Gina heard the commotion behind her as she ran up the few remaining steps leading from the cavernous Metro station.

She dared a glance.

Police whistling, people shouting.

A train came to a screeching halt so piercing, she was glad she wasn't any closer to the agonizing sound of steel skidding upon steel.

She should have been okay—her rational mind told her so—yet her gut feeling insisted that she hide.

With the confident stride of a woman certain of her goal, she set out down the plaza sidewalk paved in a mosaic of ancient granite squares. Her peripheral vision informed her as to her options.

Tall, four-story apartment buildings. She could break in if she needed to.

Stores—too temporary.

Trees—she was thankful for their shade but they wouldn't lend her the cover she needed. Yet the plaza

held potential. It wasn't a city square as such, but a center of a gentle and sparsely traveled roundabout that held a park with a small lawn and trees. In its center stood a one-story building.

People milled around, forming a line. Street hawkers selling five-Euro plastic bottles of water indicated a tourist attraction.

She crossed the street and made her way over, thinking hard. Even before she saw the signs, she realized she was at the entry point to the fabled Parisian Catacombes.

A quick scan of the crowd made up her mind. Tourists, the ones with artsy jewelry from Italy. The ones wearing sneakers from the US, a country she represented in an extremely unofficial and deniable capacity. Two Germans, a British family with a well-behaved child.

She was relieved to see that tourists who had been sitting on the grass and eating lunch began to get up and queue behind her. Being in the middle of the line was a much better cover than standing at the very end.

The line moved ahead as those up the front begin to pay and gain entry. Victorious, she glanced behind her.

He stood at the end, tan blazer and dark glasses and a smirk on his punchable face.

This mission was going so well until he showed up.

She so despised being followed.

This wasn't going well, Eugene decided when he realized where Gina intended to go. The catacombs were interesting. He had been down there some years ago, and going in again would've been fine two summers ago.

But not now.

Not after…hell. He refused to think about it. Not following his target wasn't an option—all kinds of things got dropped off in the catacombs, only to be picked up later.

He'd go underground, dammit, and just suck it up and tough it out.

Options. Stay, or leave?

If she left, he was just going to follow. Gina had been to the karst caverns, which extended into impressive catacombs, before, except that had been a long time ago. Even so, she had a vague recollection of the strange twists and turns, of the pleasant coolness and the limestone smell in the air.

She could hide—she could lose him better down there than up on the street level. She could most certainly hide her cargo and pick it up at a more convenient time.

The entry building, stuccoed in pale tan and roofed in a red tile, welcomed visitors into the maw of a green-painted entrance flanked by a pair of solid steel doors. Their green paint was chipped and scarred by graffiti, some of which had been touched up in a slightly deeper shade.

Gina scanned the small vestibule, the large plastic-covered posters which stated the rules of conduct in several languages. They were entering a sacred space, resting place of many thousands of dead whose bones had been exhumed from old and sprawling cemeteries as the hunger of the city of Paris for new houses and new neighborhoods grew along with its population.

The bones had been interred under the supervision of monks and priests and, even today, guards enforced respectful silence and prevented vandalism.

The presence of guards might be a good thing.

She quipped a pleasant "*Bon jour*" to the man behind the bulletproof glass and passed him a ten-Euro note. The admission cost less than that, a Parisian act of hospitality she had always appreciated. Taking her ticket and leaving the change behind as a donation was, however, a matter of expedience rather than generosity.

She moved down the staircase fast, not running but passing older people and the slower families with children at a pace that would move her away from her pursuer without drawing undue attention.

Pretending to be interested was the worst part of going underground. Gina descended down the long, twisted staircase, giving the informational photo display only a cursory look.

The straggly line of visitors followed the arrows to the entrance of the tunnel. A sign in both French and English informed her of a long walk in a narrow, dark space. The dim emergency-type lights were encased in protective wire cages and the floor underfoot glistened under her impractical heels, wet and uneven.

She let her fingers of her left hand trail against the wall. The surface alternated between old stones and extensive mortar and cement patches. Gina felt a measure of comfort at the realization that the underground tunnel seemed to be maintained. She didn't mind being underground, per se, and didn't mind the dark. Her prior experience told her she could duck and weave and make it out the other side, making her way to a different metro line three miles away from the original entry point.

The dim tunnel took another, rather sharp turn and narrowed. She heard a splash, followed by a cold, wet deluge inside her shoe. The echoes of her own steps were followed by the shuffling of the others along with the loud, rapid breathing of someone in the back.

Somebody was having trouble.

She wondered who.

Eugene knew the tunnel would eventually widen again, giving access to the caverns created centuries ago during the process of mining chalk and gypsum. All this rational knowledge, along with his wet feet and the painful skip of abraded knuckles over old masonry, helped him breathe. It made the weight of the earth above his head less massive and marginally less threatening. It made the space around him seem larger and the walls less suffocating. He felt a small, tentative thrill of pride at keeping his claustrophobia at bay.

Labad grinned in the dark. The man before him seemed to have belonged to that certain percentage of visitors uncommonly affected by dark, enclosed spaces. That would make eliminating him easier—which would get the woman and her cargo within his grasp.

He had made spelunking his special hobby just to overcome what his mark up ahead was suffering. His special talent was just that—an ability, through sheer perseverance, to turn his weakness into his strength.

But the man before him hadn't had the opportunity to follow that path. It would only make his job of reaching the blonde up ahead easier—both her and the artwork in question.

Finally! Gina felt an unexpected jolt of relief as the corridor emptied into a tall, wide space good three stories high, supported by vaulting Romanesque arches. In a space devoid of windows, only a high-hanging lantern illuminated the simple staircase of low risers under repeating arches that led visitors to the ossuary. That's where the bones were kept. Hundreds of thousands worth of skeletons harvested from the old and now defunct graveyards of Paris, carefully arranged by monks and nuns, laid to rest by priests.

This was holy ground, a sacred space.

A safe space.

Another uniformed guard stood his post at the top of the stairs, shushing those who seemed too boisterous. The dead didn't like to be disturbed.

"Beware ye mortal, who now enter the domain of death."

Gina's Latin was decent as befit an art history PhD, and she easily translated the large inscription carved into stone under which she had to pass.

The chill air of the underground passages cooled her sweat, and she wished for more than just a flimsy blouse and a skirt. She better keep moving and fast, both to warm up and to make her getaway.

Eugene noticed Gina fall behind a married couple. She leaned against the metal railing in order to admire a scale model of several building, carved from stone. Yes, it was here all over again, and once again he could only speculate about her allegiances.

He couldn't approach her, not now. His breathing was still too loud for his own ears and even though the pressure of the Earth had lessened in the larger cavern, the ceiling still loomed low and ominous.

He tried not to think of the thousands of tons of stone and earth overhead. He hoped the Metro tunnels were underneath them and not overhead. When leaned against a stone to steady himself, he earned a glare from an older, female guard.

Gina finally moved and he trailed her, trying not to hyperventilate. Only the thought of the prize at the end kept him on his feet, his rational faculties more or less intact.

That, and the fact that the now-blonde Gina was the one and the same innocent-seeming girl who had saved his life in Yugoslavia six years ago.

Labad trailed at the very end of the group now. He was thrilled to see the visitors before him pass the blonde in her frilly blouse and the man who had followed her for so long, and to such an unlikely locale.

He wondered why she was here.

Several novels have been written of artwork that was stolen and hidden for safekeeping in the Catacombes, with the ghosts of their skeletal guardians keeping them safe from prying eyes. There was no way she'd do the same thing. It was too cliché, too well known. Every Parisian was aware of the plot and its various twists. That, however, didn't mean that he couldn't use the opportunity to get rid of his competition.

The visitors moved in a silent queue into the first chamber, all somber as they tried to decipher the Latin and the old French inscriptions on the pillars and the walls of the extensive crypt.

Gina shivered. The cool, damp air must've been getting to her.

They had made their way through several passages. The lighting was dim and somber. The walls and structures built from human bones glowed with artful backlighting in a macabre display of sculptural shapes created over two hundred years ago. Gina discreetly readjusted her wig and wiped off yet another droplet that fell from the ceiling. Somehow she had expected to see rats down here, but there were none and their absence was a quaint surprise. Just as the uniformed guards who guarded the dignity of the space indicated, this tomb was a civilized, protected space.

Gina's eyes slid toward a locked passageway. Its wrought-iron door was closed shut with a padlock. She eased closer to it, peering into the dark space beyond. There have been many such doors, and she had a good idea where those passages led. The catacombs were a vast and an extensive network of tunnels, tying into the sewer systems and the Metro itself.

She had the details of the theoretical map committed to memory. Navigating the cavernous space in the dark and by herself would be, no doubt, an entirely different kettle of fish. Her prime directive was to drop off that little piece of art to her next contact.

To do that, she needed to get out of here unpursued and alone.

Eugene passed by a structure resembling a water bowl on a plinth but was, according to a sign on the wall, an old oil lamp. Now the basin collected droplets of water from the tall, domed ceiling above it.

The knowledge that this part of the ceiling had caved in several times in the past and had been successfully repaired did nothing to ease his sense of suffocating discomfort. He hated the confined space of the underground and kept well away from the protruding femur joints locked together in an artful design, punctuated by a rhythmic pattern of skulls. Their nasal cavities had that typical, triangular shape to them and only very few had retained their lower jaw. They all looked old and small, reminiscent of elder days when all people were shorter and smaller as well.

The path opened up to yet another crossroads.

He watched Gina to his left as she peered through the grating of the metal gates that barred her way. He hoped to all that was holy that she wouldn't find an open passage and didn't slip into the darkness.

He would have to follow her, without a flashlight, without a map. There was no way he could pursue her through the rats' maze that was the Catacombes. His fine hearing picked up the high-pitched whine of supersonic rodent repellents. The sound irritated him, yet he was grateful for the absence of rats for they reminded him of that one time he had been trapped underground—no.

He wouldn't pursue that train of thought.

Instead, he'd slow down and walk on the other side of the bone barrel, pretending to admire it. If he circled just right, maybe he would get Gina behind him.

Labad peered at his tourist brochure, feigning an interest in various structures. There was the altar with a cross made of skulls, the crossed bones, the Cup… and yes, the huge, ceiling-tall structure of the bone barrel. He turned toward the dim, yellow light to better see the information in the brochure when a guard tapped him on the shoulder, hurrying him along. They were, after all, the very last tour of the day.

"Qui…merci." He nodded, his face solemn and thoughtful. With only a corner of his eye he noticed a movement right past the bones—the woman. She was doing something and he couldn't tell quite what it was, but the tall man who had been pursuing her was to his immediate right.

He checked his watch again.

Four, three, two…

Then the lights went out and people began to scream.

Gina had been trying, very discreetly, to pick a lock of the gate that led into the rest of the caverns just as the lights went out. She took a few steps back, toward the solid cylinder of bones firmly packed and settled by age. The guard yelled something in French as he fumbled for his flashlight.

A gunshot.

Its pressure and sound reverberate off the walls and the low ceiling.

Deafening, shocking.

Liked being on an indoor range without earmuffs.

The guard's flashlight cut through the darkness. More tourists screamed up ahead when another shot rang out. His flashlight clattered to the moist gravel underfoot.

Gina unfroze. She dove over the chest-high wall of bones and skulls, making use of a shallow hiding space behind it.

I'm sorry…I'm sorry…I'm sorry…

She wasn't a superstitious and couldn't understand why she kept apologizing to the old bones beneath her, the skeletal fragments shielding her.

She wanted her gun. Now.

Except she landed on top of it and turning around on a bed of bones would have causes a racket loud enough to give her away.

Eugene had seen the woman fussing with her skirt—he *knew* it had been important and he had wanted to stick around and see if she'll try to hide her message down here in the catacombs—when the lights went out.

The relative peace of the shattered, broken by the panicked shouts of the people ahead of him, the surprised exclamation of the uniformed guard.

Then a sharp pain in his shoulder.

Temporary deafness.

The guard's flashlight clicked on—finally! The darkness had been making the pain even worse.

Another gunshot reverberated through the space. The wide beam of light illuminated the face of the shooter in a bright flash.

The shooter's face…

The guard crumpled to the ground with a gasp, followed by the sickening gurgle of a man fighting for his last breath.

Yet, that *face*.

Dark, straight hair, high cheekbones, fine eyebrows. Almost too pretty for the tough guy he purported to be, yet cagey and as tough as a snake.

Eugene had run across him in Cyprus in 1991, and he'd caught a sight of him in a spice-scented *souk* in Istanbul four months later, ducking between merchants and out a shaded alley.

He'd been on his radar, off and on, for the last five years but he sure had not expected to see him here.

At the wrong end of a gun.

The wound in his shoulder began to throb. He knew he'd have to hide from his armed opponent. No shape to fight, no condition to flee.

Steps echoed on their way toward them in the utter darkness here among the bones. Flashes of electrical lights bobbed up and down the walls far away. Eugene heard light, shuffling steps sneak back the way they have arrived.

Seizing the opportunity, Eugene crawled silently to the other side of the bone barrel. He had remembered the layout of the place well. As voices and footfalls got loud enough to cover his actions, he straightened up.

He launched himself over the nearest barrier of bones to his left. Chest-high, it formed a fitting hiding place.

He expected a hard, rather loud landing, but his fall was cushioned by something soft and warm.

Gina managed to twist and wiggle until, bit by bit, she lay on her back as flat as she could be. Her 9mm composite Beretta was in easy reach on her right thigh and the little Degas drawing, its graceful dancers still poised and frozen in time, rested in a narrow roll of cardboard in one of her skirt's secret pockets.

She let air in and out with soft and quiet ease borne of long practice, silent, enduring.

The gunned-down guard's flashlight lit the ground and its light reflected off the bottom of the opposite wall of bones. The ambient light was just a shade away from utter darkness. Silence ruled the tomb again.

Just as she decided to slowly raise her head and peek, a sound of voices and hurried footfalls had her stiffen on her uncomfortable bed of bones again.

Gina forced herself to relax.

They were coming their way and she stayed low, not uttering a sound, barely allowing herself to breathe. Her right hand was on the gun in the thigh holster under her skirt. She pressed her left hand over her mouth to force herself to be utterly silent.

Few pebbles scraped against the bedrock that formed the floor.

A rustle of fabric, an inhale and a few quick steps—

A heavy body landed right on top of her.

Her back ground into the pile of skeletal remains beneath her and she bit her hand to keep her gasp of pain from escaping.

Letting go of her gun, she grasped for purchase, trying not to shift. Her fingers found only the round, smooth surface of an ancient cranium. Her fingers slipped into the eyeholes by accident and she shivered in revulsion and regret as she slowly extricated her hand from within the skull.

The man—it had to be a man—above her froze, keeping very still. They both did, waiting for the furor of guards to pass. Their compatriot's body had been found, the police came with stronger flashlights. The searchlights played on the walls of the dark, dank space as commands and curses spoken in rapid French mingled with an overlay of sputtering radios.

It must have taken hours—the beeps and unfamiliar codes, the echoes of hard-shod heels clicking on the hard rock. The commanding voices, the occasional curse of a tall policeman who hit his head on the low lintel of a stone doorframe.

Gina had kept perfectly still through it all. For all she knew, the body on top of her might be that of an innocent man. His silence was a bond. First they'd wait until the police left, then they'd figure out where they stood with one another.

Despite the underground chill, Gina was grateful for her short sleeves right now. Since her left hand was still over her mouth and her forearm was bare, she realized that the man who landed on top of her had a sticky wetness clinging to his hair, to his cheek. It was warm smelled vaguely familiar.

It dripped.

Her tongue flashed out in an inadvertent reaction. *Salty. Metallic. Warm.*

A sudden tremor possessed Gina's body. Here she was, lying on a heap of bones of the long-dead, protected by the walls made of their femurs and skulls, pressed into them by a man newly dead.

Gina was sure he must have been dead, for he was limp, didn't seem to be breathing, and in her position she had not detected a heartbeat.

She had just tasted the man's blood.

The darkness was empty now, one devoid of flashlights and sounds and the police presence. Drops of water dripped somewhere far away, echoing through the Stygian stillness.

Gina stirred in the dark.

"Hey." The word seemed too loud in the lifeless, cavernous space.

There was no reply. Resting upon the bones of the dead long gone by, she was covered by a man only recently expired.

Gina had seen men die before.

Her stomach churned at the memory, and she suppressed it.

At least the fellow who was weighing her down had not died by her hand.

Here and now. Here and now.

A guard had been shot dead and the perpetrator had been heard running ahead, back toward the entrance staircase. The police had given chase and had removed the body, but with a suspect on the run, their search of the caverns had been only cursory.

The other visitors exited through the other exit along with the remaining guards, who had flashlights.

She was finally alone.

It was time.

First things first, though. As much as she welcomed the residual heat of the body above her, she had to get free. The muscles of her back gathered as she arched up and canted her hips, letting the body slide off her in a familiar wrestling move.

She readjusted her clothing, biting back gasps of pain as her knobby knees suffered from the protuberances of bones underneath. She fished for her cell phone in her purse and turned on the flashlight app.

A cool, white glow flooded the cavern where she had been hiding for hours now. The bones under her were a veritable mess of ribs, pelvises, vertebrae and metacarpals; only the walls displayed the carefully patterned organization instilled by the monks and the priests. There would be another bare skeleton soon, especially if the squeak of a nearby rat was any indication. A sudden, curious impulse overcame her squeamishness and she aimed his light at her motionless companion.

Pale hair, a light-colored blazer, a baseball cap. An American, perhaps?

The baseball cap sat askew. It wasn't right to die looking so out of sorts. Gina reached over to straighten his hat—and almost yelped when the hair flew off his head, still stuck to the hat in her hand. Underneath, the wild, matted hair gleamed chestnut brown in the pale light of Gina's phone.

She frowned—the color's reddish undertones, the stubble, the aquiline nose—all that was disturbingly familiar. She aimed the light into the dead man's face and turned him to see him better.

Here was her tail from the Metro and he probably had picked her up at the Louvre.

Now, in the unforgiving light of her phone, with his natural hair color, with his sunglasses off, she recognized him immediately. How could she not—he had spent days in the back seat of a car with her as she had tended to his wounds. She had thought his name was Zhenia then, an Ukrainian who didn't speak English.

He went by Eugene and spoke the King's English as befit a suspected MI6 agent—but she had learned all that later, just as she'd learned the intoxicating taste of his lips.

She allowed herself a moment of sorrow.

"Oh, Zhenia. Eugene, whoever the hell you are. You fucking moron, stepping in front of a bullet like that." Her voice broke a little, a hoarse whisper full of regret. "I'll have to leave your body behind, my friend."

For he was a friend, a rare commodity in their line of work. Not that he'd trust her or she could afford to trust him—no, never. But she felt he'd never harm her on purpose.

"Now let me close your eyes, love." She'd do that after she searched his pockets.

Eugene had always carried the most interesting tools of trade.

She opened his blazer and reached for his chest pocket.

"Nnngh."

The dead man moaned, screwing his eyes shut against the bright light.

Gina pointed it to the side. Suddenly, her situation turned from a cut-and-dry scenario into a full-blown strategic dilemma.

I can't let him die. The memory of the soft press of his lips came back hard and fast. She blinked hard.

And then, *If he dies elsewhere, he won't attract attention.*

The thought alarmed her.

Appalled her.

If he dies, he won't identify me.

The last thought sat ill with Gina. He was a fellow operative. Different agency, different country, but in their two run-ins they had gotten along well.

Had covered for one another.

Had seen much together.

Whether or not the man next to her was working the case from the opposite end or not, she just didn't

have it in her to leave him underground, surrounded by old bones, destined to expire in the dark.

Besides, Gina was wearing a disguise. As long as she remained the blonde "Marie", her identity just might remain protected, and so would the integrity of her mission.

She sighed and crawled toward Zhenia, or Eugene, or whatever he was calling himself now. To her surprise, he was not only alive but his pulse was slow and strong.

"Hey," she said, nudging him. "Let's get you out of here, okay?"

He was still drowsy from the residual effects of shock and blood loss. There was a gunshot wound in both his arm and torso and since Gina had heard only one shot, she had a hard time figuring out what was going on. It seemed as though the entry wound grazed Zhenia's right bicep, but the exit wound had damaged the right side of his back.

The attacker had seen what he'd been shooting at. He must have known him.

A slight figure in a baseball cap and a black t-shirt floated to the forefront of Gina's trained memory. She remembered large eyes sparkle in the dark, long eyelashes, a straight and aquiline nose. She'd have to remember later, though, for now, her attention was upon her patient.

She surveyed the wall of bones that barred them from the wet stone path, and identified a likely place to climb over with minimum damage. "Zhenia," she said with a whisper. "Let's get you patched up some, okay? Roll over, I need to get at your shirt."

She fished a little multitool knife from a hidden pocket behind her belt, pulled out a small knife blade, and hiked up Zhenia's sports coat. The pale color was now stained with maps drawn by blood, but there was no help for that.

With a quick yank, she pulled the tail of his shirt out and started cutting. "I need this fabric, and you need a compression bandage more than a dress shirt right now," she said. The fabric was already bloody and wet, but that didn't matter much.

Keeping the blood inside him did.

She removed her thin belt, the kind made of three lengths of strong leather that looped around her slender waist.

A quick search of her designer handbag produced tampons and pads. Not that she needed them—women working missions had military-grade implants to suppress their monthly cycles—but she always carried them along.

They were useful.

She removed the wrappers off the tampons. "This is gonna hurt. Sorry, mate." Calling him mate would, hopefully, ground him. Remind him he was a guy on a mission, and that his accomplice was stuffing tampons into his wounds to stem his bleeding, not to make him miserable.

He gasped.

"All done," she murmured. "Let's get you this wound covered, and a compression bandage…" Gently, she set the maxi-pad over her work, then the folded square of what used to be a piece of Zhenia's shirt.

Her belt was just long enough to strap the improvised compression bandage to the wound and immobilize his injured arm at the same time. Ironically, the bed of bones helped. She was able the snake the belt under him through the crevices between them, which was a lot easier than having to roll him.

"Hey, man, wake up!" She shook the uninjured shoulder; a groan was his only reply.

Suppose he couldn't make it.

Suppose he got stuck behind and die here overnight and this would be all her fault.

And she couldn't even call the police. Her cell phone didn't work this deep underground.

Desperate, she stroked his hair. "Zhenia, please. I need you to come with me. Come to a safe place, okay? Breathe, and wake up, and come on."

This panic she felt, that had nothing to do with the code on the back of the Degas drawing. Nothing with delivering it to the next party.

And everything to do with Zhenia in Limassol, where he had let her escape the rest of his MI6 team. Where she'd realized that, with his high-brow British accent, he was a lot more than just another hired Ukrainian thug.

Thinly, as though his voice was just a dream, he whispered. "Gina."

He knew her despite her disguise. He was onto her, onto everything and yet all that mattered to her now was hearing his voice.

"Yes, Gina." She wondered whether he remembered her with a halo of immense fondness.

She wondered whether he, too, had left their brief liaison out of his debriefing.

"Okay, Zhenia. Put your arm around my neck. We're climbing over."

She used cell phone light as a guide. They really needed it on to climb over the wall that was only one foot high on their side and dropped off about four feet onto the path. A lot of their time was spent on their bellies, and they had dislodged a number of bones despite their best efforts.

Once Zhenia was securely slumped on the path, Gina repositioned the bones as best she could without spending much time. Then she returned to his injured ward.

"Okay, Zhenia. Let's go."

Just to confirm her memory of this silent place, Gina consulted the tourist brochure and the simple map within in. Yes, going back would take a lot longer than forging ahead. She peered at it. Since the passages leading to other parts of the catacombs were gated off, she couldn't really get lost. Besides, the man with the gun had run the other way, and had drawn the police after him.

She helped Zhenia stand. His long, left arm was draped over Gina's shoulders and she pressed her own shoulder under it, wrapping her right arm around his waist, grabbing the waistband of the trousers. Gina's purse was slung across his chest bandolier-style, and her phone was in her left hand, illuminating the way.

Zhenia plodded on next to her, step after a painful step. Gina felt rather than heard the occasional gasp of pain and a shudder.

A rat ran over her foot—she ignored it.

"You need a break?"

"…No…I'm fine."

"Okay." She wished she knew the extent of his damage, she wished she had brought a better first-aid supply.

"Do you want to go to the hospital?" she asked, and had Zhenia replied in the affirmative, Gina would have put him in a cab and would have instructed the driver accordingly.

A moment of silence passed. "No. No hospital."

"Okay." Gina's concern yielded to relief, because now neither of them would be exposed to the authorities.

They trudged on for the next two hallways, which brought them to a small room of polished stone. It opened before them with a place where tourists were allowed to take pictures. Gina looked around at the structure resembling a sacrificial altar and the numerous inscriptions in the walls, making up her mind about which way to go, when her phone battery failed, and the light went out.

It was Gina. Not Marie, which was her current cover name, but Gina. The sweet grad student who had gotten stuck behind the lines of the Balkan war five years ago.

Stuck with him, apparently, having waltzed into a situation and a world she hadn't known even existed, and here she was now.

Dr. Gina Francesca Migliore. An international expert on the smuggling routes of art objects in the Middle East, and now a CIA asset. She might've gotten recruited over the last few years.

If she had joined the Company, he hadn't been informed. He hadn't been tracking her either. He'd been following that piece of carefully coded paper.

Who would receive it, and where would it go next?

Running into Gina was a happy coincidence, a reminder of a pleasant event in his past. He had been wondering, every so often, what she was up to.

And here she was—Gina with an unmistakable contour of a gun strapped to her shapely thigh under her fluffy skirt.

Helping him.

Because he wasn't the only one on Gina's tail. He had made Labad as fast as Labad had made him. Except Labad's gun had come out first.

Eugene would've left the wet work for later, for a dark alley. A park. Not a cavernous catacomb filled with civilians.

Not a sacred space.

Eugene clenched his jaw against the pain in his arm and his side and focused on his breathing. Gina's warm arm was wrapped around his waist and her firm shoulder supported him. He was coming to, becoming more alert as they stumbled on, but regaining his senses also accentuated his pain. Thoughts fluctuated between fuzzy and clear in his head as he tried not to lean on the babe under his arm too much. Then the light went out.

Panic flooded him.

His arm tightened around Gina's shoulder as she stood still, the sound of his ragged breathing bouncing off the low ceiling. Space seemed to close in on him, the walls no longer kept at bay by the bright iPhone light.

"Breathe, Zhenia…just breathe."

He felt rather than heard her light voice against his chest. A wave of dizziness passed over him and he stood there, refusing to yield yet holding on to his smaller, intrepid guide for dear life.

"Fuck," he said as the waves of helpless terror began to abate. "Fucking tunnels. I hate tunnels. I hate cave-ins. I hate old bones. FUCK!"

The expletive bounced around, skipping from grinning skull to grinning skull, the long-dead mocking his distress through their sightless oculars.

"Sorry," he said then, mindful of his company. "Got carried away." He cleared his throat, breaking into a painful cough that make the wound under his arm greet him with sharp pain.

"Zhenia. Do you have a phone we could use for light? My battery's dead."

"Check my right pocket." Eugene hated saying that. He didn't want her going through his contacts. Yet she had ignored the icons on the screen of his flip phone completely. She just opened it, aiming its modest glow in their intended direction.

"Let's go. According to the map, we'll go through several more hallways and then there'll be a staircase to the surface."

"We'll get lost," Eugene said.

"All the turn-offs are gated. There's only one way to go." Gina seemed to know what she was doing so he left her to it, focusing instead on breathing the air.

It smelled heavy, like the moist clay he struggled not to recall.

They made their way through a chamber lined with inscriptions and a stone basin. Then a left into another hallway full of bones. The grisly walls were barely visible in the dark. The going was slow through the occasional puddles, with bits of gravel on the floor that had an unfortunate tendency to trip Eugene up.

They passed another dark hole in the wall. Only the bright padlock gleamed against the dark, wrought-iron grating. A rat squeaked somewhere near.

"Gina. How much longer?"

"I…don't know," the woman replied, pressing her body closer into him. Her thin blouse stuck to her skin and he thought she was only too glad for his body heat.

"You…would you care to use my jacket?"

A most unladylike snort had been his reply. "It's soaked with blood, so that would be a no." They moved on, passing three more wall pillars. "But it's nice of you to offer," she said, her voice softer than before, and Eugene had to smile. Injured or no, even while fending off waves of hard-earned claustrophobia, he could still be charming with the ladies.

Gina shuddered again but not from cold this time.

No, this time his snort of glee almost gave him away. Poor man had tried to be nice even while injured. The warm, dry heat rolled off him in waves, heat which Gina gladly gleaned to warm her goose-fleshed skin. Inhibitions against socially unacceptable behavior warred with a sense of practicality, keeping her from wrapping her chilled, underdressed body around Zhenia.

The pleasant sensation of his touch and his body heat felt good in an elemental, atavistic way. Yet it disturbed her, too. Gina was in no position for a relationship, not even a fling.

Yet down here, among the dank stones and the darkness that shrouded the bones of the dead, the rules of the world above didn't apply and this man's body heat was attractive and enticing on a primal level she had never experienced before.

His cell phone flickered a bit, went dim, and they were in utter darkness again.

"Um…your phone's dead. Here, I'm handing it to you." Gina folded the small unit shut and had, presumably, waved it in front of Eugene for some time before he realized the man's other arm had been immobilized. "Oh, sorry," she whispered. "I'll put it in your coat pocket, okay?"

That was easier said than done. The darkness that descended upon them once again seemed thicker this time around, and this thickness made the layers of the Earth above seem denser too.

Heavier and threatening, weighed down by the mass of buildings and cars overhead. Gina squeezed his shoulders as though she never wanted to let go. Then she ran his hand down his chest to the right. Finally, after much touch-and-go, she found the sports coat's pocket.

"Here. I'm sliding the phone in your pocket," she said, following words with action. "There's just a few hallways. We'll be out soon."

Few minutes of stumbling and tripping later, Gina pushed away her reticence. "We need to walk in a straight line," she said in a voice so quiet it barely carried. "We need to get closer to the wall."

The wall of bones. She didn't want to say it aloud.

Just a bit of guidance—just enough to walk a straight line a little faster—and to do that, she needed to touch the wall. A wall with a surface corrugated in a rhythmic pattern of knobs that used to be human knees. Her fingers skimmed over the rough joint, its worn surface no longer protected by slick cartilage.

"I'm sorry…I'm sorry…I'm sorry…"

"What are you sorry for?" Zhenia's voice cut through the dark, and Gina realized she'd been mumbling under her breath.

"I'm touching the dead." Her admission came as a silent whisper, its syllables filling the stygian darkness, bouncing off the low ceiling and the pillars and structures made of life long unlived.

Zhenia stopped and wavered in place. "Why?"

"So we can walk in a straight line. You know, follow the wall?"

A few beats of silence preceded Zhenia's reaction. "You mean you're touching the wall of the bones and skulls?"

"Yeah…" Gina took a few slow steps forward and Zhenia came along like a big tail that wagged the dog.

The arm around her shoulder tightened. "Our guardian angels, they don't mind. Heh! They…they probably like the company."

Gina's fingers skimmed along the joint surfaces roughened with use and the tooth of time. Her finger slipped in an ocular and she gasped, jumping.

"What?" Zhenia asked.

"Nothing…an eye hole." She heard Zhenia snort, but refrained from comment as she focused on her own problems in the dark, enclosed space.

They turned a corner to the right and felt the cold wrought iron of the gates protecting those passages not open to the public. Then, like mice in a maze, they got turned the other way, resuming their trek down the main corridor with Gina stroking the bones of the dead and Eugene keeping his own terrors at bay. A good half-hour of shuffling through the wet gravel of the underground passage had brought them to a more open space. The air smelled drier, the bones had ceased and the texture of the wall had gained a newer feeling.

"Zhenia," Gina said, hating to break the silence, "feel this wall. It's different."

He let go of Gina's arm and reached out. "It's painted."

The passage had narrowed to a small hole in the wall and Eugene hit the masonry before him head-on, howling in pain.

"What?" Gina's cursory exploration had confirmed his suspicion. "Oh. This has got to be the staircase to the surface. Yeah…here, feel this. It's a metal banister, and here's the first step."

His escape-the-dark-hole instinct made him wish he could go up the narrow stairwell first, but then his innate sense of caution overruled his turbulent emotions. "I'll follow."

That was easier said than done. Eugene wrapped his big hand around the thin metal railing. His senses, amplified by the dark, told him the old tubing was painted some time ago and the paint was peeling now. He stepped up the high, steep riser, using his left arm to pull on the thin rail. Gina's steps were receding somewhere up above him and he stumbled, feeling his hurt shoulder brush the other side of the narrow passage.

A sudden panic came over him and he felt like he was being buried alive.

Like before

Alone and in the dark, injured, in pain.

His heart raced out of proportion to his effort and Eugene stopped to do his breathing exercises once again.

"Ten…nine…eight…seven…"

The ragged inhales became longer, the forced exhales flowed smoother and his heart was no longer the hammer against the anvil of his ribcage.

"…six…five…four…"

Gina's footsteps ceased in the dark; he forced the panicked thought out of his mind.

"…three…two…one."

"Hey, Zhenia. You okay down there?"

He exhaled once again before he answered. "Ye… yes. It's just…slow."

"Okay," he heard her voice reply from above. "I'm just a little ahead of you. I'll wait until you get here."

Eugene felt his face split into a grin. "Thanks." He pulled himself up with his good arm, and one step at a time he scaled the steep risers, knowing that she was waiting.

The coded message had become secondary—at least for now—and the gunshot wound just an inconvenient ache in his side.

Getting out of the enclosed spaced was paramount.

He felt the way his voice, the sound of his very breath, bounced off the nearby walls and his feet fumbled on the corkscrew staircase, whose tread was narrower than half his shoe.

He forced himself not to think about where he was. The only way out was up.

Eugene grasped the railing once more and pulled himself up, biting back a grunt of pain.

Flesh wound. Just a fleshwound.

He barrelled into something warm.

"Gina?" he asked, out of breath.

"I'm here. How's your wound?"

"Fine. Just…slower than I'd like." The less he thought about the cave-in, the better.

"You lost some blood back there. I figure if you made it all the way here, you can make it all the way up. Let me know if you need to rest. I'll go slow."

And that's how they crawled out of this old, elaborate hole in the ground, step by painful, countless step, taking a break every few risers so that Eugene could catch his breath once again.

The staircase emptied into the vestibule of a small building. Gina knew it to be a vestibule because the sound echoed, and her light-deprived eyes squinted against the lights of the streetlamps on the other side of the small, thick-paned windows below the ceiling.

"Shit. Fuck. I'm not ever going down there again. Not by all that's holy—you couldn't pay me enough to stick my nose into those tunnels again." Zhenia's voice spelled both outrage and relief, and Gina noted that no mention was made of having been shot.

"You don't care for tight spaces?" She asked, arms wrapped around her bare shoulders to keep the chill away.

"Not particularly." Eugene cleared his throat, and Gina had a distinct impression that he was, for reasons of his own, focused on his breathing.

Her heart went out to him. An occupational hazard—they all ended up with something that brought the comfortable present to a grinding halt.

To her relief, Zhenia continued. "A steel door, eh? And what shall we do about that?" The handle was located in the middle of it. She saw him feel it, a lighter shadow falling over a dark panel. She wondered if that door was painted the same faded green.

He had found a handle and pressed it. It gave a metallic jostle and click on its way down—a pleasant surprise.

The door itself was locked—a typical setback.

"Well then." Zhenia stepped back. "We can surely get this door open. I'd rather not stick around for the kind *gendarmes* to show up in morning."

Gina was tempted to come back with a wiseass remark. Instead she unzipped her purse and felt around. "Here, let me give it a try."

Eugene stepped to the right. He felt Gina right next to him, their shoulders almost brushing. A metallic something slid into the lock. Little scratching sounds followed.

And followed.

And followed.

"Crap." Gina stood and whirled at him. "Don't hover. I can't work if you're breathing on my neck." Her voice had almost been a snarl, and Eugene grinned in the dark.

"It's harder in the dark. I know."

Gina paused next to him. "You know?"

"Yeah. I'd offer to try, if I had both of my hands working." The silence grew awkward. "C'mon, Gina. Take a deep breath, stretch out your arms. Then give it another try."

"Lots of unwanted advice, Zhenia."

It cracked him up she called him by a cover name five years out of date. He wondered if they told her his real name.

He wondered whether she'd told her Company about him.

"Just speaking from experience. If you get that belt off my arm, I'll give it a try."

Gina let her breath whoosh out. "No, I got it. Thanks."

It took four more tries, the second of them coached by Eugene, whose knowledge of locks didn't seem all that surprising to her.

Finally Gina did something right. The tumblers aligned and the large, steel door creaked open.

Once their eyes adjusted to the glow of streetlamps outside the building they exited, Gina realized they were on a small side street where absolutely nothing looked familiar. It was late enough for the Parisians to be done with their suppers. Lights were on behind the sheer curtains of quaint apartments, but the ice cream store across the street was dark. Cars sounded louder up the street. If they could only find the Metro…

"I think we should go up this way," Gina said to the man leaning against the stone wall. She looked him up and down. His formerly white button-down shirt bore streaks of mud and grime of the underworld. His left arm remained strapped to his body by her thin belt. His face gleamed pale and drawn in the shadows and he could barely stand up straight.

That little cardboard roll with its coded message just about burned against her skin in its little secret pocket.

I should just leave him…he'll probably make it.

She didn't like herself for thinking that, but she had work to do. That work even precluded her from getting his number.

Dammit, life wasn't fair sometimes.

"You have any cash on you, Zhenia?"

"Why, you need some?"

"So I can put you in a cab and send you to your hotel."

Eugene's eyes widened in panic. If Gina sent him off, he'd never see her again. His only lead would be gone—there'd be no way to recover that stupid drawing and whatever message it now bore.

He extemporized. "No—don't let me go, Gina. They…they'll be waiting. They won't miss this time."

He should tell her about Labad. No, he *would* tell her about Labad and he'd do all he could to keep him off her scent. But that would have to come later. For now, he had to stick to her like glue, make sure he knew what she was up to. Make sure she didn't disappear from his life again.

"Gina, please."

Gina thought a bit. He sounded like a coward right now and begging wasn't like him at all. The Zhenia she'd known was a man of adventure, of substance, and of exceptional skill.

He had a motive.

An operative could never get attached. The rule stood for a reason, but fuck the rules.

She'd been thinking of this man for the last five years. Thoughts of him got her through training, through assignments she'd rather forget.

The life of espionage wasn't a pretty place for a pretty woman and she had known what she was getting into at the time. No regrets, but…but she wasn't ready to give up the company of this man, one she had met as a grad school kid, the one whom she'd known as an Ukrainian arms dealer.

The one she had then later seen in the company of his MI6 counterparts, dressed and speaking the English of a man who served at the pleasure of Her Majesty the Queen.

She smiled. "Well, I've ushered you this far."

"Keep your friends close, keep your enemies even closer."

The words of her mentor came to her and she suppressed them, producing a carefree grin instead. She knew exactly what Old Walter would have thought of this newest development.

Zhenia eyed her with a calculating glance. "You sure?"

She nodded. "We'll walk, slowly, until we can hail a cab."

It took another half hour before they saw a white car with the lit "Taxi" sign on the roof. Gina hailed it, swaying her hips. Only when it stopped, she dragged Zhenia from the shadows, draping her arm over his shoulder as though he was a poor woman's drunk boyfriend. They settled into the back seat, Zhenia turning his body so that injuries weren't quite so apparent to the driver.

"Rue Saint-Michelle metro, s'il vous plait," Gina instructed the driver, asking for a metro stop two short blocks from her safe place.

Because the best way to shake a tail was to not acquire one to start with.

Eugene had said no to a hospital and no to a hotel, and Gina was taking him to a quaint part of town near two metro lines. That much he knew.

He trusted her—to a point. He trusted her not to hurt him on purpose. If she dumped him somewhere due to what he thought of as a "work conflict," good for her. He smiled as the taxi forged on through the quiet Paris streets.

Gina was, in his mind, still that kid who chewed off more than she could chew. He now realized this image of her was woefully out of date. She's been doing well so far.

Maybe he could recruit her as a MI6 asset. The thought amused him.

It was good to have friends in this tough business.

"Hey, wake up!" Gina's voice roused him immediately.

Eugene straightened up, aware of the gun that was trapped between his trunk and his immobilized arm.

Aware of being somewhere strange, a location outside of his sphere of control.

He heard Gina pay the taxi driver, thank him, and bid him good night. He heard the taxi driver laugh over the sound of his car's engine and say something encouraging regarding the temporary state of her husband.

Oh, that's right. He was supposedly drunk and not shot. And they probably made a lovely couple.

They made an army of two.

Biting back a gasp, he let Gina pull him out of the cab. He even gave the cabbie a jaunty wave before she took his arm at the elbow. "This way," she said.

The tall, stately trees lined only Rue Saint-Michelle, not the street that ran tangent from it. Here, the houses were old and fairly basic, with few architectural decorations that Eugene could see. The stucco peeled off a corner of one, and he wondered how much money it must cost to redo a whole six-story building.

The slight uphill taxed him.

They passed an alley so narrow, only an economy-size car could pass through. It was one way.

The next block, Gina tugged on his arm. "Here we turn right. This is *Alleè du Chats*."

The name amused him even though he was too exhausted to produce a smile. "I guess that makes you an alley cat."

"Kind of. Second house on the left."

They crossed.

This row of houses was shorter, just three stories, as though they used to be family homes despite be-

ing stuck together like swallow's nests. A flight of stairs rose to the double door.

Gina glanced over her shoulder, then up the street. "Okay," she said in a low voice. "You get to stay with me. I trust you with knowing where I live. Please do not disappoint me." There was no fear in her voice.

Eugene thought of the gun under her skirt, of the skill she has shown. Of her picking a lock in the dark.

No. Gina wasn't a lost, adventuring grad student anymore.

"I'll behave," he promised.

"Down these steps," she said, and led him down a small staircase toward a door to a basement apartment. He saw a spiky iron fence, the waist-high kind to keep people from falling in. A gate creaked open, then it clicked shut.

She could've oiled it but a creaky gate was a good alarm system.

Gina unlocked an ordinary-looking door next to an ordinary-looking window, which seemed to have sported a window box overflowing with flowers. "Come in. Stay here, I'll get chair."

He did.

She did.

"Sit."

She took his shoes off, then unstrapped his arm and removed his blood-soaked sports coat. "You'll want to undress and take a bath. No shower here, sorry. It's a small place." With three steps she reached the window and pulled down the shades. Only then did she turn on the lights.

The foyer was a small space for shoes and coats and a door that seemed to lead into the house above. He got up, barefoot, and stepped onto the wooden floor of Gina's living room. "Just some sleep would be great. Really." He looked around. "That little carpet looks just right. I can sleep there." He'd slept on worse. They both knew it.

"Bullshit," she said. "You'll get taken care of like one of our own. If you need to talk to your own people, you can leave to do so." The hard edge in her tone softened. "Although I'd prefer if you would stay. The bed is big enough for two."

Their eyes met. "I don't know that I'll be good company for a while," Eugene confessed. "But thank you."

She laughed. "I don't expect much. Let me start your bath." As she disappeared into the bathroom, he saw her pull out the phone out of her pocket.

Dead, just as before.

Once the water was running, she beckoned him on. "Here's the bathroom and the toilet is behind those doors to the right. My bedroom is across from it." She opened the door, revealing a dark and cavernous space.

She clicked on a reading light.

Indeed, a large bed. "Looks like an antique with an old-fashioned straw mattress," he hazarded a guess.

Gina plugged her phone in. "Do you need help getting undressed? I don't want to pull those tampons out of your wound yet. It needs to be stitched up properly."

"Oh? And you can do that?"

"No. Well, yes, but I'm not really good at it. But I have a friend." She watched him unbutton his shirt. "You haven't changed."

"You have," he said with a nod. "There is…there's more of you somehow."

"I don't care about my weight," she said easily. "I know I'm fit."

"That's why there's more of you. More confidence, more skill." He paused. "More gun, too. Although I thought you had been against those."

"An acquired taste," she said with a smile. "Do you need help undressing?"

He nodded. "Yes, if it's not too much trouble."

"Not at all."

She was brisk about it. Professional, as though she'd done it before.

She waved him along, checked the water temperature, turned the water off. "I'll help you get in. No soap, no products. I don't want anything in your wounds for now. Just scrub off the blood and the mud—and let me know if you need help, will you?"

He had been seated on the bathtub's rim. Now he turned and smiled.

They were close enough to kiss.

She hesitated. He hesitated. They didn't.

Then they were. His eyes closed, and despite the darkness he didn't feel enclosed or trapped but exhilarated. Because her lips were on his, and then his tongue was skating across hers, asking for entry.

His good arm rose and he slid his hand up into her hair, now completely free of any wig, holding her to him as he devoured her mouth, rediscovering why his instincts screamed she was safe. His.

They eventually came up for air and Gina tutted, muttering something about him not overextending himself to cover her sudden vulnerability. She helped him ease down into the water. "I'll help you with your back in a bit," she said gently. "And I'll put up tea. That's what you'd like—tea, right? You can't eat until you get patched up. I won't have you retching."

He didn't disagree.

She continued. "Let me do just one more thing."

She walked away. As Eugene applied a fresh washcloth to the insults the catacombs had dealt to his body, he heard Gina through the open door. She wasn't trying to be quiet while dialing on her landline, which was a relief.

"Hi Jean-Marc," she said in French. "If you'd have an hour or so…" A pause. "I brought in a stray. I need a vet. One that can patch up a badly torn ear." A few pleasantries, one which may or may not have been code.

A good-bye.

And, miraculously, a hot cup of tea prepared in a perfectly delightful manner.

Gina was a perfect woman, one who had just one, tiny flaw.

Her apartment was underground.

But he'd get over it.

Copyright © 2020 by Kate Pavelle.

Find Gracie Wilson in the trees enjoying nature's won-ders, traveling to see the latest animal conservations, or at aquariums all around the world. This girl loves nature and all animals. She has many pets and is al-ways adding new additions. The more the merrier in her mind. Sitting under the shade reading a book, letting the world around her pass by, while she is safe in her bubble of imagination. Well that is where she'd love to stay. She is a #1 Amazon Bestselling Author from On-tario, Canada. She is a first generation Canadian living in Ontario. Her family is from Scotland, so finding her in the hot sun for very long is unlikely, but give her rain and thunderstorms and she's golden.

DEVOTION (PART TWO)

by Gracie Wilson

CHAPTER SEVEN

Emery

Jace is pacing in the backyard and Cole has been upstairs for the last hour. Luckily I used that time to get the kids to bed without too much excitement but I didn't expect them to still be brooding. Some-thing is going on and I want to know but it isn't really my place to ask. When I can no longer handle just sitting here waiting, I decide to go and see Jace. He seems like the safer of the two right now.

"I don't want to talk to you right now. Screw off." Jace says, and when he turns to see me his eyes go change from the anger I saw to pain. "I'm sorry. I thought you were Cole. I wouldn't talk to you that way. Not on purpose anyway."

His reaction takes away the sting that I'd felt when he told me to screw off. These brothers have some serious baggage. "This is my fault isn't it?"

He looks at me with perplexity.

"This is about the money, right? I'm sorry, I already told Cole, so maybe he didn't tell you, but I haven't touched it. Any of it. It's all been split up into ac-count for the kids' education and such. I didn't use a penny for myself. The money I am using is what my mother had left us from when our dad passed away." Rage is all that I see in Jace's eyes right now and I'm not sure what I've said to cause such a reaction.

"He knows all this?" I nod and he turns kicking the porch. "Sorry," he says looking down to make sure he didn't leave a mark. "I'm not asking you for the money. You shouldn't give it to Cole or my Mother either. I can't believe he knows this and is still trying to get that money from you."

I let out the breath I was unconsciously hold-ing. The fact that Jace isn't after the money anymore helps me breathe a little bit easier.

"My mom is a piece of work Emery. She is not someone you want to go toe-to-toe with, trust me. But legally she doesn't have a foot to stand on be-cause Annabelle is my dad's child. They have been divorced a long time. She has no right to the money."

So their mom wanted to live off of this money. Why am I not surprised? "I'm not giving it up with-out a fight."

He grins at me and I smile back. Talking with Jace is something I've not experienced before. May-be it's because I'm not the same person I was when I used to have conversations with people other then my siblings. Part of me thinks it's because this is an actually meaningful conversation and not just talk-ing about random things.

"He will help her, Emery. Don't let you think he won't. My Mom did a real number on him. Dad and him didn't have a good relationship, either. I'm sure seeing you and the kids doesn't help his resentment."

I'd never thought about how Cole would feel with us having his dad fulltime and him not having his dad at all. "Why don't you resent him like Cole?"

His fingers touch his chin as if he's thinking about what he wants to say. "Honestly, I never listened to half the shit my mom says so that might have something to do with it. Cole feels like it's his job to make my mom happy."

I know the urge to make someone else happy so I can't fault Cole for that. "You don't want your mom to be happy?" Even though I know she can be pretty ugly to people, she's still his mom.

"It's not that. It's that even with the money she still won't be happy. She will blow it like she always does, whereas I know you will use that money the way my dad would have wanted it done. Cole just doesn't get that. Everything she wants he gives her, hoping that one thing is the thing she's missing. I know better."

Jace's words make complete sense to me. Not just because I'm not a fan of their Mom from what I do know, but also because every day I try to make Matty happy and give him everything he wants or asks for. My brother isn't anything like Sandra, but the principle is similar.

"What am I going to tell the kids?" I say aloud but it was more for my own thinking then his. His eyes glow. Something about those baby blue draws me in every time.

"What do you mean? They don't need to know about the money." When he sees my head shaking he only looks at me with more confusion.

"You came here for a reason. When that reason is no longer here and you leave, they won't understand and I will be left to deal with telling them a story of how it's better this way." The shock and hurt on his face only make this more uncomfortable. "They know who you are now, they have faces to put to those bedrooms and to have it taken away.… I just hope this can be solved as quickly as possible before they get too attached." I should have said we, before we get too attached, but my mind is racing with the thoughts of letting someone—anyone—in again. It only leads to more pain.

"She's my sister, Emery."

I can't help the heartache that brings. Not that I'm not happy that there is someone else to look out for her, but that he only mentioned her. Not Matty or Breighlyn, even me. It was nice having a grown up to talk to even though they came here trying to take the money James left for us.

"Emery," he says softly and I look up seeing sadness in his eyes. "You really have been doing this all alone, haven't you?"

"There is no one else. Matty. Breighlyn. Annabelle. They are my life." His gaze shifts and I turn to see Cole standing behind us by the door.

"This looks cozy."

With those words I slide as far away from Jace as possible.

Cole smirks and I look away. He just got what he wanted.

"This is *my* house. I will do whatever the hell I want." Oh my goodness. The surprise on Jace's face is clear, but Cole just stares at me as if I'm something nasty he stepped in.

"I beg to differ. It's *our* dad's house. Try and remember that, little girl."

Who the hell does he think he is? Walking right by him, I go into the desk in the kitchen opening the envelope. As soon as I'm in front of him again his eyes go wide. I push the papers into his chest and he steps back, putting his hand over mine. Instantly I pull away, but something changed in his eyes.

"That says all it needs to. The house is in my name. So you may have come here for the money but this house has been in my name for five months. It was my mother's house too. I'm only letting you stay here because I believe Annabelle should at least know you, but if you for one minute think I'm going to let you stay here with *this* behaviour, you've got another thing coming. I protect them, I love them—all of them *equally* and without hesitation. That's how I know I've become the parent. So no, this isn't your dad's house. It's *my* house. If you don't like it, leave."

Both brothers look between themselves, unsure what to do. I want to run and hide but everything I said would have been for nothing.

"If you'd like to get to know Annabelle, then you can, but please don't make Matty and Breighlyn feel differently. Breighlyn and Annabelle were very happy with you here today. Matty is too—he's just got a lot going on. If you put in the time, you will never regret it, but if you're here for the money only, take a hike. Those kids need dependable people in their lives. If that can only be me, then I will make sure you are out of their lives. Permanently. Do you understand?"

Jace smirks, putting his hand over his heart, and I want to yell at his tendency to make light of serious situations, but I can't help the smile that is trying to shine through. He is trying, in his way.

Cole doesn't say a word, but nods in response before leaving the room. That's a good thing, right? It means he's staying? Yes, he wants the money, but he's staying because he wants to know the kids too?

"I knew there was more to you then you were showing." Jace is behind me and his hands go to my shoulders. He lightly squeezes them and it takes every piece of me not to tense. "Don't let him intimidate you. Just keep him on the ropes and you will do fine." His fingers trails down my arms and I can't help the shiver that comes from me. "Goodnight."

Jace walks around me and leaves me completely stunned. Not just at a loss for words, but the way my body's responding, I'm frozen for a good minute. Needing the freshness of the night air, I go sit down on the steps just outside the door, looking out at the moon that has now cast it's cool glow over my backyard.

The sounds of footsteps alert me to someone coming outside. I don't turn. The way my days been going, nothing good can come from this. When Cole sits next to me, I want to move away but I remain frozen.

"You know I don't want to be doing this."

His words are heavy with emotion but I can't let that get to me. I'm not being stubborn for my sake. This is about what's right and what's best for the kids.

"Then don't. Stay, get to know the kids, but if you think you can just wear me down and I'll give you the money, you're wrong. I'm not being selfish. This isn't about me at all. If it was just me, I'd hand it over."

His hand lays on my thigh and I close my eyes at the contact. I haven't been touched by anyone since my mom died. And now Jace has done it, then Cole, in the space of one day. I'm feeling overloaded. I haven't let anyone near me but my siblings. They needed *all* of me. That's the only reason my body is confused now. I'm lonely and I'm so very tired.

"She's not going to let this go."

"She isn't, or *you* aren't? I don't get it. Jace listened, understood, and he backed off. Why can't you? Why not just let me fight your mom?"

His hand grips my leg, not in a rough way but like he's trying to hold on to me. "Emery, you think you have this all figured out, but you don't."

Those words have me fleeing. I stand up, take a few steps away to get some much-needed space from him, from all of this. Doesn't he think I know that? All of this is more than I can possibly figure out, but I have to do it. People are depending on me. Mom and James are depending on me taking care of the kids.

He continues on. "I'm straightforward when it comes to things like this. We both have a game to play and I just don't think you understand that. Which only means you're going to get hurt."

I feel him standing behind me but I don't step away. Looking up into the moon-lit sky I can't imagine what my life is going to be like. Six months ago I had everything figured out and now I don't think I'm every going to feel that way again.

"I'm not playing a game." I tell him. "I'm not like you."

He must have taken a step forward closing the space between us because I can feel him everywhere. His breath, his warmth, everything I need to stay away from.

"Then there's Jace." His hands brush some of my hair back into place. "We all have a part to play."

He was talking about Jace? Could he be trying to wear me down as well? No, I don't believe it.

Cole continues. "He's just better at the game than I am. Always has been." His hands wrap around me, hugging me tightly against him. When his lips touch against my head I feel it everywhere. A simple kiss that could be taken as nothing more than a harmless show of caring, has my body in a tailspin. He holds me a moment longer before letting go and walking back into the house without another word.

"Mom," I whisper. Looking up at the moon I hope she can hear me. Hear my pleas for her help, for her love. "I don't know what to do." About what Cole just told me, about everything to do with James' ex-wife, but most of all, about these feelings in my heart that my life has just turned into chaos. With tears running down my face, I wrap my arms around myself. "Mom, I wish you were here to tell me what to do."

CHAPTER EIGHT

Cole

I know I'm being an asshole. No one needs to tell me that my actions are cold and callous. When I agreed to come here, I thought it would be simple. Get this brat to hand over the money my mom wanted so she would stop calling me about being broke. Jace doesn't know, but I cut mom off. The house was paid for and she was still getting money from her last husband in alimony. That was what made her do this. I think she thought that if I got more money from dad, I'd let her back into the accounts, but when I did she started with this.

At first I was against it, but then Mom told me all about this nineteen year old who was using the kids to keep all the money. She was pissing it away and those kids where going through hell. She said Emery was just like her mom who'd gotten pregnant to trap my dad in a marriage that had him move across the country. Deep down I thought the move had more to do with my mother than anyone else but he left us there. Mom had custody and Dad got visits.

The day my mom told me about Annabelle, I lost it. He was starting over and Jace was in his own personal hell. Dad wasn't there to help me pull him out of it and Mom was oblivious. She didn't care because she was getting money. He bought her a car and she just let it all slide under the carpet. No problem that couldn't be solved by money in her books.

To think that was what was going on here made me angry but not as angry as when I showed up and realized she wasn't anything like I'd been told. She was not like my Mom. She was here taking care of her brother and sisters. Giving up her life to be a mom when they needed her.

Then to find out that money hasn't been touched and was put away for the kids…. That was more than I could handle. But I'd already done things to make this worse. I'd already spoken to my mom and she wasn't willing to let this go.

Jace was doing well here but I was just waiting for him to crash. It was only a matter of time before I was back to having to watch him and take care of him too. My dad didn't know. Mom never told him and I stopped talking to him when I found out about his new wife being pregnant. Now that I have a face to that little girl's name, I'm torn. Not between my Mother or Annabelle. I'm torn because things have already been said. Things I can't take back. I can only hope that she listened to me when I told her to leave it alone.

Watching Emery every day here with her siblings, and going through the routine, was slowly chipping me away. She is more than anyone could have asked for to take care of their children. Annabelle loves her and even when the little girl slips and calls her mommy, and Emery shows Annabelle a picture of their mom, Emery thinks she's doing it so that Annabelle knows her mother, but she is doing it to remind herself too.

That's how I know everything my mother said was a lie. This girl has crawled under my skin and I don't think I ever want her to leave. There is one problem though, because each day I see the same thing in Jace.

There is no bright side to this story.

CHAPTER NINE

Emery

When I open the door and a girl around my age is standing there with a suitcase I almost keel over. "They have a sister?"

Her eyes are hazel not like either of the boys but her hair is dark brown, similar to Coles. She has a few freckles and she's just standing there smiling at me.

"Nope, they have a kick ass cousin," she says as she rolls her luggage in past me and I shut the door, still not to sure of what just happened. When I turn, she is looking around like she's expecting something.

"Boys are sleeping still."

"I'm wondering about Annabelle. I know Matty and Breighlyn must be at school but where is the baby?" she says with excitement causing me to look at her strangle.

"I'm James's brother's daughter," she says and my eyes go wide.

I've heard about her, but we've never met because her dad died while serving overseas. She lived with her mom in California, last James knew.

"Ah, there it is clicking in. Yeah, so I'm also related to you and Annabelle."

I want to correct her but something about her peppiness is refreshing. "She's napping too."

"Well then, you and I are just going to have to get to know each other without her," she says leaving her luggage before grabbing me by the hand to bring me into the living room. "Your house is beautiful."

She admires the décor. I want to tell her my mother had exquisite taste but I'm afraid to say it. I haven't spoken out loud about my mom other than to Annabelle since the incident in the backyard.

"So your Emery. I'm assuming Cole and Jace are being the same jackasses they are usually, but when I found out *why* they were out here, I came right away. Cole *didn't* tell me, like he tells me everything else.

That's how I knew something was up, so I called his mom when he wasn't answering me. She told me all about this gold-digging stepdaughter who was trying to make off with James's money." I gulp and take a step back, and she reaches out to me, patting my arm. "Oh, no. Trust me when I say I did not for one minute believe her. She's the only gold-digger in this family, Emery. You don't have to worry about who's side I'm on. Its always going to be you and the kids."

"Thank you…." I wanted to say her name but immediately realize I don't remember it, if I ever knew it.

"Oh, my heavens, I never told you my name. Wow, aren't I just ahead of the class in that one?" Something about the way she talks makes me feel relaxed. Like she just says what she wants and when she does say it she means it. "I'm Deanna Vanderwood. Just like you I hear."

"Oh, well kind of." Deanna gives me a puzzled look and I realize the boys called me Emery Vanderwood too. "My name is Emery Cecil Nichol-Vanderwood. It's long and I usually do just get Vanderwood." I don't know why I feel the need to explain but I just don't feel right taking a family name without being a part of that family. No matter how many times James told me its what he wanted. It was his idea to add it and keep my dad's name too. James always looked for a way to make all of this easier for me.

"Well that is a mouth full, isn't it? I'm just going to stick with Emery, okay?" She tilts her head watching me closely and I understand why. She's looking for my tells, the things I do to let her know what I'm really feeling.

"Deanna, if your trying to figure out where my head is, you might as well stop. I don't even know what's going on up there lately."

She breaks out in laughter, then slaps her hand over her mouth, pointing upstairs.

"Annabelle would sleep through a zombie attack. She isn't going to wake because of your laughter. If she is awake though, she might come looking for it."

Deanna smiles. Now looking, I do see parts of James in her.

My mom didn't have any family so this isn't something I would get to have, like Jace and Cole— and Annabelle.

"Emery, you have way too much going on in that head of yours. Whatever it is, just say it. With me at least you can do that without an alternative motive. I don't have one. That money is staying with you and the kids."

I let go of a breath I hadn't know I was holding and she gives me a small smile. "I'm just thinking how nice it much be for Jace and Cole to have family other than their immediate family."

"You have that now too. I wanted to come when it happened but I figured that you'd have enough on your plate and I'd give you some time. There wasn't a funeral, so I didn't have a reason to just show up. I was waiting, however. I knew something would happen and if it hadn't, I was going ti visit this summer so I could meet all the kids. Plans changed and I jumped on the next flight."

She was right. I didn't have a funeral for them. My mom hated my dad's, with me and the kids there watching it all. When it happened, I planned it all, but then the thought of having to take the kids to see her and James was too much. I went and said my own goodbyes while Aunt Hannah watched the kids. She didn't understand, but she didn't push it.

"How has the last two weeks been with the guys in the house?"

Had it really been that long? "Honestly, at first I was having a really hard time with it, but we kind of just got into a routine…until tonight. Jace hangs out with me sometimes." Her eyes tell me that she wants to say something but I just keep going. "Cole comes out when the kids are all here, but he's up in his room when they go to bed."

"Oh, of course Jace is hanging out with you. You are beautiful. Cole is an idiot with a very large brain. He just forgets how to use it. He probably isn't sure how much you want him around, and under the circumstances, I don't think I'd blame him. I'd have kicked their asses to the curb when I found out why they were here."

Having Deanna tell me I'm beautiful throws me back for a moment. No one has said that to me since my mom passed away. Having other adults around now has that happening more and more. More firsts without my mom here. I'm not sure how I feel about that.

"Look what the cat dragged in."

Turning, we both see Jace standing there in a pair of shorts. *Just* a pair of shorts. Deanna's face scrunches up in a mock disgust. In that moment, I realized I wasn't looking at him as family. While Deanna turned away, I couldn't take my eyes off of him.

"She doesn't have a cat," comes another voice from behind Jace and Cole takes his place beside him in only his shorts as well. Does neither of them own any more shirts?

"Well look who it is. Cole, are you being nice? We both know you can be when you want to," Deanna says and all I can do is continue to stare at the two of them standing there with their bare chests.

Cole makes a coughing sound and I clue in that they are watching me watch them. Instead of being the normal person that I should be and avoid their stare, I stick my tongue out at them causing them both to chuckle and I turn my attention to Deanna.

"Cole isn't being nice, is he?" she asks me and I see in the tone of her voice she wants me to play along.

"Actually, he isn't being very nice at all. He doesn't talk to me most of the time, and then when he does, its only about tea parties and which stuffed animals are invited," I say in a teasing tone and Jace and Deanna are bending over in fits of laughter.

After how broody Cole has been, I can't believe I'm trying to be playful with him. An olive branch, for sure.

He states at me, intently, then says, "You said you wouldn't tell anyone." There is a gleam in his dark eyes, so I know he isn't angry but that doesn't mean I'm safe. Before he can do anything, I take off out the front door to the safety of the public eye, grinning the entire time. I feel carefree—normal, it's been too long since I've felt this way.

Turning, I see him behind me, a few feet away and I smile brightly at him only to further tease him, looking around pointing out the people walking by and gesturing to his near-nakedness.

Slowly he walks up until he is right beside me and he leans down whispering into my ear. "You thought they'd save you."

Before I have a chance to run, he grabs me, throwing me over his shoulders while I continue laughing, but so is Cole and it's the most beautifully carefree sound I've ever heard. When he tries to twirl while I'm still over his shoulder, I try to escape and he loses his balance. Instead of both of us landing hard on the ground, I land directly on top of Cole. His arms instinctually wrap around me, pulling me closer to him.

"Excuse me." We are both started, and try to get up, knocking each other over. When Cole stands, he offers me his hand and I take it as he pulls me to my feet. He puts his arm around my waist and we both look at a guy standing there in front of us.

"Are you Miss Emery Vanderwood?" the man asks.

"Another one of your family members?" I ask Cole, but his eyes are on the man before me.

"Sign here," he says handing me a signature board. Quickly I sigh it and step out of Cole's arms. The man takes the board back and hands me an envelope looking at me with regret. "You've been served," he says walking away.

CHAPTER TEN

Jace

The smart thing to do would be to look away, but my eyes feel the need to watch every moment playing out in front of me. I keep trying to tell myself this could be taken as sibling behaviour but the way he touches her isn't as if she's just a girl. She's *the* girl and I need to watch this.

"You two never learn." Deanna says and I don't even bother turning to look at her. I just continue staring out the window, watching him hold Emery in a way I should be holding her. The way I *want* to be holding her.

"You can't do this again. Not to each other, but even worse not to Emery. She needs her family."

I know I should listen to Deanna but I can't.

"I've been better while here. Did Cole tell you?" I hear her gasp in surprise and I would too if I wasn't living it every day. Something about being here, something about Emery was changing me. Giving me a chance at life again.

"Jace, that's amazing. Not once?" Her saying it only reaffirms everything I'm thinking. It's Emery.

"She is the reason. I know it's not ideal and it doesn't make much sense, but it's her, Deanna. I know what I might be getting myself into again with Cole, and if it was any other girl I'd walk away. Damn, had I known a girl like this existed, I wouldn't have bothered until now." My words might sound desperate but I don't care. Until you know a real daily struggle you can't understand how it feels to have that weight lifted off of you and the reason for that is Emery.

"Have you talked to Cole?"

Deanna and Cole have always been closer than we are, but it never bothered me until now. Emery is going to love Deanna, just like every other person who meets her, and then she's going to be around Cole more. This isn't a game for me and I will make damn sure this isn't a game for him. The money is a different story. That's separate but if he's screwing with her just because he can or to get the win when it comes to the money, he's a dead man.

I finally speak. "He says he's only here for the money, but you're seeing the same thing I am. We are both here for many reasons, and it's not just the money."

Deanna nudges me and I look at her. There is kindness in her eyes, causing me to let a few of those walls of mine down. "I think your right, but you need to remember this isn't just about a girl. She has kids, one of which is your baby sister—"

"Matty and Breighlyn are my family too."

Deanna smiles at my declaration and I give her a wink, but when I do her face turns serious again.

"Emery is always going to be in your life, Jace. She's going to be a pivotal part of those kids lives and I know you want to be a part of that. Then there is Cole in all this too. I'm not sure where he stands on the kids."

She looks out the window again and I know she sees it all. This isn't just going to be about winning a girl's affection or the need to be with her for a short time. This is the type of girl you go to war over.

"He loves those kids just like I do," I say trying to change the topic, but she brings it right back.

"Then you both are screwing with something that could blow up in your faces." I can see the doubt in her eyes, the doubt that this is really just about wanting Emery.

"I haven't had one, Deanna. That's all because of her. She makes me want this. She makes me want everything," I say, reminding her the impact of being here with Emery has done for my life, my health.

"You better be sure before you go down this road. Make sure it's worth it all. Because your brother might be what you lose going down this path. You could lose everything, Jace."

Deanna gives me a quick hug and I know she's thinking of all the consequences of everything that could happen. I feel those same fears but I can't back down because of the chance I might lose it all. Even just having some of it with Emery would be worth it.

His cousin studied him for a long moment. "A love like this can only end one way. Either way someone is going to get hurt." The tears in Deanna's eyes tell me that she finally understands what I'm willing to risk here.

"As long as it's not Emery, I can live with it."

CHAPTER ELEVEN

Emery

The door slams behind me and I hear Jace talking to Deanna before I see him. "What the hell?" I don't stop, I just keep walking down the hall. The front door opens and I don't look back. If Cole's smart he will stay away from me. Both of them should.

"Emery," Cole calls out and I turn looking at him with every piece of disgust I can muster.

"What? You did it okay? You won."

The shock on his face doesn't stop me. I just walk into the living room where Jace and Deanna are.

"What is going on?" Deanna says and I toss her the papers. Quickly she looks down, scanning them and I see the moment she understands what is happening. Her face goes pale and I can't even look at her anymore. Turning away, Jace is standing there looking at me with confusion but I can tell my pain is affecting him. His eyes are torn, seem to be holding some form of fragility, and I do the one thing that comes naturally to me in this moment.

When I wrap my arms around him, I wasn't sure what I was looking for but as soon as his arms cradle me against him, I feel it. Cole had told me to be careful with Jace, and I believe him, but it was Cole who was doing the most damage.

"Deanna, what is it?" Jace asks, but she never answers. I can hear her softly crying behind me and it is taking everything in me not to fall apart.

"Emery," Cole says and I feel his hand try to softly pull me from Jace.

"Don't touch me," I scream, startling Cole and Jace.

Jace's arms tighten around me letting me know that he isn't going to let go.

"Cole," Jace says in a warning tone and Cole's hand drops from my arm.

"I'm sorry."

Before I lose it, I disentangle myself from Jace, bolt upstairs to my room and slam the door.

It isn't long until there is a knock at my door, and whoever it is doesn't wait for me to answer. I hear the door open.

"Emery, Jace and I just want to talk." Deanna says and I turn, looking at them with tears in my eyes. "We will fix this," she says firmly and I want to believe her but I can't. It feels like someone has ripped out my soul.

"I'm going to take care of this, Emery. You understand me?" Jace says and I look at him, seeing the pain we are both sharing.

They want to make me feel better, but nothing can. This isn't something I can live with. When I turn and see Cole standing in the doorway, a million things go through my mind. First, that he didn't leave as soon as I was served makes me believe he does feel *something* or he'd have taken off. He's won, if this letter becomes fact, but here he stands.

Jace hands me the paperwork and I remember all the reason I hate Cole right now. Anger fuels me and I get up, lunging for him to hit him, but Jace stops me. The hurt in my eyes must be apparent because he lets go. Not for the reason I thought though.

"Allow me," Jace says as his fist connects with Cole's face. Deanna gasps and Cole takes it without any retaliation. In that moment, I should feel better but I don't. Jace just saved me from making the same mistake, but in turn he just punched his brother for me.

"I deserve that," Cole says and I want to scream but calmly I pick up the papers and shove them at him.

"You deserve so much worse. Get out of my house." Without waiting for a response, I walk out and into the room across the hall. The moment I see her sleeping soundly in her little bed the dam breaks. Every tear I was holding back comes flooding out. How could someone do this to me, to her?

Sitting on the floor beside her bed, I look at this beautiful sleeping baby. My baby. Yes, my sister but she became my child when mom died and I don't know how else to describe her other than that. "I love you Anna Banana," I say, sobbing softly as not to disturb her.

When the floor behind me creaks, I turn looking at Cole standing there with a bruise in the making forming on his face. My first urge is to scream but I can't wake her. I think apart of him knew if he did this in here, he could get whatever he needed to say out.

"I didn't mean for this to happen, any of this. I promise I will fix this. You hear me, Emery. I will fix this." I want to believe him, but he's the reason I'm watching this little one sleep wondering what tomorrow brings for us.

"She won't do this," he says painfully.

"She already has."

Getting down on his knees, he sits there before me with nothing but agony written on his face. "I will take care of everything," he says handing me back the paperwork.

Taking a deep breath, I look at him trying to remember all the good things, but right now all I see is what he cost me. I wish this were just about the money.

"I need you to leave. I can't have you here with all of this too."

Leaning over, he kisses me on the top of my head and hugs me. That is the only response to my words.

Taking one last look at me he walks out closing the door quietly behind him. The sob coming from me is filled with all the fear and heartache I should be feeling in this moment, but I also have to feel it for the kids—for my mom and James.

The papers fall to the ground but those words never leave my mind. I can't look away from them, I can't get away from what I might loss because of them.

Application for Custody of Annabelle Vanderwood.

CHAPTER TWELVE

Jace

"You really are a bitch, you know that, Mom?"

My words don't even shock her. She just shakes her head. "You should speak to your mother that way."

I laugh, startling her. "A mother wouldn't do this. Not to Annabelle, not to Emery and sure as hell not to her sons."

She gets up just as Cole walks into the courthouse and I want to beat the shit out of him. Getting arrested with proof of assault would be worth it for what he's done, enabling their mom. He doesn't talk to us. Instead, he walks right by with another man in a suit.

The moment I saw the paperwork, I *knew* that he had helped her do this to Emery. I wanted to kill him. This is too far. No amount of money is worth doing this to this family. Seeing him still with a fading bruise on his face will have to be enough for me right now. I could not afford to get arrested. I needed to be here for Emery.

Walking away from my mother, I make my way to a waiting Cole. "If she loses Annabelle, I will destroy both of you. Do you understand? I don't care what it costs me or what it means for my life. Emery is the best thing for Annabelle, you both know that. No amount of lies and miswritten events is going to change that. Mom doesn't want her because she thinks she can do a better job taking care of her. Mom wants her for the money that comes with her. It's one thing to knowingly let her use *us* for that shit, but if you let her use Annabelle—we are done."

Without letting him respond I walk away to Emery who is standing on the other side of the room with her lawyer and Deanna.

"You okay?" Emery asks and I smile at her. Of course she would ask something like that. This is only one of the million reasons she should be a parent for Annabelle. My mother is toxic: we are proof of that.

The first thing I did when she got served, after knocking Cole on his ass, was call a lawyer. Deanna and I both handed in affidavits of support for Emery and I handed in one for use against my mother.

"We have this, right?" I ask and the lawyer doesn't respond. He doesn't want to do this in front of Emery.

When we get called into family court, I put my hand out and Emery takes it without hesitation. The judge is before us and I now understand the intimidation. He's elevated, showing his power, and that scares the shit out of me.

We sit and the lawyers begin talking, each telling their side. That's a laugh. My mother wouldn't have a side if it weren't for Cole.

"There are two affidavits before you from Jace and Deanna Vanderwood stating the care they have witnessed over the last month while residing with Miss Vanderwood and the child." The judge flips through it and begins to read. When he looks up the lawyer continues. "There is another affidavit that is evidence as to why Jace believes his mother, Sandra Thomas, should not receive custody of the child." There is a gasp from my mother and I look over to see her glaring at me.

"Your reason for removal is an incident with the brother, Cole Vanderwood?" the judge asks my mother's lawyer. "Yes, when the brothers made contact to get to know the child in question, Miss Vanderwood slapped Cole in the presence of the child."

I can feel Emery shaking beside me.

The judge considered the paperwork a moment longer. "I have one son saying Sandra Thomas shouldn't have the child due to neglect he received from his mother and that the child is being used as leverage for a monetary issue within the family. I'd like to hear from Cole on what transpired that day. This account of events is all from your client," he glanced down at my mother's lawyer, "and not from Mr. Vanderwood, which makes it hearsay."

Cole stands and the rage in me causes me to shake. Emery's hand touches my leg gently and everything stops. I forget where we are. I forget wanting to kill my brother. Everything melts away. But mostly, I forget that I shouldn't want to kiss her right now in a courtroom.

"The child was present during this domestic issue?" the judge asks and I stop breathing. This is the moment I was dreading. He is going to break this beautiful woman and those kids.

"One of the children were present. It was not as written. Yes there was an altercation, but it was nowhere near as violent as said. I told her to hand over my father's money because she wasn't living off of it like her mother did. She slapped the door in my face that, in result, hit me because I was in the doorway. In no way do I think she intended to harm me, only to put distance between us."

Cole just lied. Flat out lied in court to a judge that could throw his ass in jail. My mother is the first to start talking to her lawyer, yelling for him to do something.

The judge immediately silences the courtroom. "There are other children in the home?"

My breath escapes me, I can feel Emery barely being able to keep it together and I take her hand that is on my thigh and hold it tightly.

"There are three children in the care of Miss Vanderwood since the death of her parents," her lawyer says and I can see him waver. This worries him too.

"The children are what ages and names please?" the judge says, never looking up.

"Breighlyn Nichol-Vanderwood, age six." The lawyer looks back at us briefly before continuing. "Mathew Nichol-Vanderwood age nine. This child is deaf," the lawyer adds and it fucking pisses me off. Why should that matter?

"And you are only asking for custody of the two-year-old because?" he asks my mother's lawyer and she goes pale. She has nothing. No reason other than to admit the money.

"This child shares the same father as her sons. She felt the need to put this plan forward before she contacted social services about the other children."

Emery goes still next to me and in that moment I've decided I am never talking to my mother again.

"So, your client would see a sibling group separated due to the fact that they are not fathered by the same man. I'm tempted to believe this situation

is as I have written here by her son, Jace. This seems to be about money, which is a waste of this court's time. Have there been any incidents or reports from the school suggesting Miss Vanderwood could not adequately parent her brother or sister?"

This time he's looking at our lawyer and I'm so damn glad I made Emery go to the school and get letters.

"No. In the package before you, you will see that the school supports this current familial arrangement and has no concerns. There is also a letter from Mathew's specialist stating that he is in a fragile place and removal from his sister's custody would be detrimental to his well-being. He has documented visits prior to the death of the parents where Miss Vanderwood was present, and she has continued the appointments following the passing of their parents."

The judge flips through the package and pauses, re-reading something. It must be something important because he goes over it a few times.

"As there is no documentation from the school or doctors stating they have concerns, I feel it would not be in the best interest of any of the children involved to be taken from the care of Miss Vanderwood."

I breathe for the first time in what feels like forever, but he said it. The kids stay.

"However, I will be making a recommendation to social services to do a follow up with the family."

CHAPTER THIRTEEN

Cole

Standing here, outside of Emerys' house (funny, I don't see it as Dad's house now), I feel like a damn fool. This could go to shit and I wouldn't blame anyone but myself. The door opens to a beautiful Emery standing there smiling. When her smile only slips slightly at the sight of me, I take my chance. I kick the bag in front of me, showing her my suitcase that I had taken with me when she asked me to leave.

"Hi," I say lamely. My eyes almost bulge out of my damn head. I just said hi? All I can do is shake my head. "Oh, all the things I could have said. I should first have said sorry."

She smiles, a little tentatively, obviously reminding herself I'm not all bad, if I can lie under oath to help her and the kids

She opens the door wide, waving me in.

"I can move in?" I ask praying this isn't come cruel joke where Jace is waiting to beat my ass once behind closed doors.

"Annabelle misses brother *Ole*."

Hearing her talk about Annabelle brings it all back. The thought that she almost lost Annabelle because of me has been eating me up inside. "Just like that?"

"You lied for me. You could have told him the truth and then he would have possible taken them all. You took a huge risk. I won't forget it," she says and I grab her by the hand, leading her to the couch to sit down.

"Where is everyone?" I ask, looking around. Her eyes go wide and I drop her hand suddenly.

"Crap. The protection worker is coming soon. Jace and Deanna took Annabelle to the park. She wanted to talk to me without the kids here," she says, explaining, and I hate the because of me she even has too.

"I can leave," I say getting up, but she grabs my hand, pulling me back down to sit.

"It's fine. I won't have to do it alone." The fact that she wants me here after everything is a shock. I thought I'd be getting a door in my face for real this time. Forgiveness wasn't what I was expecting.

"You won't ever have to," I say without thinking and her eyes widen. "You *shouldn't* have to." I mean, quickly trying to dig myself out of this hole. Words like that imply things. Things I'm thinking but that's the last thing she needs right now. "I'm their brother too."

Her hand goes to her mouth, covering it, and I see tears fall from her bright green eyes. Even with tears running down that face, she is still the most beautiful girl I've ever known. Inside and out, this girl is the complete package. Brushing a piece of her hair behind her ear and out of her face, I use my other hand to pull her face up so I can get a good look at her. These past few weeks have been torture but I had to stay away until everything was settled.

"You said *their*," she whispers and I give her a confused look. "You said I'm *their* brother too."

My mind is racing. I hadn't realized I'd left her out of it, but saying I'm your brother too felt wrong.

"You love them just like Annabelle," she cries, and now I understand her words.

It wasn't that I left her out. She hadn't noticed that (not that Emery would. That's what makes her Emery). It was the fact that I now saw Matthew or Breighlyn as no different to me than Annabelle.

Taking a deep breath, I bring my hands up as she watches me closely. "I love them all. We're a family," I say while signing the last part and she pulls away from me sobbing.

I don't move. I wasn't sure what reaction I was expecting by learning to sign the past three weeks. I'm by no means fluent, but I was practicing talking about family and such so that I could tell Mathew myself that he's my brother too.

Suddenly her lips are on mine, and she is in my lap, and I don't pull away. The moment hers touched mine, I was done. I pull her close, holding her while I pour everything I can into this one moment. Kissing her, devouring her, was something I'd been imagining since she slapped the shit out of me for being a dick, but my imagination couldn't compete with this.

Just as I begin tipping her back onto the couch, so I can deepen this moment, the doorbell rings and it all comes crashing down.

"Oh my god," she says, sliding out from under me and the horror in her face only shatters me to the damn bone. The bell goes again and she runs to it opening it quickly. "Sorry I was downstairs and didn't hear you."

The social worker steps into the house. She's my mother's age and I can tell she isn't too sure about Emery. Straightening myself out before she sees me, I get up and walk to the foyer where she is still standing with Emery.

"Hello, I'm Cole Vanderwood." Her eyes light up and I take a step towards Emery instinctually.

"So the complaint about violence in the house was from yourself?" she asks and I realize she thinks I'm here to talk about this. Oh, hell no. I'm here for Emery. To be here for her when she needs me.

"That was my mother trying to use a misunderstanding in her favour. Nothing of what was written happened. I was rude and came off threatening, as it was a tense situation. The way we met, I would have shut the door as well. Once we all talked it over, we cleared up the misunderstanding," I say but she points to the couch. She wants to sit and talk. I just want her to get the hell out.

"Sorry. Yes, let's have a seat." Emery says and I follow them, taking a seat next to Emery.

Every part of me wants to put my hand over hers, but this worker would be all over that. Technically I am her stepbrother—and I also know my brother has feelings for her. There are many reasons I shouldn't be touching her, especially after what just happened between us.

"So we have everything on file, but I felt even after our conversation on the phone I should come out here and speak with you. Thanks to you allowing me to speak with the school and the children's doctors. We have no concerns as to the care the children are currently receiving here but—"

And it all goes downhill from here. I don't even need to know what she's going to say. What she is thinking is written all over her face.

"My question to you, Emery, is do you believe that you are the best possible option for the children? We have other options that I think you should consider."

Consider: that's just a nice way of saying I think you need to do this. I hate this woman already. I want her out of our house—Emery's house.

"Other options?" Emery asks. She has no idea what this woman is about to say. Neither do I.

"Well, there are long term foster homes, but we also have adoption homes that would be interested in adopting a group who needs a mother and a father."

This girl has some nerve. She thinks she can just walk in here and corner Emery.

When I look over to Emery, I'm shocked. She's not getting teary, she isn't falling apart, she's pissed the hell off. "So let me get this right. You have paperwork from everyone in the children's lives, along with a judge saying the kids can remain in my care, and you're saying I should just give them up? I'm sorry but if this is what this meeting is about you can leave." She stands and I stand right along with her.

The woman stands, startled by Emery's firm stance, but still trying to make her case. "I'm asking you to think about what's best for *them*."

"What is best for them is to be with their family. *We* are a family and *we* do not need anyone coming

in insinuating otherwise. I have custody papers, soul custody, and I think that's enough for you to leave. The judge wanted you to check in and you have. I think I've been very forth coming with all the documentation, but if you believe I'm going to just let them go—"

"It would be good for you as well."

My eyes turn to this woman in utter shock. "Excuse me?" I say and her gaze darts nervously to me. "I think you need to leave. Now."

"I'm just saying that she could go back to school and have a life of her own."

This was the one thing I was supposed to be talking to Emery about other than kissing her.

"Emery *will* be returning to school next semester." The social worker's eyes bulge and I feel Emery go stiff beside me.

"How? She has primary care of the children."

For a moment I think I might have given her something to work with, but I won't let her bully us. She's leaving.

"As I said it's time for you to go. The children will have my brother and myself residing here. Along with the help of our cousin, we should be able to handle it all. There are daycares as well." Putting my hand up to stop her as soon as she opens her mouth I continue. "Every day parents put their children in the care of family members or daycares. As long as they are suitable, which we all are, you have no grounds to object. As Emery has stated, you came, you spoke with the school and doctor, and now you've insulted us. If you have anything more, please contact our lawyer."

Leaving Emery in the living room, I walk the social worker out of the house, closing the door behind her.

Turning, I see Emery break down sobbing on the couch and I rush to her.

"Did I just stop them from having a real family?" she asks and her words break me. Only someone like her who was truly thinking about the children's best interests would ask that.

Without another thought, I slowly press my lips against hers not bothering with the consequences of what could happen. This moment is ours. This moment needs this. I need Emery.

When I pull away, she just stares at me a moment before she speaks again. "Why did you kiss me?"

"Why didn't you let her take the kids?"

The hurt on her face cripples me but I nudge her, trying to get her to answer.

"Because no one will ever fight as hard for them as I will. They are my life. The reason I get up in the morning and the reason I thank God every night before I go to sleep. They mean everything to me. I will never just give them up, not when I know that they need me more than ever."

This is the reason Emery is worth all this pain of being so close to her. The risk and the consequences of fighting for her are worth it.

"That is the reason I kissed you."

She doesn't react the way I expected her to. Yes, there is warmth in her eyes, but she retreats. "I think we need to pause. I just got so caught up in the moment, in the happiness of knowing you valued and protected my children. But Cole—Jace and I—I don't know what's happening, but—"

"Say no more."

CHAPTER FOURTEEN

Jace

These past few weeks with Emery have been the best weeks of my life. I know that's strange, but I finally feel free, I've never felt better. It's like she wiped my slate clean. She took away all the pain and suffering. Getting up every day and seeing her with those kids warmed me through. The cold walls I'd built up using sarcasm and other means to keep people out came crashing down. Damn, if it didn't feel good.

Each morning Emery and I would get the kids ready for school and we'd all take them, minus Deanna who we let sleep in. It was like we were our own little family. Which, I guess we are, but it felt like we were *together*. Not siblings who were just stepping up, but a family who loved each other. Emery would laugh at my jokes and cuddle up on the couch with me. When she'd fall asleep against me, I'd carry her upstairs to her room and tuck her in.

Some nights the need to hold her was too much so I would just fall asleep there on the couch with her. I was not sure if she realized how much that time meant to me, but each night I set an alarm on my phone to wake up before the rest of the house. The past week neither of us had slept in our beds. Deanna was starting to watch more and I knew she saw how deep I was in this, but she never said anything. Emery, too, saw the difference in me. To mess with that could be catastrophic—life ending.

Certain people walk into our lives for a reason and each morning I wake up with Emery in my arms, even if the arrangement is not formal, I know she's the reason I'm still here. The reason I get a few more nights in this world. Most of all, she's the reason I want a hell of a lot more than a few more nights. Deanna sees that and right now she's using that to keep me level. The irony, that a girl whose life has been more tragic than mine, is the one bringing balance to mine, is not lost on me. Her heartbreak makes me want to fight like hell to help turn her life around, as she, in turn, turns my life around.

Cole hasn't spoken to me since he walked out of the house, after Emery asked him to leave. He barely acknowledged me at the courthouse and I have to say that hurt the most. When I thought he'd betrayed not only me, but Emery as well, I wanted to kill him. I'd warned him I'd do as much if he hurt her. Thankfully, I didn't have to keep that promise when he stood up there and lied for Emery— For our siblings and for me.

The shit he must be dealing with from my mother has got to be insane. Luckily the crazy bitch hasn't called me. She won't, not until she has to start kissing ass to get at my trust fund. Little does she know, I've already seen to that. She won't get a damn penny.

When I walk into the house and see Cole sitting, beside Emery, I should be happy. My brother is back, and in one piece, meaning Emery had forgiven him. But that's also the part holding me back. Emery— him being here with her and me not knowing what happened.

"The worker?" Deanna asks and I want to smack the shit out of myself for not remembering the reason I was not with Emery. Now that I remember, I'm only further pissed off with Cole for showing up at a critical time like this.

"She tried talking me into foster care or adoption." My mouth drops open and Emery quickly continues. "Cole told her to leave. That it wasn't happening and since she had no reason to try and take the children, she wasn't needed."

Looking to Cole, I could fucking kiss him right now, in a brotherly way. I wouldn't have known what to do, had I been here, but he seemed to handle it.

"She won't be coming back?" I ask and both of them shake their heads. "So it's over," I say and they both look at each other before nodding.

I'm getting the feeling that something happened and I don't like it. If she was telling him off, I'd have liked to have seen it. "Are you staying?" I ask Cole who looks at Emery. That pisses me off but it's her house.

"Of course you're staying," she says smiling, then changes her tune. "If you want to, I mean."

"Well if you are going back to school you are going to need some help," he says and she looks annoyed with him, which makes me smile inside.

"I'm not happy about the ambush on that, by the way. Nor do I want you to feel like you need to help out so I can go back to school. It's a lot to ask."

He steps in front of her and I want to yank him away from her, but I refrain myself. This is all innocent and if I go all crazy caveman over her, I'm going to scare the shit out of her.

"They're our siblings too. You shouldn't have to be the only one doing all this. Not that we are doing this because we should, but because we *want* too."

He turns, looking at me and I glare at him before Emery steps out beside him.

"Absolutely," I say and Deanna is watching me closely from behind Emery with a knowing look in her eyes. Emery walks over to where a sleeping Annabelle is in her stroller and just smiles down at her. The warmth I get from watching her adore that little girl could melt icebergs. Her love is lethal and I fucking hope to God I get to have the final dose.

CHAPTER FIFTEEN

Jace

School will be starting soon for Emery, so we've been trying to show her it's all going to be okay, that she deserves it. Fuck she does, and more. One day we can work on more. Due to my constant trying, I got in the habit of doing my own little things with the kids. We all sort of got into a routine. Adulting

and shit. Emery is better at it than me and Shithead Cole though. The first day I had Annabelle by myself all day, I hit that pillow and it was lights out. I honestly don't know how Emery did it daily, alone, with three of them before we arrived.

I never tell her that though, but I wanted her to go to the orientation information sessions for restarting college. It took a few nights of me crashing, but now I can keep up with Annabelle and not need two naps and be in bed by seven.

At first I was worried there had been a moment between Cole and Emery. Hell, I'm sure there had been. There was an awkwardness for a couple of days, then they stepped away for "a talk," and things seemed to fall back into sibling mode between them.

Cole has started seeing a girl who works at a coffee shop, I think. He seems to really like her by his sneaking around, but you never know with my brother. He just goes and sits there with his computer, spending time at the café. Yet, almost daily, he disappears to see her. Sometimes twice. He's gone out the last seven days at night for hours. Getting some, or maybe like me he's falling in love.

As long as it's not Emery and I don't lose her, I don't care, either way. Still that nagging feeling he doesn't want her to know he is dating creeps in my brain. You don't walk away from a girl like Emery, if you can help it.

I make my way to the kitchen and see Annabelle right away. She opens her hands and motions for me to come to her. When I see the fridge door open, I know someone must be in here with Annabelle who is sitting in her highchair covered in ketchup. "Well, you look like you've just come from war."

Smash. "Argh," Emery yells, jumping out from behind the fridge door.

Instantly I feel like an asswipe for scaring her, but I wasn't even sure who it was. Maybe that's why I should have waited. Fuck. Now, on the floor, is a casserole dish in pieces with stew scattered around the kitchen.

"Emery, I'm so sorry," I curse out as I bend down and start picking up the pieces of smashed casserole dish.

"It's fine, my own fault really. I should have expected things like this from you," Emery says, almost with a flirting tone that makes my heart race, trying to escape from the place it's been buried deep inside my chest for many years now. She's slowly clawing it from me and I'm pretty sure I don't want her to stop, even though I know this could really blow up in our faces. There is no such thing as harmless flirting in this situation.

"Emmy Lemmy, boom." Annabelle giggles as she points at us.

"We are okay, Annabelle. I just scared Emmy Lemmy, that's all."

"Bad," Annabelle says with a stern look and her finger waving back and forth. "Not nice."

Emery and I both burst out laughing at Annabelle's "adult" reaction, and she starts giggling with us.

Emery is laughing so hard she's almost in tears and she swats me playfully, causing me to grab her.

The moment she's in my arms, I knew I shouldn't have grabbed her, because it's that taste of heaven you know you won't ever have for life, but you don't ever want to miss a moment you do get a taste of it.

She must feel my apprehension because she stops laughing and just stares up at me.

For a few moments we just stand there, with her in my arms, but like always kid's say the darnedest things.

"My Emmy Lemmy, no *Ace*. Mine."

We both pause and look over to Annabelle who is now trying to squirm and get up from her highchair.

"Well, how do you compete with that?" I jokingly say hoping this doesn't become something that pushes her away. "Emery?" I say when she just continues to stand there in silence.

Emery shakes herself and goes and grabs Annabelle, who has now started putting the ketchup in her hair. "Be outside at 7pm. We're going to dinner."

Without another word, she walks out the kitchen and right up the stairs, where I can hear the bath begin to run.

Dammit. Why do I always do this shit? I need to learn not to talk sometimes. Was she wanting to dress me down, for being in appropriate with her? She had sounded so firm. Had I overstepped her boundaries?

My watch says I have several hours to dwell on my bad timing of jokes as a deflection for my feel-

ings, and I stress so much I shower twice before the appointed hour.

When I walk out the house and shut the door, Emery turns to face me. As I continue down the path to the drive where she's standing beside my car, I notice she's in a royal blue flowy dress thing that makes me wish she'd have stuck with her usual look. Her mom look, as she calls it. It makes me wonder if there is a reason for the change. Maybe she's celebrating school, who knows, but damn she is stunning. All I want to do is stand here and watch her, but I'm at the end of the line. Only a few feet between us now and I'd love to make it less.

"What's going on here, Emery?" I ask because something's up. I knew this isn't usual. Where is her car? Emery is standing before me and I am having a hard time remembering what we are doing again. Other than my mind wanting to remove that dress.

"We are going to dinner," she replies shyly, as she brushes a strand of hair back into place while the rest of it cascades down her back in curls.

"I get that; you told me to be ready. I'm early, I guess. That's a first." I shrug, "not like I have anywhere else to be at the moment."

"You aren't early," Emery says, never breaking eye contact, only heightening my worry.

"Emery, I'm confused. Where are the kids?" I demand now, panicking for a minute and I start scanning the street. Nothing out of the usual, and she appears happy, but with everything that my mother has tried to pull, I can't help but fear shit.

"They are fine, Jace. They are with their oldest brother. We are okay now, remember?" she says confidently.

Emery's eyes shimmer in the setting sun's rays and it's hard at times like this to remember I came here with a mission, one I failed happily and would again and again. Nothing will happen to Emery and the kids. "Oh uh, yeah, sorry." I scuff my shoes on the pavement. "So, Cole is meeting us there?"

She huffs and blurts out, "Wow, you really are the most difficult guy to try and give hints to." A piece of her hair falls into her face, and Emery blows the hair from her eyes, crosses her arms in front of her boldly, and her grin is one of annoyance almost.

Her tone wasn't something I liked at all. I straighten myself up a bit and defensively say, "What the hell does that even mean, Emery?"

"God, relax, Jace. You aren't early because *I* am the only other person going to dinner tonight and I kind of hope we can do it again," She replies with her words laced with playful intent and taking a step towards me, still never breaking eye contact.

All I can do is stand here because I'm scared to move and wake up to find out this has been nothing more than some cruel-as-shit nightmare. That would be my fucking luck. If I didn't have bad luck, I'd have none at all for fuck sake.

"Emery," I say in almost a whisper, scared to startle her or awake from this dream.

"Jace, just listen," she says silencing me. "We've come a long way from this front yard and the first time we've met. Honestly, we *all* have so much more to go, until we're a more functional family unit, but," she's now almost in front of me directly now, "just because you saw me tell Cole to stay, doesn't mean what you think it does. He did something that I'm not sure I will ever really understand, even though I'm trying to tell myself I do. But even then, aside from that: even though he's fixed his mistakes, it changes nothing." Emery grabs my left hand pulling it into both her warm small fair hands. "He's not you, Jace. He's never been you."

My heart stops beating for a moment and then is instantly racing. "But Cole—"

"Cole is someone I could eventually love, I'm sure. He'd try to make me very happy. But you, I'm already there and it's scary. However, with everything with our parents and life being nothing like we imagined, I realized I can't wait. Because tomorrow isn't guaranteed."

I know, even more than most, that she's braver than I've ever been.

"Do you love me, Jace?" she asks gently, quietly.

"It's not just about love. It's more complicated than that," What the hell am I saying?

Her eyes roll to the heavens as frustration wrinkles her face again. "No, it's the fuck not. It's simple, actually. Do you, Jace, love me, Emery? It's easy: my answer is yes. Whether you ask me today, tomorrow, or in twenty years. My answer is always yes. I love you, Jace. I really hope you love me too."

"Well how do you compete with that?" I say with a smirk on my face, and her exasperated expression melts away.

Without hesitation, and before either of us change our minds, I pull her to me. Our lips collide and it's everything. She's on her tiptoes trying to get as close to me as she can, only furthering our connection. I lean back a moment, softly biting her bottom lip. I've always wanted to do that to her since she first lipped off at me.

"I, Jace, love you, Emery."

The words cause a wicked grin to spread across her face and mine. She tries to kiss me, but with my height, if I don't bend, she's shit out of luck. When she realizes what I'm doing, she slaps my chest and I laugh.

Before she can do anything else, I wrap my hands around her waist lifting her up and kissing her softly for a moment, her legs swinging in the air, before putting her back down on her own feet.

"So, where were we?" I joke.

"Dinner?" She raises one eyebrow.

"Is it bad if I say let's eat and then go find the kids? Get them ready for bed and curl up watching that new movie they wanted to see?"

"No. I'd say that's why we are perfect for each other." This time she doesn't wait. She hops up on me, pulling me down with her own weight, giving me the sweetest and softest but most possessive kiss I've ever had.

The dinner was amazing, but as it went on, we both started talking about the kids more and more. We wanted Matty to try her mac-n-cheese; you know, the small things. They've taken over such a big part of my heart. I might not be my dad, but I'll be whatever is needed for them all.

The park is only a few blocks from the restaurant, and when we pull in, we can see the kids off in the distance, playing. The three are chasing each other, with Cole watching closely, protectively, nearby.

I might not have understood the natural instincts of a parent when I first arrived on Emery's doorstep, but that has dramatically changed.

I get why she would move heaven and earth for those kids. Why we all now do it together. The three of us, fully devoted to the three of them.

Copyright © 2019-2020 by Gracie Wilson.

T. Thorn Coyle is author of the nine-book paranormal Witches of Portland *series, the alt-history urban fantasy series* The Panther Chronicles, *and multiple non-fiction books including* Sigil Magic for Writers, Artists & Other Creatives, *and* Evolutionary Witchcraft. *Thorn's work also appears in many anthologies, magazines, and collections. An interloper to the Pacific Northwest U.S., Thorn writes in cafes, loves live music, and talks to crows, squirrels, and trees.*

THRESHOLD OF THE HEART

by T. Thorn Coyle

She would always be the one that got away. The one I lost because of my stupidity. My short-sightedness. My arrogance.

My pride.

The bakery windows were steamy from the combination of cold and wet outside, and the cozy warmth inside. The Saturday morning rush was ebbing, but the clatter of spoons and the hiss of cappuccino being made continued. I slid a fresh tray of carrot and sunflower seed morning muffins into the display case, rotating my right shoulder as I stood. I never made enough time to stretch, despite warnings from my massage therapist. Who had time?

The chatter of regulars catching up over coffee and brioche with homemade ginger jam—today's special—was a happy counterpoint to the "yacht rock" playlist my millennial barista insisted was "cool." In an ironic way, of course. Steely Dan was the current selection streaming through the bakery-slash-café-slash-community hub that was Rise and Shine. I was barely old enough to remember when the songs were fresh, but not old enough to have listened to them in any kind of earnest.

But this morning? The words cut through my interior rain. I was the loser they were singing about, drowning my sorrows, not over scotch whiskey, but my third espresso of the already long day.

"Stop me if I order another coffee," I said to Andreas, who worked the big Italian machine as if he was born to it.

"As if," he replied, expertly stacking foam into the white interior of our signature black cups. The bubbles formed themselves into the shape of a puffy cloud, dripping rain. I still had no idea how he did it but admired his artistry. Moments when I had to make drinks? People were lucky if I managed the classic heart shape. Mostly, they got a blob of white in a sea of toasted brown. My talents all lay behind the swinging kitchen door.

Through the huge, steamed-up windows I swore I glimpsed white-blond hair peeking out from beneath a black tweed cap. Were those blue eyes? My heart stopped in my chest, waiting. But the door didn't open. No bells chimed.

Just as suddenly as I saw her, she disappeared. She was long gone. Too many years ago. It felt like forever, and like yesterday.

"You okay, boss?"

I rolled my shoulders again and turned. There was a frown on Andreas's usually sunny face.

"Yeah. Just woolgathering. I'm fine."

"I'm just woolgathering," she said, when I had asked her the same question, five years before.

A painter, Marcie was always staring out windows or gazing into high corners of rooms, visualizing surrealist landscapes only her eyes could see. But usually, her blue eyes looked dreamy, maybe pensive…not upset.

"Are you sure?"

I'd been slammed. I was expanding Rise and Shine, talking with other local businesses about carrying our pastries and specialty bread, and—already head of the Southeast Business Association—ready to tackle running for city council. Everyone told me I'd be a natural, and as a lesbian, stood a good chance with the liberals who liked to think of themselves as open-minded.

Everybody encouraged me except Marcie, who told me it was too much.

I tried again. "Are you still mad I was late for your opening?"

Her latest one-person show at Light, Image, and Sound downtown was just another in a long line of successes. At least, that's what I thought. And I *had* made it…arriving an hour late, bubbling with excitement from meeting with my campaign manager. I mean, it was just another gallery opening, and she had those at least once or twice a year. She always complained about them, actually, claiming she only did them because they were good publicity for her online gallery, which is where she made the real cash.

And it wasn't as if the Portland Museum had come calling, was it?

"You know I love you," she said, "but I feel like I barely know you anymore. You're so wrapped up in…"

"Myself. That's what you mean, isn't it?"

Not too much longer, after a few more stupid fights, the love of my life had finally called it quits.

Standing behind the counter of the business I'd built by hand, I winced at the memory. What an ass I was. As if doing anything other than supporting my lover's dreams mattered. I mean, my dreams mattered, too, but Marcie had always supported the business, One hundred percent. She just had misgivings about the city council, wondering where in the world I'd find the time. She rightly pointed out that I constantly kvetched about the business association, and that city council would be more of the same, only leaving me less time to do anything else, including running my business.

But my ego had shouted her down, not wanting to hear reason from someone who loved me.

And love me, Marcie did. More than anyone ever had. And lately? It seemed like more than anyone ever would.

I glanced at the display cases and saw that we were out of brioche. It was always a good sign when we ran out of the daily special. I took the small black display board from the counter and wrote "Sold Out!" in green chalk beneath the special.

Then I walked back through the swinging kitchen door and into the bakery. At least I could throw myself into my work. That was the only thing that seemed to help.

Two hours later, stomach growling, I looked up from the dough I was prepping for the morning's bake. Andreas was snapping his fingers.

"Earth to Levana!"

I wiped my hands on a towel and ran the back of my hand across my forehead.

"What's up?"

"First of all, it's been hours since you surfaced. Gabriella already took her lunch and I'll take mine in half an hour."

"Right," I said, heading to the pocket sink in the corner of the kitchen to wash my hands. "I'll be out in the minute."

He stood there, still blocking the door, a weird look on his handsome face.

"What, Andreas?"

"You need to eat, too. You're getting grouchy. And there's someone here to see you."

"Who?"

He shook his head. "Just come see."

My body flashed hot, then cold. That white-blond hair in the window…. No. Much as I missed her, I wasn't ready for it to be her. Besides, what were the odds?

I grabbed a paper towel and wiped the rough brown paper across my hands. "I'll be right out."

The place had emptied, leaving only a few tables occupied. One person was reading on their phone, two men were engaged in quiet discussion. A group of teenagers played Magic the Gathering in one booth, the table strewn with hot chocolate, coffee, muffins, and croissants. It was our usual Saturday crew; they came in after the rush had ebbed, happy to be out of their parent's homes for a few hours, in a place that wouldn't hassle them to leave.

The rule was no yelling or horsing around, and they had to buy something for every hour they played. This was a rule we enforced during the week for folks who used the bakery as their office space, too. Discreet "No Camping Out" signs were posted around the room, beneath the rotating art display. This applied to everyone. Teenagers. Writers. Small business owners. And the local houseless population who took advantage of our "free cup of coffee and a day-old muffin" program.

I saw nothing out of the ordinary for a regular Saturday. The bakery looked the same. So, who was waiting for me?

And then I smelled hyacinth perfume. I hadn't smelled that in five years. It *had* been her I saw through the rain-streaked, steamy, window.

She was here.

There, tucked into a corner by the community bulletin board, back toward the hall leading to the single washroom. Cup of plain coffee at her right hand, sharp face tilted down towards a book.

Well, damn.

I pumped a cup of coffee from the just-filled thermos, added some creamer, loaded two chocolate mocha muffins onto a plate, and sauntered over.

Or I pretended I was sauntering. Pretended I still had the swagger she always said she loved, until it turned hard and too self-centered, finally driving her away.

"Hi." I stood at the booth, looking down at the soft swirls of her white-blond hair. It was longer than last time I'd seen her, and the blue eyes that looked up from her book were clear, not streaked and puffy with tears.

"Hi, yourself."

"I brought you a muffin."

A smile flicked across her pale pink lips, just for an instant.

"Chocolate?"

I nodded. "Mocha. Your favorite."

She nodded back as if I'd said something worth considering. "You going to sit down?" she finally asked.

"I didn't want to presume…" I slid onto the wooden bench, looking at her hands. Colored paint specks marred the cuticles and hid beneath the short tips of her blunt filed nails. I was always crazy about her hands.

"So…" I cleared my throat. "I'm surprised to see you." I could see her face change, grow uncomfortable. I held up a hand to show her I wasn't finished. "Glad though. Really glad. Actually, I missed you."

She shrugged with a small smile and tore an edge off the top of muffin before popping it in her mouth. The scent of chocolate, coffee, warm yeast and sugar filled the space between us. I waited while she chewed, then took a sip of coffee and a bite of muffin myself. She finally looked up at me again. I couldn't read her blue eyes anymore. When had that happened? When I'd given her up in favor of a political career it turned out I didn't even want.

"You wrecked me, Levana," she said, voice soft among the clatter of dishes, the snap of Magic cards, and the damn yacht rock station. "It took me two years to recover."

She fell silent again. Ate more muffin.

"And then?" I wanted to know, but I didn't want to know. My heart was up in my throat. I tried to swallow it back down with more coffee. Should've gotten water.

"And then I started to miss you too."

"I'm so sorry, Marcie. I was an ass."

"Yes. You were." And there was the smile I remembered, like the sun breaking through Portland clouds on a gray October day.

I hesitated. Begged my tapping feet to be still. Wiped my suddenly sweaty hands on my apron. I waited. Finally, I couldn't bear it anymore. "So, what are we going to do about it?"

She shrugged again. "I don't know. I just…needed to see you again. Needed to let you know life was good. See how you were doing. All that."

Sweat ran down my back, and I could see Andreas signaling behind the counter, but I couldn't let this go. Couldn't let her get away. "I need to get back to work, but I'd love to see you again. Catch up properly."

She studied me for a long moment but didn't speak.

"You said you wanted to see how I was doing, and I want to hear what's up with you, too." I spoke rapidly, into the void of silence, before she decided she'd seen what she needed to and enough was finally enough.

She slid her hand into her bag and slid out a shiny postcard. I recognized it immediately.

It was a gallery card. One of her paintings graced it, bold and stark, with the Steel Bridge melting into the Willamette River as a woman stood on the banks, waving a handkerchief in the cold, gray air.

"A do-over?" I asked.

"We'll see," she said. "Don't be late."

I paused next to one of the ubiquitous Portland bubblers pushing a continuous cheerful stream of drinking water from a brass spout. The gallery was just across the street, all lit up and shining.

I exhaled, then adjusted the cuffs on my fancy red blazer, worn open over black jeans and sharply pointed shoes. I'd even splashed on cologne and a slick of tinted lip balm. Running my hands through my hair, I tried to recall what my therapist had said in the emergency phone call I'd made the day before.

"Just be honest," he'd said. "You can't change who you were then. Be who you are right now."

But who, exactly, was that? Other than loving the feel of freshly risen dough beneath my hands and enjoying my banter with the steady stream of regulars in and out of Rise and Shine? I really didn't know. I mean, just being a baker wasn't enough.

Was it?

People milled around behind the floor-to-ceiling plate-glass windows, strolling past paintings that were more massive than the ones she used to paint. Marcie's art had gotten bigger. Had she?

Would she even want or need someone like me? Contented with running my business and playing racquetball with my friends? Seeing the occasional movie? Shit. I was boring now. The woman she had known before had been exciting.

Hadn't I?

"Just cross the damn street," I said out loud, and, pressing the button, waited for the light to change.

The green stick person flashed, and I headed across, wiping my hands on my pants, eyes trained on the big, bright windows, and then I was pushing through the doors. Into the murmuring crowd. The low music. The massive paintings.

And Marcie, who turned just then, whose face startled, then settled into a slight smile as I threaded my way toward her.

"You look gorgeous," I said, inhaling the scent of her hyacinth perfume.

And she did. The dress patterned in royal blue with black and white swirls draped beautifully about the hips I used to love to rest my hands on. It set off her eyes, lined with black tonight. She wore silver drop earrings and a necklace of black glass beads.

"Thanks." She gestured to the long table set against a sidewall. "Wine?"

"Not tonight, thanks. Your art has changed. I like it. A lot."

Marcie smiled. "Yeah. I guess having my heart broken busted something open inside. And all of this just grew, you know?"

I laughed.

She waved at some people who'd just come in the door before turning back. "What's the laugh about?"

Shaking my head, I wasn't sure how to answer at first. *Just be honest.* Right. I'd paid my therapist two hundred dollars for those three little words yesterday. I may as well make use of the advice. "It's just that we've grown in opposite directions, looks like. I've scaled back, and you've scaled big."

Her smile was genuine this time, not a tight, polite thing, but a broad grin that lit up her blue eyes. "You seem just the right size to me."

Heart pounding in my chest, I watched her lean, closer and closer. I didn't dare move. Didn't dare to breathe. If I moved, the moment might shatter, and I didn't want that. Couldn't bear it.

And then her soft lips were on mine. And my lips pressed back. Just a quick, warm, meeting. Almost chaste. When she pulled away, I found my eyes were closed. I blinked in the gallery lights. The sound of wine being poured and people's conversations rushed in.

"Look." She turned me, gently, one hand on my back.

And I looked. The painting was easily five feet high and three feet wide. A giant heart, floating inside a starry sky. It was ringed with flames of yellow and blue, orange and red. And at the center of the heart was a doorway, with an iron runged ladder propped against the threshold.

I heard myself sigh and blinked back tears. Throat tight, I reached for one of her small, strong, hands.

"It's beautiful," I finally said. "The best thing I've ever seen."

She leaned into my side. I leaned back, the slightest pressure of hips and thighs along one thin line, as if we could hold each other up with this smallest cantilevering of black jeans against a swirling, patterned dress.

"I made it for myself," she said. "But standing with you now?"

I looked down at her, seeing the lights trained on the painting reflected in her face, her white-blond hair, her eyes, looking up at me.

"What?" I whispered.

"I think I painted it for you, too."

Then she kissed me again. This time for real.

Our columnist, Julie Pitzel, has been a receptionist, radio DJ, bill collector, telemarketer, administrative assistant, community college instructor, and an expediter (a.k.a. professional nag). She's been involved in the Houston writing community for many years including two years as president of a local Romance Writers of America chapter. She writes paranormal fiction from a geodesic dome south of Houston, where she lives with her husband and a pair of cats. Most recently, her story "The Dance" was published in The Death of All Things *anthology.*

YOU READ THAT?: EXPECTATIONS

by Julie Pitzel

During one of a thousand recent conversations about Hallmark Christmas movies, a friend commented that she liked them for the romance. To which someone chimed in "unreasonable expectations!"

This isn't the first time I've heard or seen that phrase in regard to romances, but I do wonder why it's not applied to other genres. Do they think the women who enjoy reading or watching romances are incapable of differentiating between fiction and reality? If so, apparently that inability only happens with romance and not any other type of fiction. The same person who likes romance could say she really likes crime dramas and no one will exclaim "unreasonable expectations!" And yet, most of the crime dramas match DNA or run toxicology screens at speeds no laboratory in the country could match. They tend to pinpoint time of death with an accuracy impossible to replicate in the real world, they only seem to work on one crime at a time, and they solve every crime they investigate—unless there's going to be a sequel. Talk about unreasonable expectations.

But, yeah, tell me how two people falling in love and committing to a relationship is unrealistic. Of course it's possible that's not the part they find improbable. I will admit there are some scenarios and tropes I have a problem with in romance, but I'm not going to discount the entire genre for the sins of a small percentage of stories.

What do I consider unreasonable expectations?

My biggest eye-roller are the couples who have sex four or more times in one day. People are quick to point out that few guys can perform twice in one hour, let alone six times in one night. But I wonder about the women. They never seem to lack for natural lubrication. From the first kiss to the twentieth orgasm, things slip slide along without any help from K-Y. Sometimes they're "a little sore" but that doesn't stop them from being down with anything. This is especially hard to believe with a woman who was a virgin or practically celibate before meeting the hero. A switch got flipped and she's suddenly always "on" without feeling raw or hypersensitive. Sometimes I want a character to yell "don't touch me!" and slap his hands away when the hero comes close. Of course my frustration could be an indication the author has spent too much time on sex scenes that don't advance the plot or deepen the relationship.

Another *oh-please* situation is the character who can do everything. She cooks, writes computer code, and rides a horse without a problem; and when the hero hands her a pistol, she hits the target the first time. Or the hero who can pinpoint exactly what's wrong with an engine based on the sounds it's making, play multiple musical instruments, perfectly braid his niece's hair while babysitting, and bake a flawless soufflé. It's not just that they're capable of doing multiple tasks, they're *exceptional* at all of them. We do want our heroes and heroines to be accomplished and capable, but it's unreasonable for them to be the best at everything they try. It's not only unreasonable, it's kinda boring. Because as much as we want them to be masters at a few things, we also enjoy those moments when they are humbled. We like hearing the self-deprecation when they admit they can't swim or cook or whistle. We want to see the shock they experience when someone beats them at their specialty—especially if it's the other romantic lead. We even appreciate the calm acceptance that they failed but expect to work long hours to improve themselves. Perfect characters are only interesting when that perfection gets stained and bent. It may not be destroyed, but it'll never be quite the same.

When it comes to romance tropes, I have my favorites but there aren't any I just don't like—as long as the author sets up the motivation and conflict well. But I have picked up stories where they throw in multiple scenarios until it becomes one trope too many: A secret baby, friends to lovers, amnesia, love triangle, billionaire story that winds up with marriage of convenience—or some other over the top plotline. Sometimes the complications become so twisted and complex I wonder if the author is simply trying to hit a certain page count. It becomes especially tiresome if the story appears to be complete, and suddenly there's a new plot twist that wasn't foreshadowed. I become tempted to look the writer up and suggest they save the excess tropes for the next book.

Romance stories aren't reality. Those of us who read and watch them know this. We also know that *Star Trek*, *Criminal Intent*, *Murdoch Mysteries*, *The Avengers*, *Magnum P.I.*, and Saturday morning cartoons aren't reality either. It's really not necessary for well-meaning friends, relatives, and internet strangers to warn us that the real world doesn't work that way. Although in some ways they may be right, most of us will never meet the man of our dreams while taking care of a maiden aunt at her tree farm in the Pacific Northwest.

The people who look at romances and think "unreasonable expectations" are missing the point. Most romances are about being true to yourself. The characters must overcome conflicts, especially the nasty internal ones that stop them from being happy. It's not unreasonable to realize that we all have the ability to face our fears and doubts and come through the other side. Romances usually also have a strong message about respecting ourselves and counting on our partners to respect us and our dreams. Again, not an unreasonable expectation. And one of the biggest things they're missing is that immersing ourselves in the fantasy of a romance novel or show is enjoyable. Sometimes we need a feel-good story and that's something romance can deliver. The basic premise of all romance stories is the idea of happily ever after, and that idea is not unreasonable.

Copyright © 2020 by Julie Pitzel.

C.S. DeAvilla writes award-winning science fiction, fantasy, and romance under another pen name. She has been a romance fan since she sneaked a peek at her mother's massive historical romance bookcase and fell in love with all the characters. She reads every romance genre—as long as two people are falling in love, she'll give it a read. Her favorite authors are Jennifer Crusie, J.R. Ward, Darynda Jones, Suzanne Brockmann, Sarah MacLean, and Christina Lauren. But she always has room for one more.

RECOMMENDED BOOKS

by C.S. DeAvilla

Title: *Well Met*
Author: Jen DeLuca
Publisher: Berkley (Penguin Group)
ASIN: B07L7RYYF7
Release Date: September 3rd, 2019

It's delightful when romance books have a fresh setting to explore and *Well Met* has that with pizzazz. Emily drops her non-existent life—after losing her boyfriend and her carefully planned future—to take care of her sister and niece when her sister is in a car accident. She promises to slip into any and all responsibilities her sister had signed up for, including a volunteer position as the tavern wench in a six-week renaissance fair school fundraiser. Emily, not one to be in the spotlight, is out of her element pretending to be a flamboyant bar maid. But she *does* know a heck of a lot about bartending, and staring at hot men in kilts for the summer can't be that bad. Except Simon, the high school's English teacher who runs the fair, is constantly picking on her. She doesn't do anything to his high standards, and they rub each other wrong at every opportunity. However, he turns into a flirtatious pirate on the weekends, one she suddenly can't stop fantasizing about. When they find themselves handfast as part of the show, she starts to wonder how much of their fair personas are real and how much is all for show. This debut was the best thing about the autumn season for me. I read it in a few days despite a busy schedule. There is humor, chemistry, and quick dialog beats, but this story has soul and a lot to add to the conversation of grief. I want to live in this world a little longer and now I'll have to wait a year for *Well Played*, the next book in the series. It looks like readers will be transported back to the renaissance fair once again. This one is a must read.

Title: *The Edge of Obsession*
Author: Diana Muñoz Stewart
Publisher: Sourcebooks
ASIN: B07XP8FPKX
Release Date: September 8th, 2019

If it's romantic suspense you fancy, Diana Muñoz Stewart has a series that will feed all your reader cookies. Strong female leads, hot sensitive partners—this is part of the new wave of romance where the couple works together and nobody is saving damsels in distress, but they do save each other. Dada Parish is a member of a vigilante family and she's on a mission to stop a human trafficking ring. Sion Bradford is a sexy soccer player who just might spoil her assignment. Sion doesn't believe for a second she's the nun she pretends to be and when her cover is blown they must work together to make it out of this predicament alive. Good thing Dada has a knack for luck… or is it talent? I hadn't read a romantic suspense for a while and searched for one that would fill the void. Ms. Stewart's *The Edge of Obsession* has quick pacing and at novella length it was the right sample to lead me into the series. I'll definitely be trying some more!

Title: *The Play*
Author: Elle Kennedy
Publisher: Self Published
ASIN: B07NF2BDFZ
Release Date: October 7th, 2019

I've got a soft reader spot for sports romance and I love authors who can write a good athlete. One that isn't so alpha that the romance feels saturated with toxic masculinity. Elle Kennedy is an author that knows the perfect balance for her heroes. I love her strong couples and hot, hot chemistry. Hunter and Demi were dripping in slow burn magic. After last season's out-of-control partying that lead to his team losing the playoffs, Hunter Davenport swears to live like a monk as team captain. After his last rejection he'd gone on a self-destructive streak and recognized the harm done in his immature reaction. He doesn't want to become his narcissistic father. Demi is struggling trying to live up to her parent's expectations. Her father put himself through medical school and he wants Demi to follow in his footsteps, but she'd rather be a counselor. Instead of disappointing her parents she goes to great lengths to keep up the image she's on board with their plans—all the way down to the hoop earrings she can't stand. She's got a boyfriend that fits perfectly in her family—and both their families are best of friends, except she can't seem to keep his interest. When she paired with hockey start Hunter Davenport for a class assignment, she's instantly intrigued. She discovers he's no threat with his vow of celibacy and considers him safely in friend territory. However, Demi's world is turned up-side down when her boyfriend is out of the picture and she's got her sights set on Davenport for her rebound. Only problem is, Hunter doesn't want meaningless sex anymore, he wants Demi for keeps or not at all.

Title: *The Bookish Life of Nina Hill*
Author: Abbi Waxman
Publisher: Berkley (Penguin Group)
ASIN: B07JFJXXLS
Release Date: July 9th, 2019

Abbi Waxman's books kept getting recommended to me because of my reading history, so I investigated her list. *The Bookish Life of Nina Hill* had a lot of reviews and an interesting premise and a character I knew I would care about. The first chapter had all the hooks and so I dove right in to the rest of the story easily and read it quickly. Nina Hill likes her introverted life as a bookseller at a quiet independent shop. She's got everything figured out—thank you very much. Except when she learns that her biological father left her something in his will—she didn't even know she had a father (right, she knew she had one, but didn't know he knew she existed or that her mother knew who he was). Then all of a sudden, she's plunged into a big family with lots of siblings and cousins and nieces and nephews. It's all so overwhelming! And perhaps the worst development of all is when someone from her quiz group community takes an interest in dating her, and she can't help but like him. Pushing herself away from those feelings only snaps her right back into his pull over and over. What will happen when being with Tom feels as good as being alone with a good book? Nina has trouble understanding it herself. This was a fantastic character-driven novel where all the characters were quirky and well fleshed out. I felt like I could step in and know them—I *want* to know them in real life! The omniscient narration was a welcome fresh angle on the storytelling. It added a fun tone to the whole story that carried me through each chapter and left me thirsty for more.

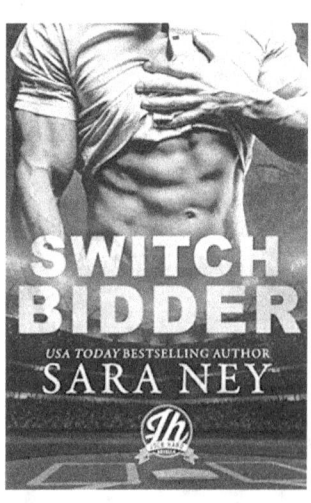

Title: *Switch Bidder*
Author: Sara Ney
Publisher: Three Legacies LLC
ASIN: B07T9QQBXG
Release Date: June 27th, 2019

Sara Ney's novels are spectacular and even though I tend to skip novellas because I want something meatier, I can't help myself when it comes to my favorite authors. *Switch Bidder* is one Ney-fans won't want to miss. Piper has a huge crush on Ryder Williams and when he's up for bid at a jock auction to raise money for a good cause, she chickens out and hides in the bathroom. But a good friend outbids the competition for her, which means Piper goes home with a date. She avoids collecting her prize and Ryder is determined to find out, because it turns out, he's had a crush on her for a long time. This was a cute, quick read. A bite that can satisfy Ney readers for a short while in-between books.

Copyright © 2020 by C.S. DeAvilla.

CLOSING EDITORIAL

by Lezli Robyn

As the weather starts to grow warmer here at Myrtle beach, and the season of love falls upon us, *Heart's Kiss* would like to thank the readers, first and foremost, for supporting our magazine for so long, and for the excited reception our diverse format has received over the years. We literally could not have published so many issues without you, our readers, valuing our efforts. Secondly, we would love to thank our writers for sweeping us off our feet, again and again, and for showing us love really is worth taking the leap into the unknown.

What's next for us? Stay tuned to our website, at *www.heartskiss.com*, for updates on our romance anthology series we'll be bringing to national distribution in bookstores near you! We'll be updating the website with our progress (and dedicating a page there to display back issues of this wonderful magazine) and we look forward to bringing you more romance in all forms, in a book format that is much easier for us to distribute around the country. *Thankfully in Love*, the first in our exciting new anthology series, is due for release in later 2020, ahead of Thanksgiving, and we cannot be more excited to share it with you all!

Until then, farewell, and thank you for all the words we've shared, for the love we've celebrated.

www.ingramcontent.com/pod-product-compliance
Lightning Source LLC
Chambersburg PA
CBHW082050220626
47052CB00006B/1200